HORN RIVER
HORNETS SERIES
book 1

USA TODAY BESTSELLING AUTHOR

K WEBSTER

Horn River Bully

Cover Design: All by Design
Photo: Adobe Stock
Editor: Emily A. Lawrence
Formatting: Champagne Book Design

Dedication

To Mom—
Our mutual love for romances about boys who kiss boys inspires me to write more MM just for you.
Thanks for always loving and supporting me, no matter what I do.

From *USA Today* bestselling author K Webster comes a MM high school bully romance called *Horn River Bully*!

Horn River was supposed to be the change I needed.
A fresh start.
An escape from my painful past.
Better in every way.

I'm a popular guy. Approachable. I make friends easily.
Cool car. Nice clothes. Good attitude.
Everything will be fine.

School is school.
I'll keep my head down until graduation and try not to stick out.
College will be here before I know it.

Yet my first day proves to be anything but easy.
The Horn River Hornets—our school's most notorious group of bad boys—have put a target on my back.
Their leader, Roan, hates me.
He calls me Rat.
To him and his friends, I'm a loser who doesn't belong at their school.

I could pretend I don't care about their hate.
If only Roan wasn't so hot.
He's mean, cruel, and sexy as hell.
My nemesis is impossible to ignore...and a secret part of me doesn't want to.

Here I thought being gay was the worst of my problems.
Turns out, being gay and crushing on your
enemy takes the cake.

Enjoy the entire Horn River Hornets series today!

Horn River Bully (Book 1 – Roan's Story)
Little Hornet (Book 2 – Jordy's Story)
Mr. Angry Hornet (Book 3 – Cal's Story)
River Knight (Book 4 – Trey's Story)

*** The Horn River Hornet series all have interlinking storylines. They shouldn't be read as standalones. The first book in the series, Horn River Bully, is the only MM story. The others are MF. The Horn River Hornets is now a complete series!***

Horn River Bully

HORN RIVER
HORNETS SERIES

book 1

Chapter One

Hollis

Guilt is a ravenous beast. One I tend to feed on the daily. Not because I want to, but because it demands it. With every sad smile my mother gives me and each emotional meltdown of one of my little sisters, the beast begs to be fed.

I did this to them.

I ruined my mother and uprooted my sisters.

I'm a selfish, selfish boy.

A shudder ripples through me as my father's words repeat inside my head. *You ripped apart this family, son. You.*

I'm gay.

Being gay shouldn't be a problem. This isn't some era or a foreign country where this isn't deemed acceptable. It's on television, movies, commercials, and books. Friends and teachers and family. Someone is gay. No big deal.

But to Dr. English, Vermont's most revered surgeon, being gay was an embarrassment. Having his oldest child come out to his school and it make its way to the hospital where Dad works was the shock of his life. Never mind the fact that Vermont is really accepting of gays. It was my father who was not. Rather than being a normal fucking human about it, Dad blew up in the worst way. Threatened to kick me out. To disown me. To take away my car, my trust fund, my college savings.

Yet…he was unsuccessful.

Mom stood in front of me and took his wrath. Chose me over him. Ended a twenty-year marriage because protecting her son was more important than protecting her marriage.

I love her for that.

I also hate me for that.

She shouldn't have had to choose. She shouldn't have had to leave her cushy life as a surgeon's wife to move out west to Oregon. Away from her friends. Away from her life. Away from everything. Sure, we could have stayed and continued our life there without Dad, but Mom said she needed the support of her sister.

"What's wrong, honey?" she asks, sipping from her coffee mug, her hip propped against the countertop in my aunt Karen's kitchen.

I stiffen, hating that she caught me deep in my self-loathing thoughts. She's so perceptive, so normally I do everything in my power to keep that from her. My mother has enough to worry about with Charlotte and Penny.

"Nothing, Mom," I tell her with a bright smile. "Just thinking about school."

She sets her mug down and walks over to me. Her fingers ruffle my dark blond hair that matches hers exactly. "I can read you better than I can read myself. You're nervous."

"Yeah," I lie. "New school, new friends. It'll be fine."

Her lips press together. "I can try and get you in the private school, but you insist on public. I can manage a way to pay for it."

But she can't.

Again, because of me.

Mom now works as a bank teller and we live with Aunt Karen until she can get on her feet. Dad will eventually have to pay obligatory child support and alimony, but it's not enough for Mom to buy us a house and pay for private school. And until the divorce goes through, she's scraping by just to feed us.

"I swear," I assure her. "It'll be fine." This time, I mean it. I came from a school where I was well-liked and popular. Most of my friends I had since kindergarten. I'm an easygoing guy and tend to make friends without having to try too hard. That's not what I'm worried about.

I'm worried about Mom.

"Promise me you'll let me know if the academics aren't what they should be. I want you to still have all the same opportunities you had back home."

"The academics are better at Horn River," Aunt Karen says in her no-nonsense principal voice. "We've gone over this, Kelsey."

Mom sighs and steps away, shaking her head at her sister. "I know. I'm just worried. They're starting in the middle of the school year."

"Garrett knew what he was doing when he gave you that ultimatum," Aunt Karen tells her gently, stroking her fingers through Mom's blond hair. "And my strong sister stood up to him, even if it meant a little chaos for her children. You did the right thing."

Once again, the guilt threatens to drown me.

"Hollis is the most resilient kid I know." Aunt Karen smiles fondly at me. "And if anyone gives you grief, I'll give them detention." She shrugs and chuckles as though she's teasing, but we both know she's not. I'm not sure having my aunt as the principal is a good thing or a bad thing.

"I really will be okay." I give them both a reassuring grin. "Four months and I'll graduate. I've got this."

As they set to preparing breakfast for my little sisters, I flip through my phone. Dad canceled our phone plan, so Mom got us new ones once we got to Horn River. I had to input all my old friends and text them from my new number. Some haven't responded back and I don't know what to make of that.

This will just have to be a fresh start. I'll skim through the next four months unnoticed and when I go off to college, I can be the Hollis I was meant to be. Guilt-free and gay. At Horn River, I plan to be invisible Hollis.

"My hair won't act right," Charlotte wails as she stomps into the kitchen. Her blond hair is sleek pulled back in a ponytail and doesn't look bad, so I don't know what her deal is.

"You look beautiful," Mom assures her.

"I look gross and no one will want to be my friend." She turns on the waterworks, making my mom's shoulders hunch with defeat. It kills me.

"Toughen up, Char," Aunt Karen barks out. "If you go into middle school crying, they're going to make fun of you. Your hair is beautiful and so are you. That's enough."

Mom winces at Aunt Karen's harsh delivery, but she doesn't correct her. This only makes Charlotte cry harder. I don't remember being so emotional in the eighth grade.

"My iPad is broken," Penny complains, walking into the kitchen shoeless and still half asleep. At twelve, she's more worried about her stupid apps than school.

"Your iPad is going to go into the trash if you don't get ready for school right now," Mom threatens, pointing upstairs.

Penny pouts and stomps off.

"Right," I say with a sigh. "Who wants a ride to school?"

"I'll take the girls to their schools," Aunt Karen says. "Just get yourself settled in. When you get there, ask for Ms. Sommers. She's the counselor and will have your schedule. If you need anything during the day, come see me."

After kissing my mom and hugging my aunt, I slip back to my bedroom. It's Aunt Karen's office, but we were able to add a twin bed to give me my own space. My mom took one of Aunt Karen's guest rooms and the girls share the other. Since this is all my fault, sleeping on a twin crammed behind a computer desk feels fair.

Especially since I kept my car.

I'm both relieved and sickened. On one hand, it'll be nice driving my 2018 Ford Mustang GT Coupe to school and not having to rely on my aunt to get me there. On the other hand, though, it was a gift from my father, which leaves a bad taste in my mouth. When I turned eighteen last fall, he paid cash for it and put it in my name. Some rite of passage being a man bullshit. Whatever the reason, it kept him from being able to take it away when we left. Insurance is fucking expensive, but I'll get a job and worry about that later.

"Everything will be fine," I mutter to myself as I glance at the mirror Aunt Karen hung on the wall in an effort to make the office feel more like a bedroom. At least I look nice. It's not like I'm some loser going to a new school who'll get bullied. I'm Hollis English. All-American boy with a happy smile and a friendly attitude. Teachers love me. Students want to be me.

It's fine.

Totally fine.

Though I'd wanted to go for comfort—a hoodie and

sweats—I decided on something more reasonable to make a first impression. Dark slacks. Dress shoes. Button-up shirt. I'd thought about grabbing a tie, but then wondered if it would seem too preppy. At the last minute, I decide preppy is fine if I want my teachers to take me seriously so I can get the scholarships I need. I can't rely on Dad anymore. I snag a deep purple tie from the closet and quickly put it on like my father taught me. With my dark blond hair styled neatly and my approachable smile affixed, I deem that I look better than good for my first day of school.

Plus, my tie nearly matches my car, and that's a small win I'll take for the day.

Letting out a heavy sigh, I grab my gray pea coat, my black leather Michael Kors messenger bag, and the keys to the 'Stang.

I'm fine.

This is fine.

My new high school is insanely different than my prep school back home. For one, there are hardly any cars in the parking lot. Everyone at South Burlington Prep drove. And most of them drove something equally expensive to mine, though theirs was probably more snowy weather appropriate in comparison. Either I'm really early, or there are twelve people who drive.

A bout of nerves makes my stomach clench painfully. I've been having these pains when I'm stressed. Like someone grabs my stomach and squeezes it. A few times, I've even puked over it. Mom says it's nerves and for her sake, I try not to tell her anymore. She looks sick herself anytime I mention it and the last thing I need to do is make my mother sick.

I park on the first row between an old Ford Explorer with the paint peeling off and a gray minivan. I still have twenty minutes before school starts, so maybe more kids will show up and fill up the parking lot. As I get out of my car, I cringe slightly noticing how obnoxious my vehicle looks in comparison.

I'm just grabbing my messenger bag from the backseat when a car door slams. I dart my eyes up to find a guy in front of the Explorer staring at me. His eyes look black and wild, and coupled with the cigarette hanging out of his mouth and shaved head, he looks borderline criminal.

"Nice purple car," he says, his tone mocking, his cigarette bouncing between his lips.

"Uh, thanks." My voice sounds high. Nervous.

"Wasn't a compliment."

The guy starts walking toward the school, flicking his cigarette into the grass, when the other car door slams. I drag my stare from the wannabe convict to another guy. Rather than bored and slightly unhinged, like the first guy, this guy looks pissed.

Dark brown hair that's grown out long enough to hang over one of his intense eyes. Flaring nostrils. Sharp jawline that clenches. All that aggression is directed my way, but couldn't possibly be for me considering I literally just got out of my car and have never met the guy.

I look over my shoulder to see who he could possibly be glaring at. When I find no one, I realize all that boiling hatred *is* for me.

Fucking great.

"Hi," I squeak out, hating how much of a pussy I sound like. "I'm Hollis."

"Don't care."

He walks off and I gape after him. What the hell was that all about? The guy is wearing the outfit I wanted to wear—black sweats, white sneakers, and a gray hoodie. It's too cold not to be wearing a coat, but he doesn't seem bothered by it.

I shoulder my bag and lock my car before hurrying after him. "Hey, man, wait up."

He stops abruptly. It gives me time to approach him. The guy's big, at least five inches or so over my five-foot-eleven frame. His shoulders are broad and he looks like he could fuck up someone like me.

Since he won't turn around, I slowly circle him like one would a rabid animal. Calm. Soft tones. No quick movements.

"I think we got off on the wrong foot for some reason." My breath comes out in a rush. "Can we start again?"

His head cocks to the side, his hair shifting to reveal a barbell through his eyebrow, and his honey-brown eyes bore into me. I can't help but squirm under his scrutiny. He takes a step toward me, forcing me to take an awkward step back. His upper lip curls in disgust.

"Are you a teacher?" His deep, sultry voice startles me stupid for all of three seconds.

"W-What? No, I'm just a kid like you—"

"I'm not a fucking kid," he snaps, his brows furling with anger.

I hold up a hand, hating that I'm already fucking this up. "I just meant…I'm sorry." My hand shakes and of course he zeroes in on it. Quickly, I shove it into my coat pocket. "I'm new here and just wanted to introduce myself."

"You did. Now move out of my way." He takes a threatening step toward me, but I stand my ground this time.

"Listen…" I utter. "I'm not trying to piss you off, I'm—"

He grabs my shoulders roughly and physically moves me to the side. Then, he storms past me and into the building.

What. The. Fuck.

"Oh, man, you screwed up," a voice calls out as he trots my way. "Take note, new guy, don't piss him off."

I slouch and scrub my palm along my cheek in frustration. "I didn't mean to. I was just introducing myself. Trying to make a friend. You know, be a normal human being."

He snorts. "Spoiler alert, everyone here sucks. Except me. And apparently you. The name's Gio Montoya."

I size him up quickly. Dark hair. Glasses. Small gap in his front two teeth. He's dressed nicely, albeit a little nerdy, but he's friendly.

"Hollis English. Moved here from Vermont."

"Welcome to Hell, Hollis." He grins. "Joke!"

I can't help but laugh. "Joke's on me. I was not expecting this."

"Expect the unexpected around here. And stay away from guys like Roan Hirsch."

Roan.

The psychopath's name is Roan.

A tiny thrill shoots through me knowing I now have his name despite him refusing to give it. It's a nice name for a not-so-nice guy.

"Don't worry," I grumble. "I've learned my lesson."

"His minions are just as bad. Avoid them at all costs. Trey, Jordy, and Cal. Jordy, though, he's a mean ass motherfucker.

Touch his stupid car out there and he'll break your nose. Just ask my buddy Richie."

"Thought you said you were the only one who didn't suck around here. What about Richie?"

Gio's features darken. "Richie's mom moved him the fuck out of here after that fight. I'm telling you. The Hornets are vicious."

Hornets?

"Right," I say with an exasperated sigh. "I'll stay away. Gladly. Can you show me to Ms. Sommers? I need to pick up my schedule and figure out where the hell I need to go."

"Ms. Sommers?" Gio waggles his brows. "She's so damn hot. It'd be my honor, man."

So today got off to a bad start.

No big deal.

Everything is going to be okay.

That lie feels extra sour in my stomach today.

Chapter Two

Roan

"You have to come," Sidney pleads, twirling a strand of her silky brown hair. "I know we're broken up or whatever." She rolls her eyes as though she doesn't believe it. "But we can still be friends. You know it wouldn't be Campfire Chaos without the Hornets."

"I have shit to do," I lie, ignoring her no matter how much she tries to shove her tits in my face.

"Ugh," she hisses, shoving my shoulder. "When did you become such an asshole?"

I snap my head her way and narrow my stare. Sidney tries too fucking hard. She's been whoring herself out to the whole student body since at least the eighth grade. I would kill Roux if she even looked at a boy.

My little sister is never allowed to turn into Sidney.

Fucking never.

"I said I have shit to do." I lift a brow, waiting for her to challenge me.

The bell for second hour rings, making several people drop into their seats.

"Maybe I'll just ask the new guy," she sneers, turning back in her seat to text someone.

Her comment boils my blood and not in the way I'm sure she hoped. I'm not jealous. Fuck no. I'm pissed. Who the hell was that guy rolling up in his Mustang like he was fucking royalty?

Mr. Henley starts to work out a problem on the white board even though no one is paying any attention. Two minutes in, the door creaks open.

Mustang Motherfucker walks in, making my skin burn. He has a forced smile affixed on his pretty-boy face and he saunters into the room as though it's no big deal to be dropped into this school. *My* school. He looks like the kind of guy who's used to being the big man on campus. I'd enjoy the fuck out of knocking him down a few pegs.

"Sorry," the guy says. "I got mixed up on where I was supposed to go."

"Not a problem, young man. Find a seat." Mr. Henley waves him off as he goes back to his equation.

The new guy—*Hollis*—glances around the room, looking for a place. Our eyes meet and he freezes, his smile slightly falling. He quickly darts his blue eyes away from mine and rushes to the seat in front of Sidney. She must find him cute—or the prospect of making me jealous—because she leans forward and taps him on the shoulder.

I'm still glaring at him when Mr. Henley says my name.

"Mr. Hirsch," he says again, finally dragging my attention to him.

"What?"

The whole class sniggers.

"Don't what me? I want you to come solve this problem."

I stare at the board in irritation. Fuck no. I don't know how to do that shit.

"Pass," I grumble.

"Which is exactly what you won't be doing if you don't get up here and attempt this problem."

Hollis glances over his shoulder at me, a frown on his face.

"Look somewhere else," I snap.

He jerks his head around, but I don't miss the way his neck blazes crimson.

"That's enough," Mr. Henley grumbles. "Apologize to this young man."

I snort. "No."

"Son, I will not have you—"

"I am not your son." I pin Mr. Henley with a dark glare that has him taking a step back.

He huffs in exasperation. "Get out."

Unbelievable.

"Hirsch, I said go," he barks. "To the office. Now."

I stand with an exaggerated sigh and storm up the aisle. The preppy new fucker has some fancy bag on his desk. For some reason, I make a stupid decision my dad would be proud of and shove it off the side of the desk.

"What the fuck?" Hollis howls.

"Both of you!" Mr. Henley yells. "Out of my class. I will not tolerate these disruptions."

I cast an amused look over my shoulder at Hollis. His features go from angry to surprised to horrified. I'm quite pleased with myself by the time I make it into the hallway. It's stupid to continually get kicked out of class, but it sure beats doing the schoolwork. I start down the hall and then footsteps follow after me.

"My laptop is in my bag," Hollis tells me snippily as he approaches.

I turn on my heel and glower at him, forcing him to stop right in front of me. "So?"

"So, it's expensive."

It annoys the fuck out of me that he's barely been at this school half a day and I've already encountered him flaunting his money twice now.

"Get the fuck out of my face," I sneer.

He gapes at me. "What is your problem with me, man?"

"I don't associate with your kind."

My words hit their intended target because he flinches. His blue eyes flash me a wounded look before he averts his gaze. I scrutinize him openly for a moment since he's standing right in fucking front of me. Shorter than me but built enough that he might take me in a fight. Dark blond hair that makes him appear sort of innocent. And sad eyes. How the hell a rich kid who drives a purple Mustang could be sad is beyond me. If I were rich, I'd be happy as fuck.

He's a rich prick and I'm me.

Our kinds don't play nicely together.

I shove past him, clipping his shoulder. He lets out an annoyed groan. Stalking down the hall, I try not to think about how pissed Ms. Frazier will be. Last time I got sent to her office, I thought she was going to skin me alive. As soon as I make it to the front office, I smirk at Miss Fields, the office secretary. She's young—fresh out of college. My buddy Cal is positive he's going to fuck her before the year is over.

"Frazier," I clip out to her.

Miss Fields gives me a snooty once-over. "Have a seat. She's with another student."

I plop down in one of my usual chairs as Hollis enters. Her face lights up at seeing him.

"Hey, honey. How's your first day going so far?" she chirps, smiling fondly at him. "Ms. Sommers said you got into all the classes you wanted."

Of course she'd love the pretty new boy. If I had to guess, he has a much better chance at fucking Miss Fields than Cal does.

"It's fine," he says in a bright voice that doesn't at all seem defeated like it was moments ago. "Is it supposed to snow today?"

While they start talking about the fucking weather, I slouch in my seat, stretching my long legs out in front of me. We have basketball practice after school and then I have to haul ass to my after school job. Mondays and Wednesdays are always long ones. And now that winter break is over and I'm no longer on vacation, I'm back to work this week.

Ms. Frazier's door opens and Trey storms out. I lift my chin at him. We fist bump as he walks by, neither of us saying a word. He's pissed, though. When Ms. Frazier sees me, she lets out a heavy sigh.

"It wouldn't be a Monday if I didn't see all my favorite Horn River boys," she grumbles. "Were you involved with the vending machine incident?"

"Nope." I pop the 'P' in an obnoxious way that makes her nostrils flare.

"What then?" she demands. Her eyes drift over to Hollis, who's gone quiet, and she gives him a concerned smile. "Everything going okay?"

He shakes his head, briefly looks over at me, and then forces a smile. "I got kicked out of class."

Ms. Frazier blinks several times in confusion. "Why?"

"I cursed in class."

Her face turns red with anger. "And why did you curse in class?"

His eyes dart my way and then he looks at his feet. "I don't know."

Ms. Frazier sees right through bullshit, though, and doesn't believe him. "Roan," she barks out. "What happened?"

I clench my jaw and shrug.

"Both of you. In my office now. You both know me well enough to know I'm not going to let this go until I have answers."

How the hell does rich boy know?

It's his first damn day.

With a huff, I rise to my feet and stalk past her into her office. I plop down in a chair. Hollis takes the one beside me. Where I'm all sprawled out and uncaring, he sits rigid and straight like he's here for a fucking Harvard interview. Unbelievable.

Ms. Frazier glares our way as she takes her seat. Without missing a beat, she launches into her lecture. "I won't stand for disrespect at my school. Mr. Henley is fair and only asks that you show up, shut up, and do your work. It's not that hard. Hollis, you excel at math. The fact you're getting kicked out of algebra on your first day is uncharacteristic for you." She hardens her eyes at me. "Roan, what happened?"

I would get mad and accuse her of blaming me of being the perpetrator, but I know better. Ms. Frazier is one of the few people who cares about me. Mom sure as hell doesn't. Ms. Frazier wants my account because she trusts me with the truth.

"Henley wanted me to do a problem, but I didn't know how to do it," I admit with a grumble. "Then he got pissy."

"And how did Hollis get involved?"

For just fucking being there.

Annoying me.

Looking perfect and rich. Reminding me I'm not.

"I pushed his bag off his desk." I challenge her with an evil stare.

Her brows crash together. Disappointment. Fuck. I'm screwing this all up. I can't get on Ms. Frazier's bad side. She's too important to my family.

"And you cursed for that reason?" she asks Hollis.

"My laptop is in there," he says bitterly. "It's expensive and it's probably ruined."

Tattletale. His words boil my blood.

"Fuck off, rat."

"Roan!" Ms. Frazier bellows, slapping her palm on the desk. "Enough of this."

I curl up my lip and give Hollis a look of disdain before turning to regard Ms. Frazier with a cool expression. "I'm sorry."

She rolls her eyes. "No, you're not. But you'll be sorry if you have detention."

I wince at her words. She's right. I can't get detention. Detention is after school. I can miss basketball, because even though I love it, it's not a requirement. My after school job is.

"Listen," she says, leaning forward. "I need you to be someone Hollis can turn to. He's new and doesn't have anyone yet."

Hollis groans in embarrassment. "Aunt Karen—"

"What?" I snap, frowning at her.

Her lips thin out. "Hollis is my nephew. He doesn't gain

favor because he's family. You of all people know I'm fair, Roan."

She's right, but it's still annoying as hell.

"I'm not going to give you detention with your friend Trey, though he could certainly use the help cleaning off the horrible words he wrote on the vending machine," she tells me. "You have basketball…and everything else." She lets out a heavy sigh. "I need you to remember to stay focused, okay?"

I let out a defeated sigh. "I get it."

"You're not like him." Her eyes sear into me, but I don't believe them. I'm more like my father than she'll ever know.

"Can I go?" I clip out, ending this line of conversation.

"You both can. I don't want to see either of you in my office again. Make nice with each other. You're both adults, so act like it."

Chapter Three

Hollis

Lunch time used to be fun. I had friends. Lots of them. Plenty of guys and girls I could sit with. We laughed and joked and talked. Sometimes we studied. Mostly we planned whatever parties were coming up.

It wasn't like this.

Not even when I came out to everyone that I was gay.

This is weird.

Fucking creepy.

People eye me curiously, but don't offer a seat. The room almost comes to a hush—the air crackling with electricity as they wait.

Wait for what?

I scan the crowd looking for the kid Gio I met this morning. Nothing. I'm seconds from abandoning lunch altogether when someone sidles up beside me.

"Hey, new guy," the brunette girl from my algebra class chirps. "Looking for a place to sit?"

She's pretty. If I were into girls, I'd find her attractive enough to want to date. I can definitely tell she's interested in me. It'd be smart to come right out and tell her I'm gay so she doesn't waste her time.

But…

Things are weird around here and I will take what I can

get right now. If that means befriending a girl who thinks I'm potential boyfriend material, so be it.

Turning on my charm, I grin at her. "I would love that. This school is bigger than my old one. It'll take some getting used to. Call me Hollis. And you are?"

"Sidney." Her green eyes brighten as she grabs my elbow and points. "The girls and I sit right over there. Wave to Wendy." A girl with blond hair and a big smile waves goofily at us. I wave back. "So let's get food and talk about the next Campfire Chaos."

I allow her to lead me to a line. "Campfire Chaos?"

"Everyone who's anyone goes. It's something the Hornets started when everyone was in middle school and it's been going strong ever since."

"We camp?"

She laughs. "Among other things."

What other things?

"I'll have to ask my mom."

Her brows lift as she blinks her long lashes at me. "Aren't you adorable?" Then her lips part. "Oh, wait. You're serious? You really have to get permission?"

I cringe at her words. It's on the tip of my tongue that our family has been going through some shit and I'm just trying to give my mom the respect of asking. Sure, I'm eighteen and can technically do what I want, but I don't know if she needs me to babysit or has family stuff planned.

"I'll see, okay?" I say, winking at her.

Her cheeks turn pink and she nods. "Okay. I really want you to come. You can share a tent with me."

Oh crap.

Back up, Hollis.

Slow your fucking roll here.

"I, uh," I start, but then I'm shoved out of line. I stumble a few steps and knock into some kid who barks out something in annoyance. When I swivel around, I come face to face with the guy from this morning who was with Roan. The stomach pains I'd been managing just fine come back in full force. I almost double over and have the urge to puke.

"Jordy!" Sidney screeches. "Don't be an asshole!"

Jordy cracks his neck, his dark, nearly black eyes searing into mine. The guy is a bit bigger than Roan. Meaner too, it would seem. Violence ripples from him and I don't want any part of it. I've never been in a fight in my entire life.

"Back of the line, fuckface," he sneers, gesturing with a nod of his head in that direction.

"You can't do this," Sidney whines, but loses her fire when he peels his stare away from me to glower at her.

He takes a threatening step toward her. My stomach pains and the fear of a fight dissipate as I worry about the girl. I stalk over to him and step in front of her.

"Don't." I say the word quietly but laced with warning.

The crowd hushes.

"Or what?" Jordy bites out, bumping his chest to mine.

I want to swipe the spittle off my face, but I'm staring at a venomous snake. One false move and I'll regret it.

"She's just a girl," I grumble.

"And so are you." His grin is wolfish and evil.

"Let's go, Hollis," Sidney utters, grabbing my elbow.

I tug my arm free and don't take my stare off Jordy. "We were here first. He can't take our spot in line." It's not right.

Jordy laughs. "You have no idea whose goddamn school you walked into, do you?"

"This is my school now too." I may not say them as vehemently as he does, but there is fire in my words. I believe them. I'm here for just a few months, but I'll be damned if I let a couple of bullies make my life hell for no reason.

Before Jordy can go off, I feel his presence. Roan. Like a tidal wave of hatred growing so high it blots out the sun before obliterating everything below it. He's about to crash into me and drown me.

"You heard him. Back of the line, rat. I won't say it twice." Roan's stare is seemingly bored, though I notice the tick of his jaw and the way he has his hand fisted in Jordy's hoodie.

I could maybe take one. But two? Hell no.

"Whatever. I'm not even hungry." I shove past them, clipping Roan with my shoulder like he did me and away from the crowd of weak bystanders. Everyone just stood around and watched. No one intervened. That dude was about to kick my ass and no one cared. What's wrong with these people?

"Hollis, wait," Sidney calls out.

I ignore her until I get into the hallway outside of the cafeteria. She regards me with a pained expression.

"Are you okay?" she asks, reaching for my hand.

I cross my arms over my chest to avoid contact. "Yeah. Just another shitty thing to add to my already shitty day." I let out a heavy sigh. This is not me. I don't feel sorry for myself. Normally, when faced with a craptastic situation, I'd find the good in it. Forever an optimist. But now that we've been displaced and I'm in some level of hell, I can't find it in me to try. "I'm sorry, Sidney."

"It's just Jordy being Jordy. He doesn't hurt girls. That was all show for you."

I let out a sigh of relief. "I don't know what their problem is with me."

"They're Hornets," she says as if this explains everything. "They're used to telling people what to do and them listening. Once you get used to them, they grow on you. They're not bad all the time."

Another sharp pain seizes my stomach as my skin flushes with a cold sweat.

"I'm going to head to the nurse. I don't feel so hot." Not a total lie. I feel like shit, but I'm not going to go to the nurse.

"You know where to find me and Wendy. They'll leave you alone now," she promises, but I can tell by the flicker of her green eyes she doesn't believe it.

I flash her my widest, albeit fakest, grin. "I'll be back."

"Oh good. And ask your mom about Campfire Chaos. Friday night after the basketball game, everyone heads over to the river. Cal's dad owns a campground over there and we have permanent access to part of it. As long as we don't trash it, he lets us use it. It's really fun," she promises. "Everyone drinks and roasts hot dogs. In the summer, we swim. In the winter, we cuddle up and stay warm." Her smile is flirtatious and hinting of ways we could stay warm.

The thought of sharing a tent with Sidney really makes me feel sick.

"I'll ask."

"Goodie! Now give me your number so I can fill you in on the details."

After we exchange numbers, she gives me a hug. The girl is shorter than me and feels right tucked against me. Right in a "just friends" kind of way. It's selfish of me to want to latch onto her knowing she's interested in me for other reasons besides friendship. Regardless, I hug her tight anyway, thankful of her kindness, no matter her motives.

We pull apart. She bounces back into the cafeteria, pleased at having gotten what she came after, and heads over to Wendy. I feel an angry stare on me. I'm ready to back out without finding the source of the stare when my eyes lock on his.

Roan.

He sits hunched over his plate of food, eyes on me, as he eats like it's his last meal. I'm reminded of how a lion looks as he tears into a gazelle he's just slaughtered.

A chill that has nothing to do with my stomach issues ripples through me and I visibly shudder. One corner of his lips quirks up in satisfaction.

Fuck him.

His eyes seem to glitter with challenge.

I hate backing down to these assholes, but in this moment, I do. The last thing I want to do is puke my guts up in front of the whole school. So, rather than running off with my tail between my legs, I shoot him the bird.

And then I get the hell out of there.

I sit in the driveway, my forehead against the steering wheel for a long time. Probably an hour. Maybe two. When I walk in that house, I'll have to deal with Charlotte and Penny and Aunt Karen. Today, I don't have the energy for it.

A coldness settles in my bones the longer I sit without the heater on. There's snow in the forecast for this evening, but not enough to cancel school tomorrow. Pity. For someone who always loved school, I've done a complete one-eighty. This school sucks. I want to blame the Hornets for being assholes or Mom for bringing us here or Aunt Karen for not getting a handle on those monsters. But I know better.

It's Dad who's to blame.

He ruined our lives.

Hot, angry tears burn at my eyes. I squeeze my lids closed, hating that wetness escapes, streaking down my cheeks. I'm so tired and I've only just begun. In minutes, I'll have to go inside, put on a fake face for my family, and pretend everything is okay.

My stomach clenches violently, reminding me nothing is okay.

Sitting back, I swipe at the stupid tears and swallow down bile in my throat. I should have eaten, but the Hornets made that impossible. My stomach churns at the prospect of eating anything at this point.

I climb out of my Mustang and slam the door too hard. It feels good to release a little tension. I'm just walking up to Aunt Karen's front door when I hear a loud engine echoing down the street. Stopping in my tracks, I whip around to see a familiar Ford Explorer pull up in front of the house.

Shit.

How do they know where I live?

Did they follow me home?

Dread consumes me, making all my bones feel like jelly. I know Sidney said they wouldn't hurt a girl, but it still worries me considering I have a houseful behind me. Jordy's dark eyes lock on mine from the driver's side through the window, but he makes no moves to get out. The passenger door flings open and Roan hops out.

Fuck.

He has a bag slung over his shoulder that's seen better days. Sweat clings from his hair and his face is slightly red like he's been running or working out. All I can do is gape. It's cold as fuck out here and he's wearing basketball shorts and a T-shirt—the hoodie and sweats from earlier long gone. I hate that the motherfucker who's been nothing but an asshole to me sparks a physiological response in me. My dick twitches as I rake my stare down his muscular form that glistens with sweat. Thank God I have my messenger bag slung across my front hiding my semi.

Our eyes meet and Roan's flash with gold fire.

Hate. Anger. Bitterness.

Not violence.

I don't let my guard down, though. If he's going to try to kick my ass, I'll be ready.

"Who's that?" a voice says from behind me. Charlotte.

"Go back inside," I grind out, glancing at my little sister. "Now."

"No," she sasses, her blond ponytail swishing back and forth.

Roan is no longer looking at me as he opens the back door. A girl with brown hair and glasses climbs out. She sort of stumbles, but he steadies her. Confusion washes over me. What the hell is going on around here?

"Roux?" Charlotte exclaims. "Oh my God!"

My sister tears off in a full sprint to go hug the girl about her age. Roan scowls, shooting a glare my way like I'm some accomplice to whatever the hell is going on.

"Char," I call out.

She grabs Roux's hand and tugs her toward me. "This is my new best friend Roux. We're in most of the same classes together. And now she's here!" Then she frowns. "Why are you here?"

Roux fidgets, her face turning red, and looks down at the dead grass. "I, uh, I—"

"It doesn't matter," Charlotte chirps. "Now you can see my room. I have to share with Penny and oh my God she's such a slob, but we can still hang out. Oh! Do you like birthday cake ice cream? Aunt Karen bought some and it's so good."

Roux seems relaxed at my sister's nonstop rambling. Roan cracks his neck. If I had to guess, he wants to kill me for unknown reasons. What else is new today?

"Why are you here?" I blurt out.

Charlotte scoffs. "Hollis! Don't be a butthead!"

Roux flinches at my words, which makes me feel like an ass. It sets Roan off, though. He stalks over to me and pokes my chest with his finger. "Watch the tone you take around my sister."

Charlotte blinks in surprise. Back home, we were well-liked. Popular and revered. She's never seen such animosity from anyone before. The tension between Roan and me is so thick and cloying you can taste it.

"Ms. Frazier tutors me," Roux explains softly. "I'm sorry."

Guilt swells up inside me. "Don't be sorry, kid," I say, injecting lightness into my voice for her sake. "I was just confused. Aunt Karen is inside. Go on in."

The girls hold hands and walk inside. Roan stares after them, an unreadable expression on his face. He turns, waves at Jordy who takes off, and then looks down his nose at me.

"Stay out of my way, rat."

Chapter Four

Roan

I should get great satisfaction each time he flinches at my insults, but it only makes me feel dirty inside. Is this how Dad feels when he asserts dominance over anyone who isn't him? I hate my dad and don't want to be anything like him.

But I also don't like Hollis.

He's already seen too much of me.

It was one thing for him to see that me and Ms. Frazier have an agreement. It's a whole other for him to see Roux. Roux is a vulnerability not many are allowed to know about. I protect her at all costs. She has no one but me. Sure, she has Jordy and Cal and Trey and Ms. Frazier and a couple others, but that's it. Her father is in prison and her mother's a fucking addict.

"Close your mouth, rat, or you'll catch snowflakes."

The promised snow has just started to fall. Tiny flakes of white dust his features that look as though they're carved in porcelain—not unlike the dolls Roux used to have when she was little. Guys aren't supposed to look so perfect. Perfection isn't real anyway. It's unattainable and fucking ridiculous. Still, I can't look away from his face.

Why not?

My skin heats in an uncomfortable way I don't

understand. All I know is the sight of the snowflakes dusting his long, dark blond lashes and settling on his slightly pink cheeks is one I can't look away from.

His brows furl together and his blue eyes flash with anger. I'm not like Sidney or Miss Fields. I can see right through his façade. He wants everyone to think he's as perfect on the inside as he is on the outside.

He's not and we both know it.

I hoard this secret just like he knows about Roux.

I'll be damned if I let him use her against me.

"Why are you here, Roan?" he demands, his arms crossing over his chest.

It's cold as fuck and I'm still dressed for basketball practice. We're standing outside arguing. I hate this kid.

My eyes skim over his preppy coat in disdain. "I'm here to work."

"Work?" His probing expression contorts into one of confusion. "Doing what?"

Jesus. Does this family not talk about anything?

"Doesn't matter. You don't pay me." I start for the door when he grabs my still sweaty, but now chilled bicep. His touch sends fire racing through my arm.

"It matters. Tell me."

I shake off his grip and throw a finger in his face. "You don't get to order me around, rat. Just because I work here doesn't mean it involves you. So fuck off."

His lips press together and I note that they're full and pink, like a girl's. I don't know why the hell I notice his lips, but I add it to the growing list of annoying shit he does. I've known this guy for a day and he's already the most obnoxious person in my life. That's a lot considering my mom has a revolving door of horrible boyfriends.

Ignoring his poutiness, I hurry into the house to look for Ms. Frazier. I find her already at the kitchen table with Roux with a textbook open. Charlotte, Roux's new friend she prattled on and on about today on the way here, grins at me.

"I can help too, right, Aunt Karen? I'm good at math like Hollis." She beams at me. "This is so exciting!"

Roux giggles and it causes tiny cracks to form inside of me. My sister rarely smiles or laughs. The ride home and her incessant talking about a new friend was so out of character for her, Jordy shot several worried glances my way.

"I'm not here to do schoolwork," I tell the bubbly girl. "I have other work to do."

Ms. Frazier chuckles. "You could always join us for some math problems."

"Pass," I say with a smile as I walk over to the oven to peek in at what's cooking. "What am I doing today?"

"The attic's a mess. If you want to make sense of it, that'd be a great help. My sister Kelsey brought in a bunch of boxes when they moved up here over winter break, so everything is just thrown on top of everything else."

I give a nod and start out of the kitchen.

"You're still staying for dinner, right?" Ms. Frazier asks.

The thought of having dinner with Hollis makes me see red. But life isn't about me. It's about Roux. And Roux getting a home-cooked meal is more important than having to look at some asshole while I eat.

"Duh," I tease. "We never pass up lasagna night."

Charlotte squeals with excitement and Roux giggles again.

Needing space from this new situation, I drop my bag by the sofa and then rush up the stairs. I pass by Ms. Frazier's office and groan when I realize it now has a bed. Hollis lies on top of it face down.

Messenger bag smashed beneath him.

Coat and shoes still on.

The air is thick with despair.

What the fuck does he have to be unhappy about?

A spike of pleasure shoots through me at the thought of me causing the despair. It's only fair since he's kind of fucked up my world.

And then I hear it.

A whine.

Pained and sad.

Familiar.

It spooks me because I recognize it as my own. I don't understand how this kid can have everything and hurt like I do, but I feel it. I can almost taste it. From experience, that shit doesn't come from one day of dealing with assholes like me.

That sort of pain is slashed into you over time.

Inflicted day after day.

Ongoing mental torture.

I backpedal away from his room and rush to the end of the hall where the attic door string hangs. With a quick yank, I pull down the ladder and make my way up. It's cold up here, but I know I'll sweat my ass off by the time I'm done. All the jobs I do for Ms. Frazier are labor-intensive. Basically, I work my ass off in trade for her to tutor Roux two times a week.

Ignoring the chill, I begin with her Christmas boxes that were recently thrown in one corner. Had she called me after Christmas, I would've taken it all down, but when school is out, Ms. Frazier doesn't ask for help. It's strictly a trade for Roux. Two years ago, Ms. Frazier offered to do it for free, but I hate fucking handouts. We made a bargain that I'd work to pay for it, and it's been that way ever since.

My mind lingers on Roux as I organize the boxes. She struggles so much with life in general. Mom is a piece of shit who can't keep food in the pantry. If it weren't for me forcing her ass to get her food stamps, Roux and I would starve. Her boyfriends are always worthless assholes who keep her laid up in bed, moaning like a whore, with God knows what sort of drugs running through her veins. Frankly, our home life sucks, which is why I've always been grateful for these two days a week of normalcy for Roux. We can relax, feel wanted, and eat real food.

A twist of my gut reminds me I'm hungry. Since we get free lunch, one lunch is all we get, though on basketball days, I could eat a helluva lot more than the school dishes out. This afternoon, Coach Rendell ran us hard. Jordy complained like a little bitch. Cal, the energetic bastard, just laughed at us. Trey was too busy cleaning Sharpie off the vending machines and missed practice, which means he'll be benched Friday. All that running made me hungry as fuck.

I manage to get the Christmas decorations put away in a better spot and then work on the boxes labeled "Kelsey." I open one and pull out a picture frame. A pretty woman who looks like Hollis smiles at the camera. Beside her is a man with a serious expression and three kids. Hollis grins like his mother and sister Charlotte. The other little girl is expressionless.

"You came here to snoop?" Hollis demands hotly as he yanks the frame from my hand.

Holy fuck, the guy is a silent creeper. Where the hell did he come from?

"Just cleaning the attic," I snap back. "Don't you have somewhere else to be?"

"Unfortunately, no." His words are softer this time.

I sneak a peek his way. He's no longer in his substitute teacher outfit. Wearing jeans, Chucks, and a black hoodie, he almost looks normal. Under the yellow bulb of the attic, his eyes seem haunted and dark circles are more prominent under them.

"If you're going to bother me, at least help," I grumble, hoping to send him on his way. To my surprise, he picks up the box I'd just opened and carries it over to a far wall.

"So you help my aunt? You do work and she tutors Roux?"

"Yep. Got a problem?"

He picks up another box but gets distracted by the label. When he tears it open and sucks in a sharp breath, I can't help but look his way. I get a brief glimpse of two guys wearing basketball jerseys—Hollis being one of them—smiling into what looks like an almost kiss. He throws the frame back in the box and stomps over to the corner with it.

Okay.

Who was that guy in the picture?

Were they going to kiss?

He continues to move boxes in an almost angry way. As though I'm the one who's pissed him off. I'm getting tired of his attitude. I was doing just fine without his help. When he bumps into me, I lose it. Swiveling around, I grab the front of his hoodie and shove him into a stack of boxes.

"What the hell is your problem, rat?" I snarl, my face inches from his.

"Fuck you."

"You'd like that, wouldn't you?"

He flinches and gapes at me with such a wounded look, I release him. I take a step back and study his hurt features.

"Why are you so fucking pissy?" I demand, crossing my arms over my chest. "Tell me."

His eyes roll as he shakes his head. "Seriously? Hmm, let's see. I was looking forward to my first day of school when some guy I don't even know is a total dick to me. Then, he tries to break my laptop. Then, he and his friend keep me from eating lunch. Now, this same dickhead is in my home, messing with my shit. Oh, and his sister is friends with mine now too. So not only is he an asshole to me at school, but I also have to deal with him after school. Everything's fucking peachy, Roan."

I bristle at the way he says my name. It makes the hairs on my arms stand on end. The nerves in my body electrify. My heart speeds up angrily.

"Are you going to go downstairs and cry to your aunt?" I taunt, overwhelmed with the need to put more cracks in his perfect façade.

Disappointment flashes in his blue eyes that are darker in the attic. "No, man. She has enough shit to deal with than to worry about me."

His comment worms its way inside of my head.

I've developed that mentality. I take the focus off myself and put every ounce into Roux. She's the one who needs it. What I want doesn't matter as long as she gets what she needs.

"Hey, boys," Ms. Frazier calls out. "Dinner will be ready in fifteen. Roan, don't you dare come to my table smelling like a locker room."

As soon as she's gone, I leave him without another word and head for the ladder.

Anytime I'm here, I take a shower after whatever grueling work Ms. Frazier puts me through. This is the first time I feel weird about it.

I hustle down the ladder and practically jump down the rest of the way. Like there's a fire under my ass, I rush downstairs to grab my bag and then head back up. I'm just making it to the landing when Hollis is pushing the ladder into place in the ceiling. His hoodie lifts and it reveals, pale, toned muscles that pretty boys don't get from just being pretty. Those are the kind of abs you work your ass off for.

His arms fall to his sides and his brows furrow. "What?"

Heat floods up my neck to my cheeks. I was not just checking out the abs of my new nemesis. That's not fucking weird or anything.

"Sorry, rat, but there's only room in the shower for one." I laugh cruelly at him in an effort to chase away the awkward feeling settling in my bones.

"And your ability to be a bigger asshole with each passing second knows no bounds," he grinds out as he storms down the hall and into Ms. Frazier's office.

I stop him before he can close the door. "You're just sad you won't ever get a piece of this asshole." I'm not one hundred percent sure he's gay, but I have my suspicions.

He looks over his shoulder at me, affixing a smug grin I haven't seen before on his face. In an agonizingly slow way, he makes a blatant show of skimming his gaze down my body and then back up again. He bites on his lip, not unlike how Sidney always does, and his eyes flash with heat. My dick fucking responds much to my horror.

"You wouldn't be able to handle me anyway," he says with such sure confidence, I'm left speechless.

The door slams shut, making me jump.

This rich prick has no idea who I am. He's the one who wouldn't be able to handle me. I'd dominate him in the bedroom. Make him quiver and cry. I'd make him beg for every single touch. I realize my dick is achingly hard and that I've been fantasizing about a roll in the sheets with fucking Hollis the rat.

What the fuck?

I've never even been with a guy, and if I ever entertained the idea, it sure as hell wouldn't be with some prissy bitch like Hollis.

I'm sure of it.

It's my dick that's a little confused on the matter.

And unfortunately, I'll have to tame the fucker in the shower. I just hope to hell I don't beat off to the memory of Hollis's parted lips. The image of them—plump, pink, and parted—briefly flashes in my head. My cock jolts in appreciation.

I am so fucking screwed.

Chapter Five

Hollis

Mom looks tired. Guilt coils itself in the pit of my stomach. She didn't have to work back home. Life was easier for her. Now it's too hard. We've barely gotten here and it's too damn hard.

Aunt Karen busies the girls—including Roux—with setting the table. I stay out of her way and opt for tossing the salad while I clear my head. Mom sits at the table, watching the girls with a smile on her lips that doesn't quite reach her eyes.

I turn away, unable to witness her unhappiness any longer. I'm singularly focused on the salad when my body seems to come alive. I don't have to look up to know it's Roan. I can feel him and I don't understand what to make of that. When I'd dated Lucas, one of my teammates back home, it'd been fun and flirty and hot. He was my first and only, sexually, and I really liked him, but he wasn't the committed type. Since he was bi, and mostly swung toward females, it wasn't something he wanted out there for the public knowing. Our entire relationship was a secret until he ended it not long before I came out as gay.

Seeing the picture of Lucas earlier in the attic hit me right in the stomach. I hate that I miss him, but I do. I'd give anything to see him right now, even knowing we'd never be lovers again. Today, more than ever, I crave the normalcy of my old life.

Aunt Karen introduces Roan to Mom, and no matter how much I try to ignore him, my eyes eventually creep his way. He looks too good dressed once again in his sweats and hoodie. For the girls, he smiles and it's real. I don't understand why he's such a prick to me and nice to all of them. He sits down beside Roux and playfully pokes at her. It amazes me that Roan is more comfortable at my family's dining room table than I am. It's as though he fits in better than I do.

Shame floods through me. Had I just stuck to the mold, Mom and Dad might still be together. The girls wouldn't have been uprooted. Aunt Karen wouldn't have had her house taken over by four extra people.

"Everything okay, honey?" Mom asks, her palm at my back.

I jolt at her sudden nearness. "Yeah."

"You look a little pale. Is your stomach acting up again?" Her concern for me makes my stomach roil violently.

"I'm fine," I lie. "How was work?"

It's her turn to look ill. "Great."

Yeah right.

"It's fine," she assures me with a smile, her arm coming around me for a motherly hug. "I don't like my boss, but it was the first day and we were busy. I'm sure it'll get better."

I lean my head against hers and enjoy the moment with my mother. Life is so messed up right now, but this feels right.

"Your dad texted," she says with a sigh, her voice low so the kids won't hear.

"And what did he have to say?"

"Wants to see the girls."

The girls. Not me.

"Oh," I mutter.

"He wants to see you too, I'm certain of it," she assures me, "but he's horrible at expressing himself."

I tug away from her and frown. "I don't want to see him anyway, so it doesn't matter."

We finished out the semester and then moved to Aunt Karen's over Christmas break. I'd wondered how he'd managed the past three weeks without having anyone to bitch at. Must have been a boring holiday for him.

"The divorce isn't final," she reminds me. "So if he wants to see them, I have to let him. He's not fighting for custody, and I don't want to poke the bear. I already told him he'll have to make the effort to come out here, though. The girls can't miss any school."

"Just let me know when he shows up so I can make myself scarce."

She presses her lips together but rather than defend him or argue, she simply nods. "I love you, kiddo. No matter what. I'd do anything for you."

I hate that she's already had to.

She left her husband, uprooted her children, and moved across the country for us—for me. The gnawing, burning pain in my gut flares up. Where I was hungry moments ago, now I can barely handle the smell of the food without feeling nauseous.

Mom, always able to sense when I'm not quite right even though I dazzle her with bright smiles, cradles my cheeks with her hands. "We're going to get through this, honey."

"I know, Mom."

I feel eyes on me and dart my attention to Roan, who

watches me with cool indifference. Mom notices him looking our way and gives me a silly smile.

"Friend or…" she whispers.

"Neither," I grumble. "But our sisters get along, so there's that."

Her eyes twinkle knowingly. "Give it time."

There's not enough time in the world to ever make me grow to willingly like Roan, much less want to date him.

"I met two people today. Gio and Sidney. Both really nice." I flash her my big, fake grin. "You'd really like both of them."

Two friends. I made two friends.

My smile falters.

"It's only been a day," she says. "You'll be the boy everyone loves in no time. How could they not?"

I hug her to me again, inhaling her familiar motherly scent. I'm taller than her and bigger, but she'll always be my mom. Someone who I want to lean on when shit gets tough. She can't do much about anything, but she just has an inner strength I can tap into.

"Lasagna's ready," Aunt Karen chirps, ending our heart-felt moment. "Let's eat."

It *really* bothers me that Roan is more comfortable in my aunt's kitchen than I am. We never visited her in Horn River. She always came to us. So even though we've been here a few weeks, it doesn't feel like home.

Roan, however, acts like he lives here.

Mom, Aunt Karen, and the girls have all retired to the living room to play a board game upon Charlotte's obnoxious insistence. I offered to stay back and clean, and to my surprise, Roan hopped up to help.

"You don't have to do this," I tell him, as I set down a clean plate from the dishwasher a little too hard in the cabinet, making it clang.

"It's my job," he bites back, shooting me a nasty glare.

Whatever, asshole.

I continue to unload the dishwasher while he grabs plastic containers to put the leftovers away. He hesitates for a moment as though he's unsure what to do. Before I can utter a word, Aunt Karen peeps her head in.

"Roan," she tells him lightly. "Roux loved the lasagna. Can you just take the rest back with you tonight? There's not enough for this group to have leftovers, but there's plenty for the two of you for tomorrow night."

He nods and then continues on with his task as she leaves. When I'm caught staring, he drops the container onto the counter and turns around, crossing his arms over his chest. Just three feet away from me, I can nearly feel the heat from his muscular body burning into me.

Why must horrible people be so hot?

"What?" he demands, his brows furrowing and his jaw clenching.

"Nothing."

"Say it, rat."

I take several steps toward him until my chest bumps against his arms. "Stop calling me that."

"Or what?" He smirks, an evil glint in his fiery bronze colored eyes. "You'll tell?"

"You think because you're bigger than me that I'll take your shit?"

His eyebrow hikes up, making the barbell piercing look extra hot on him. "Yep."

"I'm not one of the spineless cowards at school."

"Is that a threat?" He lowers his head until our faces are inches apart. "Because I don't take threats lightly. I deal with them."

I refuse to back away, but this close, he smells good. Too good. My gaze travels down his strong nose to his full, pink lips. His hair is still wet and hangs long and messily over his brow with the piercing. Roan is too good-looking. It's maddening.

"How?"

"How what?"

"How do you deal with threats?"

His head cocks slightly to one side as he studies me up close. I want to squirm under his intensity, but like a dog with a scent of meat under his nose, he'll hunt down my weaknesses if I show any sign of them.

"With your fists?" I taunt. "You're eighteen too, right? Fights could land your ass in jail." He flinches at my words, so I pounce. "What would Roux do then?"

He grabs the front of my hoodie and pushes me back until my ass hits the counter. I'm crowded by his massive frame that radiates with fury. His hips press hard against mine, making a strangled breath escape me.

Seconds *tick, tick, tick* by.

His anger morphs into something confusing and heady—something he doesn't seem to understand either. He roams his hot glare over my features, but rather than his eyes being filled with hate, something sparkles in them. Interest. Curiosity. Heat.

I'm imagining it.

Roan Hirsch hates me for no fucking reason.

He certainly doesn't look seconds from kissing me.

Because I feel like a rat caught in a trap, all I can do is stare down the predator before me. I lick my lips in a nervous way that attracts his attention. Then I feel it.

Hardness.

Between us.

Me? Him? Both?

His cheeks flush with a tint of pink before he releases me and steps back, nearly stumbling over his own feet.

"There are certain things you're not allowed to talk about to anyone. Roux being at the top of that list," he warns, his hands folding together and hanging loosely over his crotch.

I can't help but dart my stare there, wondering if what I felt was my imagination. "My sisters and mother are off-limits too."

He nods without hesitation. "Our sisters are friends, and for that reason only, I'll be fucking civil to you in this house."

"At school?"

"At school you're on your own, rat."

We manage to get the kitchen cleaned up without any other conversation. When we finish, Aunt Karen comes in to check on us.

"Hollis," she says, giving me a side hug. "Can you do me a huge favor?"

"Of course."

"The girls need to shower and your mom is exhausted.

I'd love it if you could take Roan and Roux home for me so I could help her get them off to bed."

He stiffens and I nearly choke at her request.

"W-What? Me? Even after today in your office?" I stammer out.

Her lips press into a firm line as she bounces her attention between us. "I think you've managed to sort out your differences today. You're both grown up enough to handle a little car ride. Be careful out there."

Defeated, I give her a nod, despite the churning in my stomach. "Sure."

Roan stalks out of the kitchen. He tells Roux to gather her stuff. Aunt Karen gives me a sympathetic look, but then she leaves me. Fuck. I grab my coat and keys, leaving out the front door without a word. The car is cold as hell, but I sit inside of it as I wait for them to come out. Snow flutters around, but nothing too heavy yet. Within minutes, Roan and Roux head out of Aunt Karen's house toward my car. Roan is normal and nice to Roux. It's interesting to see this side of him. He's a mean, hateful bastard at school and to me, but to her, he's sweet. I expect him to sit in the back with her, but once she's buckled in, he sits up front with me with his container of leftovers in his lap.

"Where to?" I ask as I back out of the driveway.

He grunts out some directions. We're quiet as I maneuver the dark, icy streets. As I near the apartment complex he named, he goes rigid.

"Pull over," he barks out.

"What? We're not there yet—"

"I said pull over now!"

I dart my eyes to the rearview mirror to see Roux's eyes

widen at her brother's outburst. Not wanting to make this worse for her, I pull over onto the side of the road.

"Roan, it's snowing," I mutter.

"Yep. Roux, get your stuff. Let's go."

"Let me pull up farther—"

"Leave it alone, Hollis," he snarls at me.

Not rat. Hollis.

Something in his burning expression tells me I need to back off. I just don't understand what his deal is. Is it because he doesn't want me to see where he lives? I've driven by this apartment complex before. It's rundown and old, but nothing to be ashamed of.

"I, uh…" I pull my phone out of my pocket and hand it to him. "Can you put in your number? I can text you and when you get home safely, you can text me back, so I know you guys didn't freeze to death or some shit."

He eyes the phone for the longest time and then he takes it from me, his rough fingertips grazing along my palm sending a tingle of awareness shooting through me. Quickly, he enters in his number before tossing my phone back at me. While he gathers his backpack and climbs out, I text him.

Me: This is Hollis.

Feels formal as fuck, but I don't know what else to say to the guy. He doesn't respond, but instead busies himself with getting his sister out of the car.

"Bye, Roux," I call out through the still open front door of the car. "See you Wednesday, I guess."

She smiles and waves at me. "Bye, Hollis."

Roan doesn't even look at me. Simply slams the door shut and walks off, his arm slung over his sister's shoulders in a protective way.

I don't drive off.

Just watch them walk away.

Alone. In the dark. Snow billowing all around them.

Fuck if my heart doesn't squeeze inside my chest with worry.

The asshole better text me back.

Chapter Six

Roan

I hate this place, but I especially hate it at night. Most everyone leaves me the fuck alone because they know I'll kick their ass if they don't. But it's dangerous for a teenage girl.

Pulling Roux to my side, we weave our way through the parking lot, steering clear of any groups of people. This complex is a haven for drug deals. A few guys call out to me. I acknowledge them with a head nod, but don't further engage.

"Charlotte is my best friend," Roux chirps happily. "We're going to have slumber parties every weekend. She said her mom will take us roller skating. Did you know she used to have a python, but she had to leave it with her dad when she moved?"

I can't help but smile as Roux rattles on. She hasn't been this excited in God knows how long. Truth is, Roux has a hard time at life. Her mom is worthless. Her dad is doing life in prison for shooting and killing three men during a bar fight. And the kids at school are fucking monsters to her. All she has is me.

And now Charlotte.

It makes me uneasy because I know how kids can be. Especially the pretty popular ones. They're vicious and mean.

What happens if Charlotte realizes Roux doesn't have any friends? Will she leave her behind for the cool kids?

That thought angers me.

I swallow it down, though, and focus on getting up to the third floor in one piece. Several assholes glower at me like they might start some shit, but I crack my neck and eyeball them back. In the end, they leave us alone. As we walk up to our apartment, I notice smoke sliding out from underneath the door.

What the fuck?

I touch the handle, but it's cold.

"Hold this," I tell Roux, passing off the leftovers as I unlock the door.

With the turn of the knob, I open the door and push it open. Thick, gray smoke billows out.

"Stay here," I instruct as I rush in. "Mom? Alexander?"

Nothing.

They're not home.

I choke and wave my hand in the air as I make my way into the kitchen. A fucking pot of macaroni is cooking, but the water has long since evaporated. It's charred to black and smoking. With a growl, I turn off the stove and then toss the pot into the sink. Once I fill it with water, I open a couple of windows and head back to Roux.

"Is our apartment on fire?" she squeaks.

I scrub my palm down my face, fighting exhaustion. "No, but it's smoky. I'm going to call Mike and have him come check it out for us. Make sure we can sleep here tonight."

Roux sits down on the dirty carpet and pulls out one of her novels. While she reads, I call one of my mom's few ex-boyfriends who was worth a damn. Of course he smartened up and moved on. It just sucked we got left behind too.

"This is Mike."

"Hey, man," I grunt out. "How busy are you tonight?"

"Never too busy for you or Roux."

I let out a sigh of relief. "Great. So, uh, Mom or Alexander left something on the stove. The apartment is filled with smoke—"

"Don't go inside. I'm on my way," he says, immediately going into fireman mode.

"I already did. Got the stove turned off and the pot in water. I opened a couple of windows."

"That was dangerous, Roan," he chides. "You could have been exposed to toxic smoke."

"I know, I know," I grumble. "You don't have to bring the firetruck—"

My words are cut off by the wail of a siren on his end.

So much for that.

As I wait, I notice my phone has been blowing up in my pocket. I wouldn't even have a phone—neither would Trey or Jordy for that matter—if it weren't for Cal getting his dad to put us on their family plan. We pay him ten bucks a month each for the added lines. Sometimes I don't know what I'd do without the added security of being able to call someone like Ms. Frazier if I need help with Roux or when I need a ride from one of my boys.

Unknown Number: This is Hollis.

I add the number in as "Rat," and it changes all the texts from him, which are a lot.

Rat: Are you safe?

Rat: Do I need to come get you guys?

Rat: I know you hate me, but just reply, okay?

Rat: You don't have to be a dick about it.

With a sigh, I reply.

Me: We're fine. Get off my nuts, rat.

The dots move and stop. Move and stop. I smile, wondering what sort of flustered look he has on his face right now.

Rat: Do you need a ride to school tomorrow?

Fuck no. The whole reason I had him drop us off was so he didn't get his car jacked by some tweaker. You can't ride around in a car like his in my neighborhood. It's a good way to put a target on your back. And if the fuckers who live at this apartment complex with us thought we had money, they might not let Roux and I just walk on by.

Me: I said back the fuck off. You're not my girlfriend, though you do have dick sucking lips.

I'm being a mean bastard, but I don't care. He needs to leave me the fuck alone. We're not friends. Just because Ms. Frazier and I have our deal, it doesn't mean he gets to saunter into my life and be a part of it.

Rat: Okay.

I'd expected fire back from him. More angry words. Maybe even no response at all. Anything other than okay. Such a defeated answer. I hate how guilt settles all around me like the smoke from the apartment—choking and tainting me.

The moment I hear the sirens, I tuck my phone away and let relief flood through me. Maybe they can clear us to go inside and then I can finally relax. It's been a helluva long day.

Minutes later, three firemen show up. Mike, tall and burly, walks over to us. The other two firemen head into the apartment while he squats in front of where we're sitting.

"Hey, kiddos. How's it going?" He smiles at Roux. "Where's your mom?"

I scoff at his question. "Who the fuck knows."

His lips thin out and he glances down the hallway. "She at Popper's?"

Popper's. The topless bar down the street. Fucking gross.

"If she was, Alexander would be home. They're both out." When Mom's not flashing her tits for money, she's laid up in bed with Alexander. If they're both gone, that means they're off getting drugs together.

"I should call this in to CPS."

I shoot him a nasty glare. "I'm eighteen, Mike. I'm looking after Roux. For fuck's sake, don't do that to me."

He softens and sighs. "Yeah, yeah, I know. I just want to know who looks out for you, Roan. Sure as hell not your momma." When I don't respond, he stands. "I'll check it out. I think you should be fine to stay, though I wish you wouldn't."

"If we can't stay, I'll call Cal's dad," I assure him, but it's a lie. I only call Cal's dad when I've called everyone else—Ms. Frazier, Jordy, Cal, and Trey.

He stares at me long enough to make me fidget, and then he walks into the apartment.

"I'm tired," Roux says. "When can we go to bed?"

"Won't be long," I assure her, hugging her to my side. "What movie are we watching tonight? *The Goonies* sounds good."

"Not that one again!" she says, giggling. "We should watch *To All the Boys I've Loved Before*."

"Dude," I playfully grumble. "We've watched that one like seventeen times this month alone. Nope. Not happening." We both know it's happening. I can recite that damn movie by heart now.

"Maybe Hollis can watch *The Goonies* with you and Charlotte can watch *To All the Boys I've Loved Before* with me at our slumber party."

I freeze at her words. There's no way in hell I'm sleeping over at Hollis's house. But would I really let Roux go without me? I take her everywhere. Even to Campfire Chaos. Thank fuck Cal's mom loves her like a granddaughter and looks after her on Friday nights. It gives me one night of social freedom.

"We'll see."

"That wasn't a no."

"It wasn't a yes either, twerp."

Our playful banter is cut short when Mike and his guys step back into the hallway.

"All's clear, but leave the windows open until bed," Mike instructs. "I want an update later. Text me."

He hugs us both and then the three of them leave. Mike was like the dad we should have had. Instead of the one who left us eight years ago in the back of a squad car and never came back. Too bad Mom couldn't get her shit together to keep him.

"Ew," Roux complains. "It stinks."

"Nah, you stink worse," I tease. "Grab a shower and we'll watch the movie."

As she scampers off, I set to cleaning up the mess Alexander and Mom left. There are clothes all over the living room floor, which is fucking disgusting. Underwear. A bra. Condom wrapper. I don't want Roux seeing that shit, so with mounting frustration, I clean it all up. When I find a burnt-up spoon barely kicked under the old ratty sofa, I lose it.

What the fuck?

Heroin?

I'm glad Mike and the guys didn't see this. He would've sure as fuck called CPS. I speed clean the rest of the apartment, including the charred pot, before closing the windows that are blowing in chilly air. By the time I make it to our bedroom, I'm tired as hell. I'm glad I already showered at Ms. Frazier's.

"*The Hunger Games*," I state as I walk into the room, flicking off the lights. "You never cease to surprise me, kid."

"I figured we needed something different." She curls up on her twin bed, hugging her pillow to her.

I kick off my shoes and sprawl out on my bed. "You okay, Roux?"

"Yeah. You?"

"I'm good." I let out a heavy sigh. "I'm gonna get us out of here one day."

"I know."

"Don't ever forget."

"Never."

I wake to laughing. Loud and high-pitched. Mom. She's fucked up from the sound of it. Music blares from the living room. God, I fucking hate her sometimes. Yawning, I roll over and grab my phone.

Four sixteen.

What is wrong with these people?

I should have just gone over to Cal's. David, Cal's dad,

would have given me hell about my mom and shit, but he would've let us stay. Now they're going to wake up Roux and she's already struggling in school enough as it is without losing sleep on top of it all. I'm just about to tell them to shut the fuck up when the door flings open. A massive body fills the doorway.

Alexander.

I tense up, sitting up in the bed.

"Where's Roux?" he slurs.

I'm on my feet in the next instant. "Get the fuck out of our room."

"Don't talk to me like that, shitstain." He laughs, swaying in the doorway. "Roux and I are gonna play a game."

"You're not playing shit with Roux." I storm around her bed and shove him into the hallway. "Stay the fuck away from my sister."

Alexander is bigger than me and is always packing heat, but he's so damn wasted all the time he's no match for my youth. He recovers and swings at me. I get clipped on my cheekbone by his fist, but I dodge most of it. Slinging my elbow up, I nail him in the nose. He makes a groaning sound and then stumbles back to the other bedroom he shares with Mom. I hear her fussing over him, which pisses me off.

"Tell your dickhead boyfriend to stay the fuck away from us, Mom."

I don't wait for an answer. I stalk into the living room to unplug all the shit making noise. An empty Tupperware container that once held lasagna sits on the coffee table where Alexander and Mom must have dug in. That small thing sets me off more than anything that's transpired tonight. They know I bring that shit home for Roux and they don't care.

Selfish motherfuckers. I grind my teeth all the way back to our room. As soon as I get the door closed, I drag our dresser over to it to keep that fucker out.

Eventually, I fall back into bed, exhausted as hell. I'm just drifting to sleep when I hear Mom's loud ass moans and the headboard hitting the wall.

Anger bleeds from me and defeat consumes me in the darkness.

Why is life so fucking hard?

I just want to be normal and have normalcy for Roux.

Thankfully Alexander doesn't last long. By five in the morning, I'm drifting back to sleep. I fall asleep imagining a life where we can relax. Where Roux is safe. Where we don't have to drag dressers in front of the door or put out kitchen fires.

And then, I think of *him*.

He's the last thought on my mind before I pass out completely.

Hollis the pretty fucking rat.

Chapter Seven

Hollis

My phone buzzes in my pocket as I pull into the school parking lot. This time, I avoid parking next to the Ford Explorer and choose a spot several rows back. Of course, in the empty lot, I stick out like a sore thumb. With an annoyed sigh, I swipe open my phone.

Lucas: Saw your dad last night. He looks like shit.

I'm irritated that when I finally get a message from Lucas, it's referring to my father, not catching up.

Me: Yeah? Why?

Lucas: I don't know. Just looked tired and angry.

Me: That's his signature look. How are you doing? How're Jamie and Wendell?

I know I sound fucking desperate, but I ache for my old life. When it was filled with friendship and laughter. Where Lucas and I would flirt all the time and most everyone chalked it up to a bromance. How we'd sneak off and make out, sometimes jacking each other off within earshot of our teammates.

Lucas: Jamie's still a dumbass. Wendell's out for the season. Broke his ankle.

I wince, knowing how much this hurts the team. Wendell was one of the best.

Me: Fuck. That sucks.

The reply back is instant, but it takes me a second to realize it's not him.

Roan: You too good to park next to Jordy?

I lift my gaze to see Roan leaned against the back of Jordy's Ford Explorer as Jordy stalks my way. My heart rate stammers wildly as I wonder why in the hell this guy is headed my way like I've done something to him.

He walks right up to my door and flings it open, his body tight with barely contained rage. This dude has serious anger issues.

"You got a fuckin' problem with me, rat?" he snarls, cracking his thick neck.

Jesus, now they're both calling me that shitty nickname.

"Nope," I grumble.

"Get out of your car." He thrums with violence.

"Nah, I'm good right here."

The fucker pounces on me, yanking me out of the car. I drop my phone in the process. Jordy shoves me to the dirty, snowy pavement. The wet, cold slop saturates through my jeans before I manage to jump to my feet.

"He's not worth it," Roan calls out to his friend, approaching the two of us. "You'd hit him and he'd break. Little porcelain doll."

Jordy's lip curls up. "You thought my piece of shit was going to door ding your gay-ass purple car?"

I try not to flinch at the word "gay," but it's too late. I've done it and Roan zeroes in on it with narrowed eyes. I'm not ashamed of being gay, but it's times like these that people make it really fucking difficult.

"I just wanted to avoid this," I hiss, waving between us. "A stupid altercation over nothing."

Jordy charges for me, shoving me again. I don't fall down this time and fist my hands. Sure, I've never fought, but that doesn't mean I won't go down without swinging at his psycho ass.

"Let's go," Roan grumbles. "You'll get your ass expelled, Jordy."

"And I give a fuck, why?" Jordy throws back.

Roan grabs his jaw, turning him so they can face off. "I need you. Roux and I both do."

This seems to dismantle the bomb. I guess underneath all Jordy's psychopathic tendencies, he has a conscience. Carting around his best friend and his little sister are what gives him purpose, it would seem.

I'm thinking I've managed to go unscathed when a loud, big black truck whips into the parking lot. The dual exhaust is obnoxious and deafening. Thankfully it cuts off as he parks crookedly right beside my car. The three of us have to step close to my car to avoid getting run over. At least there is distance between me and Jordy. He's near the hood of my car with Roan and I'm closer to the trunk. The driver of the big truck flings his door open with no regard to my car.

Thunk.

"What the hell?" I grind out, rushing over to inspect the damage.

A big ass guy steps out of the truck and slams the door shut. Someone shuts the door on the other side, but I can't see over the vehicle. I stare up at a guy taller than either Roan or Jordy. The guy has a baseball cap on, flipped backward, and his big green eyes burn into me. He'd be cute in a country boy kind of way if he didn't have the same mean look to him that Roan and Jordy do.

"Oops." He smirks unkindly at me. "My bad."

"Fuckin' Cal," Jordy says with a snort from behind him.

Our eyes travel together to the dent in the top of the upper doorframe that takes up the entire three-inch width. Unbelievable. I'm about to go off on this asshole when I feel a presence behind me. A quick glance behind me and I realize it's Roan's friend I saw briefly leaving Aunt Karen's office yesterday. Fucking wonderful. Four assholes all present and accounted for, ready to kick my ass for no goddamn reason.

And, on cue, my stomach decides to choose this moment to give me problems. Nausea burns up my esophagus, making me feel like I'm going to puke. Dizziness washes over me and blackness eats at the edge of my vision.

I'm going to pass out.

I start to collapse, falling toward Cal. He shoves me right into the guy behind me. That guy pushes me to the asphalt. Protecting my face, I curl into myself, waiting for the abuse. I don't know what to expect, but with four of them, it can't be good. I'm groaning, trying hard not to throw up, when a foot nudges me.

"Get up." Roan. "Now."

I blink back the dizziness, wishing like hell I wouldn't have turned my nose up to biscuits and gravy this morning. I should have eaten.

"Rat," Roan snaps, a little more forcefully. "I said get the fuck up."

Shakily, I sit up. The world spins around me. Roan, who's now squatted in front of me, seems to go around and around like I'm on a merry go round. I reach out, grabbing his shoulder, to steady myself. Surprisingly, he doesn't shake me away and hauls me to my feet. I lean against my car, praying like hell I don't pass out. That was too close.

"What's your problem?" he demands. "Are you sick?"

"You saw what he did to my car," I spit out. "You'd be sick too."

"Poor, spoiled baby. You have a dent in your precious car. I bet the world feels like it's fucking end—"

Everything goes black.

"Whoa, man, why are you so pale?"

I'm vaguely aware of being manhandled back into my front seat. My clothes are wet and dirty, but all I can worry about is making the world stop spinning.

I close my eyes, willing the episode to pass.

"Hollis? Are you okay?"

I blink my eyes open in confusion to see Aunt Karen standing in front of my open car door. How much time has gone by?

"Aunt Karen?"

"You're white as a ghost, honey," she says, reaching in to run her palm over my forehead. "Clammy too. I'm going to run you home. I'll call Kels—"

"No!" I bark out. "Mom just started her job. Please don't make her feel like she has to leave to come deal with me." I let out a heavy sigh. "I didn't eat anything."

"Hollis Nathaniel English," she chides. "You know better than that."

"Sorry. I just...maybe I can sit here until it passes."

"I'll grab you a soda and some crackers. Sit tight." Then, to Roan who's hovering nearby, she says, "Please stay with him until I get back. I'll write you a pass."

"Happy to help," he says with false cheer.

"Don't look so eager to get out of class," she grumbles.

As soon as she disappears, Roan opens the passenger side door and sits down like we're best fucking pals. I groan and try to ignore him.

"You look like shit, rat."

"Fuck off."

"You dropped this," he says, handing me my phone with a now cracked screen back. "Your boyfriend has been blowing up your phone."

I see several missed texts from Lucas, one of which he admits he misses me. Knowing Roan has seen this causes anger to spark inside of me, chasing away the ill feeling.

"Is this the same guy you were kissing in the picture?" he probes, his voice low and demanding. "Or a different one? How many guys do you have exactly?"

I turn my head to look at him. He's wearing me out. Instead of responding to his stupid questions, I stare at him. Dark shadows beneath his eyes that weren't there before now stand out, showing me he isn't the only one having a bad day. It makes me wonder what kept him up so late. Sure as hell wasn't studying. I don't know much about the guy, but I can deduce he's not a studier.

"If you hate school, what do you plan to do after this?" I ask, voicing my question.

It catches him off guard because for a second, he seems scared and unsure. And that's not right because he's fucking Roan. A prick who's quite sure of himself.

"We're not friends," he reminds me.

"So?"

"So I'm not giving you my life story."

"I was just asking for your future."

Our eyes meet and his amber ones blaze with intensity. It's a shame he's such an asshole. He's hot. Really hot. Distractingly so. I crave to push away the overgrown fallen lock of hair that hangs over one brow that I know is pierced. I want to see the piercing up close and wonder if he's pierced elsewhere. This guy is a dick, and yet I still want to touch him.

"I want to be a fireman."

I'm so stunned he responded, all I can do is gape. "For real?"

Anger flashes over his features. "I didn't say it would fucking happen. You just asked what I wanted. Whatever, man."

"Don't be so sensitive," I grumble back. "It was just a question."

His body relaxes. "I know this guy Mike. He's a fireman. Cool as hell. Loves his job."

Imagining Roan all decked out and sweaty in fireman gear is enough to make me want to faint all over again. Rather than embarrass myself, I close my eyes.

"I used to want to be a doctor."

"Used to?" His voice is gruff.

"My dad's a doctor. We're not speaking anymore. Trying to figure out what I want to do now."

"You look more like a substitute teacher if you ask me."

And you look like an angry underwear model.

"No one asked," I say instead.

Roan's not so bad when he's not under the influence of his friends.

"What are you doing after school?" he asks, his voice tight with some sort of hidden emotion.

"Going home."

"Nope. Pick up Charlotte and bring her to basketball practice. Roux never has anyone to talk to." He starts to get out of the car as Aunt Karen makes her way toward the parking lot from the building. I grab his arm to stop him.

"I'm not an errand boy." I huff. "Besides, what would I do?"

"Play ball with us." He shrugs. "I saw your jersey in the picture. Figured you played."

"And snooped in my texts," I grit out. "How did you even get into my phone anyway?"

"Face ID. Yours."

"You seriously broke into my phone using my face while I was passed out?"

"Yep. Held your eyes open for you and everything."

"Unbelievable."

"Believe it, rat."

"Fine."

"Fine, what?"

"I'll pick Charlotte up and bring her to the gymnasium. Penny has to come too, though."

He smiles—real and beautiful. "I like that broody kid."

"Are we…is this a truce?"

His features darken. "No. It's you helping my fucking sister be happy because it's the right thing to do."

"Which makes you happy," I bite back. "What the hell do I get out of it?"

"You keep from getting your ass kicked. I'll call off the dogs."

"For how long?"

"Depends on how long your sister stays friends with Roux."

"Feels like blackmail."

"Feels like the truth."

Chapter Eight

Roan

Defeated.

Exhausted.

Ruined.

I know the feeling. I live it every day. For some reason, I'm fascinated with seeing it so blatantly displayed on someone else. Hollis. He's still wearing the dirty pair of jeans from this morning, but it's long since dried. I track him as he walks into the lunchroom. Alone.

"That kid is such a pussy," Cal says with a laugh. "Did you see him nearly piss his pants this morning?"

Jordy growls. "The rat needs to watch his back."

"What did he do to piss you guys off anyway?" Trey asks as he shoves a handful of fries into his mouth. "Did he fuck your mom, Cal?"

"Don't be a dick," Cal bites out, whacking Trey's hand and sending his new handful of fries scattering across the table.

"He's a rich asshole who thinks he's better than us," Jordy snaps. "And he knows about Roux."

Cal and Trey sober up.

"He's messing with Roux?" Trey demands, popping his knuckles. "That's not right, man."

With a sigh, I finally speak. "He's Ms. Frazier's nephew. Hollis lives there."

"No shit?" Cal gapes at me from across the table. "Is he threatening to tell about your deal with his aunt?"

"Nah," I say, "I already told him he's not allowed to."

"If the rat tries to use Roux against Roan, he'll fucking pay," Jordy warns.

My eyes drift back over to Hollis. He's standing in line, now smiling brightly at some nerd and Sidney. Of course Sidney would be all up on his nuts. He's the hot new kid. I'm surprised she hasn't charmed him into her bed yet. Sid's fucked every single one of us at this table except Jordy. Some of us more than a few times. That someone being me.

She notices my staring and makes a deliberate attempt to flirt with Hollis in an apparent effort to make me jealous. His smile is fake as fuck, but she believes it. I'm pretty sure he's gay. Sidney is barking up the wrong tree. For some reason, this satisfies me. Not because I'm jealous of him sleeping with Sidney. I don't even like Sidney most days. I just…I don't think he needs to fuck her.

The nerd speaks up and somehow manages to engage Sidney in talking to him. Her flirtation fades as she has a serious conversation with the kid. Hollis seems to be relieved at the loss of her attention. He stares hard at the menu board, his jaw clenching. They go through the line and where the other two emerge with trays, he walks out holding an apple.

What the fuck?

I know he eats. I saw him eat at dinner last night. He barely touched the lasagna but filled up on bread and salad. I'd think he has some kind of stupid, prissy rich kid eating disorder, but now I'm not so sure. He has a muscular body. I caught a glimpse of his stomach yesterday and felt his biceps when I moved him to his car this morning. You don't get fit like that and not eat. It's like he's sick.

My heart thuds hard in my chest, confusing me.

I get that nervous, worried feeling whenever something is wrong with Roux. Not some random kid I met yesterday and whom I also hate.

They sit at a table and he waves off offerings from both Sidney and the nerd. At least they notice it too. It's strange he's not eating.

"You think he's fucking her?" Cal gestures toward them.

"Sidney is Hornet property," Jordy snaps, challenging me with a glare to argue. "We'll make sure he doesn't."

I nod, not because she's our property, but because I don't think Hollis will fuck her anyway. "I thought you didn't like Sidney."

Jordy's dark eyes glitter evilly. "I don't. She's your and Cal and Trey's little slut."

"Awfully protective of our little slut," Cal teases him, batting his lashes at him in a dramatic way.

Jordy cracks a smile. "Do you always have to be an idiot?"

"Only always," Cal says seriously, making me and Trey snort.

"We're done with her," I offer. "You seem like you could get laid. Maybe time to finally hit that."

"And catch whatever STIs you assholes are carrying? Fuck that," Jordy says, taking a bite of his burger and talking over his chewing. "She's all yours."

He's just fucking with us. My boys may like to fuck, but they use condoms. We all do.

Trey launches into a heated story about the fight he

had with his grandma over getting detention. I'm only half listening because my gaze drifts back to Hollis. He nibbles at his apple, grimacing with each swallow.

What's going on with you, rat?

As though he can hear my inner thoughts, he lifts his gaze. His long, thick lashes seem to make his blue eyes pop out like bright stones in a clear lake. Because of his episode this morning and only eating an apple, his skin is stark white. He looks tired and his hand trembles when he rubs at the back of his neck. Our eyes never leave the other. I know he's staring at me, but I don't care at the moment. When he licks his plump, pink lips, heat burns down my spine. I'm embarrassed and should look away, but I don't.

I fixate on how his lips now glisten.

I drag my stare along his pale throat, noticing the bulge of his Adam's apple and wonder if it protrudes when he takes Lucas's cock.

I'm sporting a chub in my sweats, which is fucked considering I hate this kid. I've never been attracted to a guy before. I like sex and have plenty of it…*with girls*. But my curiosity is strong. My mouth waters to taste him. To bite him. To kiss him.

Images of his mouth on mine are not bad ones. I don't feel ashamed or grossed out. No, I'm fucking turned on. With a groan, I scrub my palm down my face before tearing my stare from him. Trey is imitating his grandma, so I lose myself to his hilarious story.

Don't look.

Don't look.

I look a few times.

I'm distracted and practicing like shit. My eyes keep drifting to where Hollis sits with his sisters and mine on the bleachers in the gym. Coach Rendell is running us hard and I want to fall to the ground and die.

Trey dribbles easily past me and throws the ball to Wyatt, who shoots. They make the basket and Coach yells at me.

"Come on, Hirsch! Would you rather play dolls with the girls?"

I grunt and try to focus on the next play. I'm tearing down the court when I hear Roux's giggles. The ball falls from my grip and rolls out of bounds right over to Hollis. Coach yells at me again. Ignoring him, I trot up to them.

Hollis picks up the ball and throws it at me. Hard. Challenge gleams in his stare. Because I'm a dick, I throw it back at him, harder. Hoping to knock him on his ass. He catches it like it's no big thing. We go back and forth, throwing the basketball to each other, harder and harder. Then, instead of throwing it back, he takes off with it. Flashes right by me, dribbling fast. I turn around to see him sidestep Jordy's crazy ass, outrun Cal's long legs, and then shoot over Trey's arms trying to block it. The fucker makes the basket from the three-point line.

Everyone just stares at Hollis.

"You go to school here?" Coach asks him.

"It's Principal Frazier's nephew," Brody reveals like he's a fucking gossip girl.

"No shit?" Coach grins. "Want to practice with us today?"

I expect Hollis to shrug him off or something, but he nods, an easy smile on his face. "Yeah. I'd like that."

Jordy shoots a death glare at him. Cal and Trey don't seem impressed either. I'm annoyed as fuck. Coach is going to want to replace me with a rat. Unbelievable.

The rest of practice, Hollis annihilates. He dominates the court. It's surprising because he's shorter than anyone on the team and just looks so…pretty and breakable. And considering he passed out this morning and only ate an apple, my mind is reeling.

Who is this kid?

I always have basketball. Even with Mom being a shit parent, and me taking care of Roux, I have this. Something I'm good at and call my own. Now, it feels as though it's being taken away from me. Hollis has infiltrated my life in every aspect. School. Job. My sister's friends. Basketball. Anger swells up inside of me. I know it's probably unfair to blame him, but I do. Fuck him for being perfect at everything.

We're all dripping with sweat and dying by the time practice ends. Coach tells Hollis to hit the showers and to grab some of the extra clothes to borrow since his are drenched. I shoot a look Roux's way and when I see her happily talking with Charlotte and Penny on the bleachers, I head for the locker room.

Several guys are already undressing and talking to Hollis like he's on the fucking team. Jordy, Trey, and Cal all give him dirty looks. I know mine rivals theirs. As soon as Hollis's smiling face looks my way, he flinches.

Damn right.

I hope he feels my anger radiating from me.

Is this how Dad felt all those times before he kicked someone's ass?

The thought sobers me up and I breathe out heavily,

trying to expel some of my dad's rage. Hollis must sense my fury because he retreats toward the showers. He pulls off his hoodie and shirt, dropping them on a bench along the way. I take in his sculpted back and muscular shoulders. His hips are narrow and his jeans hang off his ass enough to reveal his black Hugo Boss underwear band. I'm still staring when he shoves his jeans down, showing off the tight globes of his ass.

"Who the fuck does he think he is?" Jordy demands, coming to stand beside me. "Coach acted like he was some basketball god. I'll be damned if he plays on this team."

I tear my eyes from Hollis when he pushes down his underwear. I'm not going to lust over my fucking nemesis, especially when I don't even understand why I feel this way in the first place. My dick may be confused, but my mind knows exactly what's up. Hollis is a little bitch who's getting in my way.

"His aunt is the principal, man," I bite out. "Coach will put him in."

"I'll make sure he doesn't play," Jordy threatens. "Hard to play ball with broken wrists."

I sling my arm over Jordy's shoulders. "We'll figure out some other way to knock him down a few pegs. Don't take this away from Roux."

Defeated, Jordy relaxes. "I never heard her laugh like that, Roan. Ever."

"She likes Charlotte a lot. Unfortunately, Charlotte is Hollis's little sister. We just need to be careful where the girls are concerned."

He nods. "I may hate that kid, but I'd never do Roux dirty. You know that."

"I do and that's why you're my best friend."

I stick my tongue in his ear just to piss him off. He shoves me away and swipes at his ear, laughing. Truth be told, Jordy's laugh is one I don't hear often either. It's a good sound. A real good sound.

The four of us cut up while we undress. Hollis is leaving the showers as we enter. I stay back and nod for my friends to keep going. My towel is wadded up in my hand, covering my junk, thank fuck, because my body is reacting to his.

Why does this asshole have to look so good?

With his hair wet, it no longer looks blond, but instead brown. Water rivulets run down his muscular pecs and down his tight abs. His obliques are a beacon, directing the eye down to where his towel is wrapped at his waist, covering his dick. The blond hair below his belly button glistens and my mouth waters wondering what he tastes like right there.

"Keep staring at me like that and people are going to wonder," he says, his voice low and meant only for me.

I walk right up to him, our noses nearly touching. "Wonder what, rat?"

"Why Roan is sporting a hard-on for the new guy."

Smug ass motherfucker.

"I don't have a hard-on, freak."

His lips twist up on one side in a half grin. Blue eyes twinkle with mischief. "But you will."

My jaw clenches. "You're fucking with danger."

"I can't help that danger looks so good."

What is this?

Is he fucking flirting with me?

I grab one of his shoulders to push him away, but my greedy hand won't let go. I'm transfixed by the way his muscles feel in my grip.

"Don't forget that I hate you," I snarl, squeezing his shoulder.

He breaks free from my grasp. "Don't forget that you hate me when you're jerking off later."

With those words, he leaves me with the hard-on he promised.

Fuck him.

Problem is, I kind of want to.

Chapter Nine

Hollis

Me: I made the team.

Lucas responds immediately.

Lucas: You told me you weren't trying out!

Me: It sort of happened.

Lucas: Of course it did. Story of your life, golden boy. All the good things fall into your lap.

Like you, I think bitterly. *But then you ended it.*

Me: So who's the lucky lady nowadays?

The dots move and then stop. I frown as I wait for him to respond. Ten agonizing minutes later, he sends me a text.

Lucas: Eric.

Eric? Eric from our team Eric? Eric, who last I checked, was dating some college chick?

Me: Ha ha.

Lucas: Truth, man. People know now…that I'm bi. I worried over nothing.

Acid burns in my gut. For months, we slept around in secret, kissed in corners, and kept our friendship turned lovers relationship on the down-low. And in the few weeks I've been gone, he's suddenly come out and openly dating someone from our team?

Me: Congrats.

"Who pissed in your Cheerios?"

I nearly drop my phone and dart my head up. Roan stands in the doorway of my room, his hands gripping the doorframe as he leans in. It does amazing things for his biceps, making them strain against his T-shirt. The bottom of his shirt rises up to reveal toned, tanned flesh.

"What?" I stammer, dragging my stare from his body and back to his face.

"You look irritated and you hadn't even seen me yet." He flashes me a smug grin.

Truth is, I saw him plenty today. I didn't have any altercations in the parking lot like yesterday, but the Hornets did give me shit. I guess my showing them up on the court yesterday didn't sit too well. The school day was almost over today when I was called into my aunt's office where Coach Rendell was asking if I wanted to join the team. It'd been surreal and I said yes, because for the first time since I'd moved to Horn River, I felt wanted.

"Don't you have attics to clean?" I grumble, the venom missing in my words.

"I'd much rather bug you."

I let my eyes skim over his appearance again. He didn't take a shower after practice today, no doubt knowing Aunt Karen would make him do dirty, sweaty chores. My mouth waters as I wonder how salty he would taste if I ran my tongue up the side of his throat.

"You should have eaten lunch, rat," he says, releasing the

doorframe to step into my room. "You're looking awfully hungry."

The air seems charged, but I don't say anything to make it spark.

"Dinner will be ready in an hour," Aunt Karen chirps, making us both startle as she peeks her head in the door. "Roan, hon, I was thinking instead of the attic, you could dismantle my desk and move it into my bedroom. I'm hoping to give Hollis a little more space." She winks at me.

"Yeah," Roan says, "I'll get right on it."

She leaves us and he saunters the rest of the way into the room. His attention is on the desk as he inspects it. My phone continues to buzz, no doubt texts from Lucas, but I'm no longer mad at him. I'd much rather watch Roan take apart a desk while I imagine him taking my ass over it.

He leaves, and I'm assuming to grab tools. I take the moment to gather my wits and reply back to Lucas's texts.

Lucas: It's nothing serious.

Lucas: You're not mad are you?

Lucas: I like Eric, but we don't have the connection you and I did.

Lucas: If you hadn't moved away, you know it would be you.

Lucas: Text me back when you're not pissed at me.

He then sends a picture of his abs as though that will fix everything. When we'd been dating in secret, we sent dirty pictures back and forth a lot. I'd enjoyed the thrill back then, but his abs are just abs to me. I don't have the spike in body temperature or the rapid beating of my heart or the instant hard-on. No, my body responds to one guy in particular now. My fuck-hot enemy.

Me: We're cool. Just have to study. Talk soon. Tell Eric I said hi.

I leave it at that. He responds with smiling emojis. I'm feeling slightly sorry for myself when Roan enters the room. He tosses the tools on the bed beside me and then sets to pulling stuff off Aunt Karen's desk.

"Need help?" I ask, my eyes roaming down his muscular back and to his nice ass.

"Nope."

"Fine, I'll just watch."

He looks over his shoulder and smirks, sending a ripple of heat rushing through my veins. "Suit yourself."

Annoyed at my eagerness to stare at him, I snatch my algebra book out of my bag and start to work on my homework. "Did you already do the assignment in Henley's class?"

Roan laughs. "No."

"Do you plan on doing it?"

"Fuck no."

"It's worth twenty-five points."

"So?"

"So you kinda need this class to graduate."

"I'll pass."

He's getting pissy now, tossing stuff onto the floor off the desk. One thing I'm learning about Roan is when you poke at his touchy subjects, he responds with defensive anger.

"I could help you," I offer.

He jerks his head my way, a sneer on his face. "In trade for what?"

"Why does there have to be a trade? Why can't I just help you?"

"I don't want your help." He snags up a small Allen wrench and kneels to start with the first screw.

"You could be nice to me. That's a fair trade," I grumble.

"I'm already being nice."

I scoff. "This is your version of nice? Maybe I ought to tutor you in that department too."

At this, he laughs. The sound is throaty and goes right to my dick. "This house is neutral ground. I already told you."

Oh, God. He's being serious. This is as nice as he gets.

"I could fix your dent," he says, his back to me.

Fix my dent?

"On my car?"

He nods and shoots me a serious look. "Jordy's brother owns a garage. Sometimes when they're overloaded, I go in and help. The money's under the table, but it helps me save it away for when Roux and I get the hell out of here."

"Where are you going?"

He lets out a heavy sigh. "Not far since I still need Ms. Frazier to help her. But an apartment of our own."

"What about your parents?"

"Dad's in prison," he states in an icy tone. "Mom is unfit as fuck."

I think about my mom and how wonderful she is. How she gave up her entire life and marriage to protect me from my father's anger. It makes my chest ache to think of her not loving or caring about me. No wonder Roan is such a dick.

"So you think you'd be awarded custody?"

"I don't know. It's not like Mom would fight me on it."

Tossing the book to the side, I stand and walk over to

him. "I can help you. Here. Whenever you finish what you do for my aunt. If you really are planning to take care of Roux, you can't fuck up school."

He rolls his eyes and his jaw clenches. "You sound like Ms. Frazier."

"Maybe because it's sound advice you need to hear."

"I don't accept help for free. So let me fix the dent and we'll be even."

"Deal," I agree. "But you can't be an asshole. Let me help you without all this grumpiness."

"No deal. I can't change who I am."

I step closer, drawn to his salty scent. "Then here, when it's just the two of us, change for me. You said it was neutral ground. Let it be neutral. Drop the tough guy act. I'm not some dick who's going to exploit you."

He grits his teeth and pokes my chest. "People aren't nice for no reason."

"There's a reason," I tell him, my voice husky. "We both know my reason."

Him.

His lips press together to form a thin line as his copper eyes study me. I take note that his skin turns slightly pink. Beneath all the asshole exterior is a vulnerable boy curious about the one in front of him. It gives me hope. If I can crack him, maybe he'll let me in.

Why do I want to be let in?

Because he's different. I'm drawn to him. He's fucking hot. So hot it hurts a little to look at him sometimes. I want his smiles directed my way. I've never wanted a guy in my entire life as much as I want Roan.

"I know you're not gay," I tell him boldly.

"You don't know shit."

My brow lifts. "Sidney said you two…er, dated."

"We fucked," he says bluntly. "Plenty of times. She's not my type, though."

"What is your type?"

"Not her."

"Are you bi?"

"I'm nothing."

His words, spoken softly and with such pain, cut into me. Not a gory slash. The kind that dives deep, slicing through every internal organ along the way. With every pulse of my heart, I bleed for him.

"You're not nothing." I step closer and lift my chin to look at him. We're inches apart. Any other guy and I would've already made my move. I feel the heat that burns hot between us, but he's too brittle. I have an urge to protect him. Even from me.

He leans in, bringing his mouth close to my ear, brushing it barely. "Careful, rat, I might think you care."

His awful nickname for me doesn't feel awful at all. It's a breathy caress. An endearment.

"Have you ever kissed a guy?" My words tumble from my lips in a whisper.

"No." Then, in a way meant to hurt me, he says, "Don't plan on it either."

I'm not scared away, though. If anything, it makes me want to taunt him further. Make him face what he feels deep inside, because clearly it's not far off from how I feel. We may hate each other, but our bodies sure as hell haven't gotten the memo.

"I kissed girls before," I reveal, my voice low. I bring two fingers to his lips and ghost them over his flesh. "Too soft."

His amber eyes flare like a ball of flames, but he doesn't move away. Simply pins me in place with his hot glare.

"But guys," I murmur. "Guys have just enough roughness. Scruff. Edge." I lift my gaze from his mouth. "Meanness. They aren't sweet like girls."

"I'm not kissing you, rat," he says in a husky tone. "No matter how much you try to seduce me."

A grin tugs at my lips. His bronze orbs fall to my mouth, catching a glimpse of it and lingering. "Pity because I've been told I'm a great kisser."

"By Lucas?"

The name has me jolting in pain, but the look on Roan's face erases it. Barely masked jealousy. I'm not sure why this thrills me, but it does.

"And others."

"Girls or guys?"

"Both."

My thumb brushes his bottom lip this time, pulling the soft flesh to the side. His facial scruff scratches against my palm. It's exhilarating touching him. I'm liking "neutral ground." His hand reaches up, gripping my wrist hard. He doesn't pull me away, though.

"Did you fuck all those people?"

"Just Lucas."

Satisfaction glimmers over his features. I want to dissect his mind. Ask him a thousand questions. Figure out every part of him that makes him tick.

His lips part, and without hesitation, I press my thumb inside. The heat of his mouth sends pleasure tingling right to my dick. I'm hard and aching with need. He bites down on the tip of my thumb. Not painfully. Just a statement. That he has me. I don't think he even realizes he stakes such a claim.

"Boys," Aunt Karen calls out. "Come eat!"

I jerk my hand back and turn toward the window, hiding my boner, right as she makes her way into my room.

"Oh, good, you've got the desk cleared and ready to be taken apart." Then, to me she says, "Hollis, hon, I made your favorite. Chili enchiladas."

"Thanks, Aunt Karen." I flash her a brief smile. "Be down in a second." My stomach twists violently at the idea of eating chili anything.

She leaves and I catch Roan watching me with an unreadable expression. His guard is back up and his features are stony. Awesome. Back to square one.

"I'm so proud of you," Mom says, reaching over the table and ruffling my hair. "And surprised. I didn't think you'd try out." She bites on her bottom lip, refraining from saying the rest. *Your dad would be so proud of you too.*

"You can thank Roan. He made it happen."

Roan nearly chokes on his enchilada. He sucks down some tea and shoots me an annoyed look.

"How wonderful," Mom tells him. "Thank you for inviting him. You've been great to my children and I can't tell you how much that means to me."

Roan's cheeks turn redder than I've ever seen them. "It's fine."

"Roan's a good big brother," Roux tells her, pride in her

tone. "When he finishes school, we're going to live in our own house."

Roan tenses and shoots her a look that has her shoulders slouching.

"What about your parents?" Mom asks.

Roan's jaw ticks and I can tell he's freaking out. So I save him. Neutral ground and all.

"Did you say you got cupcakes?" I waggle my brows at Mom.

She affixes her fake smile because she can sense the air is charged and I'm begging her to move on. "Duh," she says, rolling her eyes, looking much younger than her thirty-eight years. "There's a little bakery right next to the bank. When Karen told me about you making the team, I picked some up. There are all different flavors to choose from." Then, to Roan, she smiles. "If you let me know your favorite, honey, I'll make sure to get some for next time."

"Roux loves chocolate like me," Charlotte says, her mouth full of half-chewed enchiladas.

"I only like the icing," Penny tells us grumpily. "Like Dad."

Mom and I deflate at her words. Sometimes it's as though we're the same person. Our moods are that similar.

"You can have my icing," I offer, knowing full and damn well I'm not eating those cupcakes. My stomach is seizing violently at the few bites of spicy enchiladas.

I lock eyes with Roan. His angry mask has fallen and he seems relaxed. I try not to obsess over the fact he looks good sitting at the table with my family. Like he belongs with us. Such a dumbass thing for a guy to think about another guy he met only days ago.

His easy smile fades when he looks down at my plate.

Coppery brown eyes flash with anger, confusing me. Why the hell does he care what I do or don't eat?

"When is Dad coming to see us?" Penny asks Mom, jerking me from my internal thought.

"I spoke with him today," Mom says with false cheer. "As soon as he gets a few days off. He can't wait to see you. Maybe later you can call him and talk about it."

Penny nods, revealing a rare smile.

The food I did manage to consume roils in my gut. It feels as though my stomach is on fire. Nerves. Worry. Stress. They seem to settle there and pulsate with energy. I grab my glass of tea and gulp it down, hoping to put out the internal fire. All it does is make me want to throw up.

Dad is coming.

Sooner rather than later.

I dread that day with every fiber of my being.

Chapter Ten

Roan

"I have to pee."

I crack my eyes open and stare up at Roux's sleepy face. "What time is it?"

"Time to pee."

"Smartass."

She laughs. "I can't move that thing on my own."

With a grumble that she woke my ass up at four in the morning, I climb out of bed and walk over to the dresser. Last night, after Ms. Frazier dropped us off, we made a beeline straight for our room. Alexander was partying with some of his friends and I didn't want to deal with any of them.

I move the dresser out of the way, and she bolts into the bathroom. Leaning against the wall next to the bathroom, I wait for her. Music plays from the living room, but I imagine everyone's gone home or passed out. I'm yawning when I sense a presence.

Alexander.

"Fucking pussy decided to come out of his cage?" he sneers, taking a menacing step toward me.

"Mom!" I bark out. "Call off your dog."

Alexander's lip curls up. "She's out."

"Mom! Wake up!"

"Not asleep, dumbass. Out."

Where in the fuck would she be at four in the morning?

"Leave us alone," I warn.

Roux opens the door and steps out behind me. Alexander's eyes drop to her and he grins like a motherfucking wolf about to devour a bunny.

"Go to our room," I hiss at her.

"Roan." Her whine of terror is my undoing.

"Go!"

She scurries off and slams our bedroom door shut. I wish she were strong enough to move the dresser. Fisting my hands, I square my shoulders and glare at Alexander.

"Leave us the hell alone."

"This is my home, boy," he sneers. "My rules."

"Last time I checked, it's HUD housing under Mom's name and you're not even supposed to be here." I take a step forward, cracking my neck, ready to beat this motherfucker's ass if need be.

His dilated pupils glimmer with hate and then he rushes me. I barely get a swing before I'm shoved into the wall, something cold digging beneath my jawbone at my throat.

"I could blow your fucking head off right now," he threatens, grinding the barrel harder into my flesh. "Make your sister clean your brain matter off the wall."

"You'd go to prison," I spit back at him.

"So?"

"You don't think my old man won't find you and gut you like the pig you are for killing his son?"

His eyes narrow, but I know he contemplates my words. My dad is a mean bastard. Alexander is nothing in comparison. With a cool expression, he takes a step backward. And then with a hard swing, he pistol whips me with his gun.

Pain explodes across my cheek and I stumble. He cracks me over the back of the head with the gun, sending me hurtling to the floor. I groan and blink away the dazed feeling. When I hear a scream, I get on my hands and knees, adrenaline fueling me. I rush into the room after him, ignoring the dizziness. Alexander, with his gun in hand, swats at Roux like she's a pesky little sister and they're playing. This fucker is twisted, so I don't want him playing anything with Roux. I tackle him, sending him crashing into the dresser. He snarls as I start wailing punches on his back. I manage to get one good one to his head and knock his ass out. With a grunt, I drag him out of our room and into Mom's. Once the door is shut, I make my way back into our room, pushing the dresser back into place. I hide the gun under the mattress. The room spins and I crash into the end table, knocking over the lamp.

Roux is crying, but I'm so fucking tired.

I fall onto the bed now that she's safe and pass out.

My head is killing me.

The voice on repeat is making it worse.

"Roan! Roan! Roan!"

Roux.

I force my eyes open. My sister sits beside me on the bed, sobbing. She hands me my phone.

"Who is it?" I croak. "Hello?"

"Oh, Roan, honey, thank God."

"Mom?"

"No, baby, it's Kelsey. Roux called the house phone crying. Hollis and I are on the way to come get you."

"What?" I'm so fucking confused right now. "Why?"

"It's not safe there." Her voice is firm. Motherly. Fuck, it makes my heart hurt worse than my head. "We can bring you here—"

"No," I bark out. "I mean, we have someplace to go. The fire station. I have a friend there."

"We'll be there shortly. If it feels unsafe to leave, let me know and I'll call the police."

"Please don't," I beg. I'm eighteen, but Roux? They'll fucking take her from me.

"Okay," she says with a ragged sigh. "Be there soon. You have Hollis's cell if you need to call us."

We hang up and I frown at Roux, which makes my head throb worse.

"Why did you call them?" I murmur, hurt in my tone. I always take care of her. We don't need anyone else.

Her bottom lip wobbles. "I tried all your friends. No one answered."

"Mike?"

"He must be asleep or at a fire. He didn't answer either."

"The dresser is there. We would've been fine," I try, hating that I don't even believe my own words.

"Not you," she utters. "You're bleeding and I think you have a concussion."

"Okay, Dr. Hirsch."

She laughs and the sound is a miracle worker. "My new best friend said she's going to be a doctor like her dad when she grows up. I think I'll be a doctor too."

"Good," I tease. "Then you can take care of me in my old age."

I hug her to me and kiss the top of her head. We stay like that for a moment before we get up and pack our shit.

Everything we own fits into a couple of bags. There's no coming back here. Not after Alexander pulled a gun on me. Next time, if he's fucked up on drugs, he might just pull the trigger. I can't live without Roux and I'll be damned if I let her watch me die. I'm not sure where we'll go or how we'll manage, but I have to try. Anything is better than this. Hell, I'd be happy camping in my favorite tent at Cal's campground if it meant never having to see Alexander again.

"Let me make sure it's clear first," I tell Roux as I move the dresser from the door.

The apartment is quiet aside from the music playing in the living room. One quick look toward my mother's door and it's still shut. I walk back into our room, gather up most of the bags, and leave a couple for Roux to carry. Quietly, we slip out of the apartment. At five in the morning, no one is up. We make it out of the building and into the blistery cold just as a suped up Denali pulls up with Hollis at the wheel.

"Oh, thank God you're both okay," Kelsey cries out the moment the passenger door flings open. She rushes to the hatch and opens it. We toss our bags inside and she closes it. Before we can get in the car, she pulls us both to her for a hug. "I have you now. You're safe."

Tears burn at my eyes as I slump against this woman. She's small, but her strength is addictive. I need so badly to be strong right now. A sob catches in my throat. Her hand pats my back as she whispers assurances. I break away and quickly jump into the backseat with Roux so I don't do something stupid like cry. Everyone is quiet on the way to the fire station. Hollis keeps glancing at me in the mirror, worry evident in his stare.

I can't look at him.

I can't look at either of them.

When I try to see myself through their eyes, I see a weak brother who can't keep his sister safe. I see all of my insecurities like blinking lights for all to witness. I see the fatigue of a life that's too fucking tiring for someone only eighteen.

Defeated, I close my eyes and hope I'll find my way to a bed soon. We pull up to the fire station and park. One of Mike's friends, Frank, comes out to greet us.

"Everything okay? Do you need medical attention?" Frank asks. When he realizes it's Roux and me, concern washes over his features. "Roan, what the hell, man? You might need stitches."

I shrug. "Is April here? She can stitch me up."

"Everyone's asleep. I'll get them up, though. Let's get inside." He ushers the four of us into the fire station. The scent of coffee hits my nostrils, making me recoil. I don't normally dislike the smell of coffee, but at the moment, it makes me nauseous.

He takes us to the living area where there are a couple of sofas before rushing from the room. Hollis paces while Kelsey and Roux sit down. It makes my heart ache to see Kelsey hug Roux like she's her daughter. Roux deserves so much better than the piece of shit who gave birth to us. I stumble a bit and Hollis pounces on me. He gently guides me down to sit.

"How's your head?"

"Fine," I grumble.

He doesn't release my arm, sitting so close our thighs press together. "You're not fine, Roan, you have a huge gash on your cheek and can barely stand upright."

I grumble, but don't argue. Truth is, I don't mind his touch. It's comforting in this moment.

"What in the ever-loving hell?" Mike demands as he charges into the room, still sleepy-eyed, with Frank and April on his heels. April has her kit in hand. She's a nurse and is married to Frank, so she's always up at the station with him.

"Good morning to you, too," I deadpan.

Mike doesn't seem amused as he plops his big ass down on the coffee table in front of me and puts his fingers under my chin, lifting my head. He touches below my jaw and I wince.

"I have to call this in," Mike says, frowning.

"Mike!" I bark out, hating the wave of dizziness from this action. "You can't."

We both glance over at Roux. He grits his teeth.

"Fine, but you're not going back," he throws at me. "Ever again."

I shrug my shoulders. "I can call Cal or Jordy—"

"Nonsense. I have the garage apartment. It sits empty. You can move in there."

My heart rate speeds up. "Really? I mean, I can pay. Well, not right this second, but I can get a job and—"

"We're not worrying about all that when you've clearly got a concussion and are bleeding all over the damn place. Let April get you stitched up. We'll figure the specifics out later." He clutches my shoulder. "I'm sorry I haven't been able to do more. I always wanted to."

"I know," I choke out, hating how fucking emotional I feel right now. This isn't me. I'm hardened. The boy made of steel. I won't allow anyone or anything to hurt me or my sister. Right now, I feel every bit as breakable as the porcelain boy beside me.

Mike rises and moves out of the way so April can set to

assessing me while Frank hovers, his brows furrowed in concern. I overhear Mike and Kelsey speaking in hushed tones. Roux is already fast asleep with a big blanket on her. Hollis remains at my side. It's then I realize he's holding my hand.

Warm.

Comforting.

Secure.

I don't shake away his hold, simply draw strength from it.

Hollis swipes his thumb over my flesh. I don't know what to make of it. It's weird as fuck to hold hands with the kid I hated from the second I saw him. But the hate has evolved. In a few short days, it's melted into something dangerous and consuming. Something I've never experienced. Frankly, it scares the hell out of me. How can someone feel so inexplicitly drawn to another person in such a short time?

I want to hate him, but I can't.

I don't like him. That much I'm certain of. Yet, I can't figure out what it is about him that I crave. Friendship? Affection? His voice? The searing looks he gives me? It goes beyond some lust filled, sexual desire. If it was just sex, guy or not, I would've fucked him out of my system much like I did Sidney. This is different. All-consuming. Scary as hell.

I try to pull my hand away, unsure if I'm able to handle whatever this storm brewing between us is. I don't know if it'll end with fists and broken bones or kisses and broken hearts. It's too intense and cataclysmic to not end in destruction, though. If it's not hate, it's something close. Hate destroys and decimates. Whatever this is, it'll ruin too.

Ruin me.

Ruin him.

Probably ruin everyone in this room.

His fingers thread with mine and I fucking let him. I let the perfect, rich boy hold my hand like I belong to him. April says stuff to me, but I'm not entirely focused. I mumble out words that must calm her because then she begins stitching my cheek. Hollis squeezes my hand, reminding me he's here with me. My heart throbs hard in my chest.

She finishes and then gives me a stern look when I yawn. "You need to stay awake so we can keep an eye on you."

"I'm fine," I grunt.

"You're not fine." She frowns. "Stay awake. I'll grab you some coffee."

She stands and walks away. Frank follows after her into the kitchen area toward the nauseating smell, talking lowly. I'm so fucking tired. I don't have a concussion. I just didn't get enough sleep last night. Bitterness makes my eyes sting.

I fall back against the cushions and my head throbs harder. My eyes must close because I'm shaken awake a second later.

"Roan, man, you can't," Hollis says, an apology in his tone. "Sit up."

"No," I snap. "Leave me alone."

"I'm trying to help you." The concern in his features kills me.

"Why?"

"Because I want to."

"I'm so tired." Of this day. Of this life.

"I know."

"I want to go to sleep and never wake up."

He swallows. "I know."

"I don't know what to do."

Rather than offer an answer, he pulls me to him. The rat

of Horn River, my enemy, hugs me to his chest. Fucking holds me like he can put all the broken pieces back together again. I fist his hoodie in my hand, breathing in his scent. Tears burn at my eyes and then leak of their own accord. I cry silently, overwhelmed with life, and soak Hollis's hoodie. He doesn't offer assurances, simply holds me.

"Stay awake for me," he murmurs. "Please."

The tears burn hotter and with more intensity.

"I'm awake, rat." I smile, the fabric of his hoodie soft against my lips. "You can't get rid of me that easily."

Chapter Eleven

Hollis

All of my texts go unanswered. It's frustrating as hell because I want to know what's going on with them. Roan and I may have our beef, but there's something linking us. It would feel too superficial to say just physical attraction. It's something else—something deeper. I feel connected to the broody asshole in ways I don't understand. When he's near, I want to inhale him and look at him. Feel him. I've never wanted to just be in someone's presence before like I do with him.

It's really fucking confusing because he's a total prick most of the time.

That's just superficial too, I think.

Beneath all that hardness is a soft, vulnerable boy. Just knowing he's inside there makes me want to dig and dig and dig until I unearth him. I feel like he's mine. Like he could be mine. If I take the time and effort to find him.

Me: How's your head?

I send Roan another text. This one, like the others, goes unanswered. It makes me worry his condition has worsened. He's not at school, which is understandable considering he got the shit beat out of him by some druggie asshole, but what if he had to go to the hospital or something? My gut tightens and twists.

The bell rings for lunch and I take my time getting to the cafeteria. I'm sick to my stomach with stress and worry. The scent of pizza or whatever the fuck they're cooking today has my insides burning in protest. I bolt into the restroom and head for a stall. Bile creeps up my throat and the room spins as I push into the handicap stall. I barely get the lock pulled when I'm scrambling for the toilet. Pain lances through my stomach as I gag. There's nothing in my belly because I felt too sick after all that happened with Roux and Roan this morning to eat. I'm thankful I didn't eat anything, because I'm too exhausted and overwhelmed to add puking my guts up to shit I'm dealing with today. Acid burns up my esophagus, but nothing escapes.

Once I feel like I'm no longer going to dry heave, I stand up and rush from the stall, eager to splash cold water on my clammy face. I'm just turning on the sink and getting my hands wet when the door to the bathroom opens.

In walk the Hornets.

Minus their grumpy leader.

"I thought I smelled a rat," Jordy sneers, prowling inside with Cal and Trey behind him. Trey stands in front of the door, blocking it. Cal cracks his neck, towering behind Jordy, as Jordy steps into my personal space.

I don't like him at my back, so I turn off the water and face off with the psycho freak.

"What did you do?" Jordy demands, poking my chest. "What the fuck did you do?"

"What the hell are you talking about?" I bite back.

"We know you ratted like the bitch you are."

Cal must sense my confusion because he clutches Jordy's shoulder. "I don't think he knows."

"Knows what?" I glare at them both, imploring them to tell me just what it is they think I did.

Jordy pokes my chest again. Hard. "You told your aunt and now child protective services are involved. So help me—"

The words are drowned out as my blood turns to ice. Aunt Karen told CPS? Oh, shit. This is bad.

"You hear me, motherfucker?" Jordy roars. "We'll make your life a living hell!"

He shoves me with the strength of three men, sending me hurtling across the bathroom. I fall to my ass, bruising my tailbone on the linoleum floor. My stomach is seizing as my stress reaches new heights. Not because Jordy is seconds from kicking my teeth in, but for what this means for Roan and Roux.

Oh God.

I need to explain that I didn't know Aunt Karen would say something.

The guys are taunting me, but I manage to get back to my feet. Jordy stalks my way, his fist raised, when someone bangs hard on the door.

"Open this door now," a deep voice booms.

Coach Rendell.

We all flinch and Trey steps out of the way. Coach storms in, assessing the situation.

"You okay, English?" he asks me, clearly understanding the tension and that it's directed at me.

Jordy gives me a murderous warning glare.

"Y-Yeah. Fine. I, uh, I just need to leave. Feeling sick." I push past them and head for the office. I want to confront Aunt Karen. Ask her how she could throw Roan and Roux under the bus.

I find Aunt Karen in her office, on the phone. When she sees me storm in, she tells them goodbye, before turning her sympathetic eyes on me.

"Why did you call CPS?" I practically shriek at her. "Do you know what will happen?"

Gone is her sympathy as her stern authoritative scowl washes over her features. "As principal of this school and an adult, I have an obligation—"

"Aunt Karen," I snap, cutting her off. "They'll take Roux away."

"Perhaps it's for the best," she says softly. "Their home situation—"

"Unbelievable." I pace her office, ripping at my hair in frustration. "What happens now? She goes and lives with another family? This will destroy him, Aunt Karen."

"Honey," she says in a soothing tone. "It's best if you let people more qualified handle their unique situation. I'm only trying to help them."

"By ratting them out?" Tears of anger prickle at my eyes. "I have to go."

"Hollis! You can't just leave!"

"I'm sick," I growl. "So fucking sick. I'll see you later."

I speed the whole way to the fire station. It's snowing and the streets are slick, but I'm a man on a mission. Make everything right. But how? I don't know and that just makes me want to throw up. This day keeps getting worse and worse.

I need to explain.

I want to help.

He's going to hate me more than he already does, and it kills me. It kills me because I didn't want this for him or Roux.

My car slides into a parking spot. I barely get it turned off before I'm flying out and into the station. As soon as I step inside, I notice a woman speaking to Roux while Roan paces. The woman sees me and smiles.

"You must be Hollis? You and your mother went to get Roux and Roan last night?" she asks, her nose crinkling.

Unable to formulate an answer before seeing Roan's face, I glance over at him. His jaw clenches, but he says nothing.

"Yeah," I grunt out. "Roan, can I talk to you for a sec?"

The woman nods. "I think that would be great. Roan, go talk to your friend. I wanted to ask Roux a few questions anyway."

His nostrils flare, but I plead with my eyes as he walks over to me. He passes me and steps outside. I follow him around the side of the building. Is this where he's going to kick my ass? Finish the job Jordy clearly wanted to do?

His expression is unreadable. It's dead. Empty. A void. I don't know if he's mad or upset.

"Roan..."

"Don't," he warns, his bronze eyes flashing a yellowy gold like fire.

"I didn't—"

He rushes me, his palm covering my mouth. The brick digs into my back and his hips keep me pinned. "I said don't."

His eyes lose their fury as anguish sets in. He's scared. Devastated. Fuck. I want to wrap my arms around him and promise him it'll be okay. Has anyone ever assured him it would be?

"I can't lose her," he hisses, bringing his mouth to my ear.

"Carol is talking about putting her in a temporary home and I…" His voice breaks. "I can't fucking take that, rat."

I flinch at the name. Doesn't feel like much of a caress now.

My palms slide up his muscular chest over his hoodie. I'm desperate to hold him and make him all the promises in the world. He needs it.

"If…" He trembles, trailing off, as his hand slides from my mouth down to my neck. "If they take her away from me…" He pulls back, searing his flaming eyes into mine. "I'll fucking kill you."

I blink in confusion. "What?"

"You heard me, rat. If this all blows up and I lose my sister, then I'll have nothing left to lose. I will hunt you down and fucking destroy you." His palm tightens around my throat, restricting the airflow.

"I can fix this," I promise, though it's not my fault and I don't know how. "Let me help you fix this." My hands slide up his neck and into his messy hair. I scrape my fingertips along his scalp. His eyes flutter closed briefly.

I steal the moment.

Inhale him.

Stare at him.

Feel him.

We're on the edge of something, and it's about to be taken away from me.

So I keep the moment for as long as I can.

I grip his hair tighter, making him open his eyes and hiss in warning. He clutches my throat tighter. Despite his anger and devastation, his body responds to mine. I can feel just how much so, as his dick rubs against mine through our jeans.

His shoulders sag slightly and his hand falls away from my neck. I pull his head toward mine. Forehead to forehead, we breathe in each other's scent. Amber eyes lock onto mine—the brokenness in them causing little fissures inside my heart. I caress his scalp with my fingers, trying to convey wordlessly these intense feelings for him that have consumed my every thought.

Our mouths are so close.

I could kiss him.

Would it solve everything?

So close.

A tilt of my head.

I could make it happen.

He exhales and tilts forward, bringing his lips near enough to mine, they almost brush. "Remember, Hollis, if I lose her, I'll ruin you in every way possible."

Not a kiss.

Just cruel, hateful words that make my stomach clench violently.

"Roan…"

He pulls away so abruptly, I nearly collapse without his body holding mine up against the wall. Roan is hard in his jeans. An angry scowl paints his face into something hauntingly beautiful. Those lips…fuck. Those lips are pink and full and would feel so good pressed to mine.

"Roan…" My voice is shrill and pleading.

The vulnerable boy retreats into the shadows as the fierce one steps up, ready to defend.

"Get the fuck out of my life, rat." He cracks his neck and gives me a scathing glare. "Or I'll do it for you."

Chapter Twelve

Roan

I glower at Hollis through the window of the fire station as he slowly walks back to his car. His shoulders are hunched, utterly defeated. It's bullshit. I'm the one suffering here because of his family, and he's the one feeling sorry for himself.

His head turns, looking my way, but he can't see me from his vantage point. He fumbles for his keys in his coat pocket. They fall to the snowy asphalt at his feet. His knees buckle and he grabs the side of his car before bending to get them. I'm still staring after him, even after he drives off, when a hand clamps down on my shoulder.

"Carol's not going to separate you two. You know that, right?" Mike asks, his voice filled with fatherly authority.

I almost believe his tone.

Believe him.

But I'm not stupid.

Nothing ever goes right for me and Roux.

"She said that? In those exact words?" I challenge, shaking off his hand to turn and look at him.

Mike's lips thin out and he nods. "Pretty much. I told her I have the garage apartment."

"She's letting Roux stay with you because you're stable and can provide," I grit out. "This has nothing to do with me.

I'm only getting to stay because you like me. If it weren't for you, we'd be split."

He shrugs. "Maybe. But that's not the circumstance. You do have me and you're not getting split up."

For now.

He doesn't have to say the words because I feel them. I know them as truth.

"Come on," he says. "Carol is leaving. It's probably best I get you two settled in and back to the station while we have coverage."

Ten minutes later, we pile into Mike's big redneck truck. The drive is quiet, each of us trapped in our heads. I'm sure Mike is wondering how in the hell he managed to suddenly get himself two kids. Roux is scared. I'm just angry at the injustice of it all. He pulls into a familiar neighborhood.

Oh, Jesus.

Seriously?

"There's Charlotte's house," Roux says, pointing at a house as we drive.

My body tenses when I notice a purple Mustang parked out front. Mike drives to the end of the street and hangs a left. His house is at a dead end with a green belt behind it. The house is modest in size but boasts a big garage—probably for his monster truck—and the apartment sits on top.

We climb out and Mike helps Roux with her bags. He shows us up to the garage apartment. Once inside, I take in the small space.

"This kitchen is outdated, but everything works. I just had everything serviced up here because I was considering renting the place out," he says as he walks over to the fridge and opens it. "I'll get some food for you guys. Until then, just help yourself to whatever's in the house."

Guilt niggles at me. He obviously needed the money if he was going to rent it out, and now here we are freeloading. I'm going to have to find a job and fast.

"The television works, as does the DVD player, but if you want cable, we'll have to get a box added—"

"We don't need it," I blurt out. "We'll be fine."

He gives me a knowing nod and then shows us down a hallway. "Here's the bathroom. The sink sometimes is slow to drain so just watch that." He opens another door once in the hallway. "This was a laundry room at some point, but the plumber said it'd cost a shit ton of money to fix the pipes. We capped it off and I converted it to a small bedroom."

Roux steps inside and points out the small window. "Look! You can see the ducks in that little pond!"

Hearing her excitement does something to me. It melts a glacier-sized hunk of ice on my heart. I'll have to work my ass off to pay for this somehow, but I've never wanted anything more than to give Roux a safe place to stay. Someplace happy and homey.

"And the other bedroom is back here. It doesn't have the duck view, but you have a fabulous view of the street," Mike jokes.

Though I want to give Roux the bigger room, I like that I can see what's coming for us with this view.

"I get the duck room," Roux tells me. "Sorry, bro."

"You wound me," I tease.

"I'll round up some stuff from the house and bring it back so you guys can get your beds made up and shower. If you need anything, you have my cell. Take today to get settled, but tomorrow I want you back at school." He gives me a firm look. "Both of you."

So much for dropping out and job hunting.

"Thanks, Mike."

"No problem, kid."

He leaves and my tension hitches a ride with him. Just Roux and me feels more like normal. They can't fucking take her from me. I won't be able to cope.

I make my way back to the duck room. She's already unpacking her clothes into a small dresser that's made of clear plastic. Leaning against the doorframe, I watch her.

"I like it here," she tells me, looking up from her task. "Without Alexander...without Mom."

"I do too." I scrub my palm down my face. "I'm going to work my ass off. I'll make sure we get to stay here. Maybe even get someplace better eventually."

"You're afraid."

I let out a heavy sigh and sit down beside her on the bed, hugging her to me. "I'm afraid they'll tear us apart."

"Me too."

"They can try," I say, ruffling her hair in a playful way.

We both grow quiet because it's not a joke. If they separate us, I'll do everyfuckingthing in my power to bring us back together again. My father is a law breaker. Maybe the apple doesn't fall far from the tree. I'd do it for Roux. I'd do anything for Roux.

"We're going to be okay." My whispered assurance does nothing to calm the stuttering in my heart.

Will we ever be able to relax in this lifetime?

"I hope so," she says. "I really want us to be okay."

I walk out of Coach Rendell's office burning with anger. It's irrational, but I want to throttle Hollis. He's nowhere to be found, which is good, because there's no telling what I'd do to him if I saw him right now.

Definitely not rub my fucking dick against him like yesterday.

A shot of lust shoots straight to my dick when I remember the way he ran his fingers through his hair and worried his plump bottom lip between his teeth. I was furious, but something about his nearness made me burn hot with something else. Something unfamiliar and strange.

Attraction.

Intensity.

Need.

I've fucked a few girls in my lifetime, and none of them, naked and balls deep on my dick, ever made me feel that way. It was mindless sex to get off and pass the time.

Hollis fucks with my head.

The hate I have for him feels a lot like desire.

Strangest fucking thing ever.

In this moment, I'm unsure if I could even kick his ass. Not that I'm afraid he'd get one over on me. That's not it at all. I'm afraid I'll let him do worse. Much worse.

Images of kissing him assault my mind—unwanted and hot.

It makes my headache worsen.

Fuck this and him.

I'm charging out of the locker room when I slam into a hard body. Trey grips my shoulders and steadies me.

"Dude, what the fuck?" he mutters, his dark brown eyes assessing me. "Are you okay? What the hell happened yesterday?"

I rub at the back of my neck and let out a heavy sigh. "Too much."

Footsteps round the corner, revealing Jordy and Cal. Jordy rushes over to me and yanks me to him for a hug. I let out a heavy sigh as I sink against my best friend, desperately needing his violent strength to get me through the fucking day.

"There are rumors and shit," Jordy growls, pulling away to glower at me. "I want to know the truth."

Cal nods behind him, his normally playful features twisted into a solemn expression. "Yeah, man. Tell us what's up."

My three best friends crowd in on me. We've been tight ever since I can remember. Bad boys with a bond. They're my family.

As much as I want to throw Hollis under the bus, just to bitch about him, I can't. So, I do what they ask. Tell the truth.

"Alexander pulled a gun on me." I wince at the reminder. My heart gallops in my chest. Had he pulled the trigger…

Jordy gently slaps at my cheek. "He did fucking what? Focus, man. You're dazed right now. Are you on drugs?"

"W-What? No." I pinch the bridge of my nose and shake my head. "Alexander tried to mess with Roux. I don't know what he was planning on doing, but I wasn't fucking having it."

Jordy's eyes darken and his nostrils flare with barely contained rage. Roux is not just my little sister, she's theirs too. They take care of her like their own.

"The fucker pistol-whipped me and then started in on Roux while I was out—"

Slam!

Jordy rams his fist through a locker, crunching it inward. The sound echoes loudly down the hall. I cringe, wondering if it was loud enough for Coach to hear.

"Did he…" Trey trails off, unable to finish.

Cal's haunted expression chills me to my core.

"No," I mutter. "I woke up and beat the fuck out of him."

Jordy slides down the wall of lockers, falling on his ass. Anger is his go-to expression, but currently, his features are pinched. His eyes are glassy. I don't miss the tremble in his hand before he scrubs his palm over his face.

"So you bailed?" Cal asks, brows pinched.

"Not exactly. I got a concussion. I was kind of out of it and it scared Roux."

Jordy growls. "I'll fucking kill that asshole."

"You don't have to kill him," I assure my best friend. "We're out of there."

His menacing glare seems to argue otherwise.

"Did you call the police?" Trey asks, knowing if I did, it was a last resort kind of thing.

"No, uh, after Roux tried calling you guys, she eventually called her friend Charlotte, who woke up her mom, Kelsey."

All three guys' shoulders slouch when they realize Roux tried to contact them.

"I was sleeping, man, or otherwise," Cal tries, his voice hoarse.

I grip his shoulder. "I know. It's okay."

Jordy pulls his knees to his chest and bends down, bumping his forehead over and over again on his knees. "I should have answered."

"Kelsey is Hollis's mom." I bite out the words, hating the bitter taste on my tongue.

"What?" Trey demands, now pacing beside me. "That prissy purple car motherfucker?"

Jordy is on his feet in an instant, all despair erased as rage fuels him forward. He stands too close, assessing me. "He went with his mom to get you?"

I nod and let out a sigh. "They took me to the fire station to see Mike. Apparently I might have a concussion. It's enough that Coach doesn't want me playing tonight. I'm benched."

Cal groans. "Fucking really? We need you, man."

"You have Hollis now," I bite out harshly. "Coach says you guys will manage a game without me, especially with him on the team."

The truth of Coach's words hurt.

I've been replaced by a prettier, richer, more perfect version.

A golden boy.

I'm nothing but old news. Replaceable. A problem that needs fixing.

"So the fucker tells his aunt and CPS gets involved?" Jordy demands. "Now they're going to take Roux away from us?"

My heart races wildly in my heart. "No one is fucking taking her."

He relaxes. "Damn straight."

"We'd kick their asses if they tried," Trey grumbles.

"Make them regret the day they messed with Little Hornet," Cal agrees. "Do you need a place to stay? I bet Mom and Dad wouldn't mind."

"For now, Mike's letting us stay with him." I let out a

heavy sigh. "I'm going to have to lie low for a while. I can't get into any shit and risk them yanking Roux into the system."

All three guys nod, features contorted into angry scowls.

"Don't worry." Jordy snarls, his eyes locking in on a target behind me in the hallway. "We'll do the dirty work for you."

We all turn to see Hollis walking toward us, his head down and shoulders slumped. He doesn't notice us until he nearly runs into Trey. As soon as he acknowledges the four of us, he tenses and straightens. His eyes dart over to mine, concern glimmering in them.

I look away.

"Watch where you're going, rat," Trey snaps, shoving Hollis back.

He stumbles but regains his footing before falling. Fury turns his pale features crimson and he fists his hands, readying for a fight. As though the porcelain boy is a match for four Hornets.

"Roan," Hollis says, eyes burning into me as he ignores the others. "Can we talk?"

"Fuck no, you can't talk," Jordy sneers, stalking over to him. His chest bumps Hollis's. "If you have something to say, you say it to me."

Hollis tries to look around Jordy, but Jordy isn't having that shit. He grabs Hollis by the jaw and shoves him against the bank of lockers on the wall, pressing his head into the depressed locker he ruined moments earlier. Hollis wriggles to no avail, panic flashing in his blue eyes.

"You stay away from my boy," Jordy warns. "Or I will fucking crush you." To punctuate his words, he digs his fingers into Hollis's jaw.

Hollis cries out in pain.

The sound burns down my spine, chasing butterflies into my stomach. I don't understand the sensation, but it isn't a pleasant one.

"Not here," I murmur. "You'll get your ass in trouble."

Jordy holds Hollis in his punishing grip a second longer before releasing him roughly. He spits at Hollis's feet before stalking off down the hall. Trey and Cal saunter after him. I start to follow, but Hollis grabs my bicep before I get far.

I shake off his hold and step close, my face inches from his. "You heard Jordy. Stay away from me."

His brows furrow together. "I just want to make sure you're okay."

"You stole my spot on the team for tonight's game and your family called CPS on mine." I laugh cruelly at him. "I'm fucking peachy, rat."

I start to pull away, but he fists my hoodie, pulling me flush against him. My hand flies to the smashed locker behind him to keep from slamming my hips on his. His breathing is uneven and mine is harsh. Bravely, he stares at me as though he can project thoughts straight into my skull.

Don't hurt me.

I won't hurt you.

A shudder ripples through me. I don't like the spooky ass mental vibes he's giving me. Like he knows me. I met the guy Monday. He doesn't fucking know me.

"Roan, I'm not a bad guy." His blue eyes soften, warming the iciest parts of me.

I cool every part inside me, especially the heat flooding down to my dick. "Sucks for you then, rat," I mutter, leaning in to brush my words against the shell of his ear, "because I am."

Chapter Thirteen

Hollis

The crowd screams when I make my shot. Adrenaline races through my veins, chasing away every nervous or uneasy feeling. When I'm on the basketball court, I'm in my element. A few guys from the team slap my back in appreciation as they pass.

Not the Hornets.

Trey curls his lip up in disgust.

Cal's nostrils flare.

Jordy shoots me glares filled with venom and hate.

Besides that, still feeling pretty good.

That is, until I catch Roan's stare on the sidelines. He's benched, just as he said, watching the game with furrowed brows and sadness gleaming in his eyes.

Someone from LHS rams into me, knocking me to a knee. Coach yells at me to pull my head out of my ass. Roan now smirks at me, satisfied.

Fucker.

"We wipe our asses with Horn River trash," the Lebanon High kid mutters.

My eyes track the ball, ignoring this douchebag. He says something else, his attention diverted my way, and not on the play.

"And we embarrass Lebanon losers in front of all their

friends and family," I grunt as I dart around him, intercepting the ball that was meant for him.

The crowd screams again, numbing me with a pleasure you can only feel when everyone is rooting for your success. I storm down the court, sidestepping every LHS asshole along the way, before throwing the ball from the three-point line.

Swoosh!

Coach yells at me again, but this time he's grinning. "Way to run the court, English!"

By half time, I'm starting to feel slightly woozy. The rush of adrenaline has sapped up the last of my energy. I knew I should have grabbed more than a protein shake. We're all herded into the locker room so the cheerleaders can perform their halftime show. I get knocked along the wall a couple of times. Blindly, I reach out to steady myself. My palm wraps around Roan's firm bicep.

Oh shit.

I should let go, but I can only stare at him, hating that he makes me feel even more lightheaded than before. He grips my wrist in a punishing hold, prying me from him. But, rather than letting go, he hauls me over to his locker.

"You're going to pass out, rat," he complains as he flings open his locker. "Coach won't let me bail you out, so you're going to have to figure your shit out and fast."

Coach is rambling about kicking LHS's ass, but I'm too focused on Roan to hear all the details of his gloating.

Roan pulls out a package of peanut butter crackers. My stomach recoils. His features darken when he notices my reaction. Before I can open my mouth to protest, he rips open the package and shoves a cracker at me.

"Eat this. Now."

I shake my head. "I…"

"So help me, rat. Eat it or I'll make you."

Anger pulses deep inside me. It makes my gut clench hard and painfully like a fist. Rather than get into it with him, I snag the cracker and make a great, messy show of eating it. He smirks and hands me another one.

"Good little rodent."

"Fuck off," I grumble.

His eyes dart to my mouth, chasing away my irritation with a shot of heat. When he lifts his hand, I stop mid-chew. Oblivious to the chaos around us as Coach says something that makes everyone cheer, Roan lifts his thumb to my mouth. My breath catches in my throat.

"Crumbs." He utters the word. I see it tumble past his lips more than I actually hear it over the noise. His thumb brushes along my bottom lip.

Time slows like molasses hanging thickly from an overturned jar.

The moment almost passes, but lingers.

Barely.

Seconds drag by, the heat of his thumb on my lip scarring me.

He pins me with a hot stare for what feels like an eternity. I'm no longer breathing. My heart doesn't beat. I simply stare at him.

He kills the spell when he shoves the pack of crackers into my chest. "Eat so you don't fuck up the game."

With those words, he's gone.

I'm left feeling even more fucked up than ever.

Why does Roan get inside me and strip me bare every

damn time? Being so stupidly affected by him is becoming an issue. It's overwhelming and exhausting.

And exhilarating.

Thrumming with adrenaline, this time the Roan induced kind, I run out of the locker room with the rest of the team to go kick some Lebanon loser ass.

"Keep kicking ass out there, English, and you might just lead this team to the state championship," Coach says, slapping me on the back. "Awesome work out there."

He turns to shower praise on a couple of other guys. I'm left grinning.

"You played so well!" Sidney exclaims as she bounds over to me. She throws her arms around my neck for a hug. "Ew, you stink."

"I just ran my ass off," I say with a chuckle, hugging her back. "You walked into this sweat trap."

She pretends to look offended but makes no moves to peel herself from me. Gio walks up, winking at me.

"You two are so cute," he teases, batting his lashes. "Future prom king and queen."

"Pass," I grumble.

Sidney pouts. "But we'd be such a cute couple."

I manage to pull her away from me. "Yeah."

"So convincing," she groans. "Well, I can speak for everyone when I say we'd be adorable. Right, Gio? Back me up on this one."

I smirk as he placates her in a teasing way. Gio clearly likes Sidney. From what I've gathered this week, she's on a totally different social rung than him, but they get along great regardless. Maybe if she wasn't so hell-bent on trying to date me, she'd give a guy like Gio a chance.

"Hello, Earth to new kid," Sidney whines. "You're always in your head. There's a whole world out here with me in the center of it."

Gio snorts. "Give him a break, Sid. He just scored most of the points for our team. I wouldn't be surprised if he passed the hell out at any second."

"Save the passing out for my tent later," she whispers, fluttering her lashes at me. "You're going, right? To Campfire Chaos? I've only begged all week."

"I, uh," I start but then snap my mouth shut when I feel an intense presence behind me.

"What's happening?" Roan's smooth rumble ripples down my spine and makes the hairs on my neck stand on end.

"We're inviting Hollis to Campfire Chaos," Sidney says bravely, staring past me with fiery challenge in her eyes.

"Me too," Gio throws in. "Packaged deal."

Sidney's lips twitch. "Duh."

"I don't remember inviting the rat to the river," Roan says in a menacing tone. "Do you?"

I don't have to see them to feel three more guys flank Roan. Having them at my back makes me nervous, but knowing we're in front of a shit ton of parents, students, and teachers helps.

"It's fine," I mutter.

Sidney's face tightens with fury. She opens her mouth to speak when my mom pushes her way into the group to hug me.

"You did amazing, honey," she praises, kissing my sweaty head. "I was so proud."

I close my eyes, ignoring all the bullshit, and focus on my mom. So strong. So loving. So kind.

"Thanks, Mom."

She pulls away to grin at everyone in the group. "Hi, Roan." Her smile is sympathetic and motherly. Then, she regards the others. "I'm Kelsey."

Roan sheds his asshole attitude and introduces his friends. Trey and Cal shake hands with my mother, both wearing matching good ol' boy grins. Jordy grunts out a hello and manages to somewhat smile for her, which feels crazy to me since I've never seen him do it before. Gio hams it up for her when he introduces himself, making sure to kiss the back of her hand. I kick him in his ass, aiming for his balls, but he manages to thwart my attempt.

"I'm Sid. Hollis and I might go to prom together."

Mom's brows lift in amusement. She knows I'm not into Sid, but she plays along anyway. "That's wonderful, sweetie."

Sidney preens and then sidles up to my mother, her eyes flashing with victory. I don't know what she thinks she's won. That is, until she opens her mouth. "We invited Hollis to go camping with us. Cal's dad owns a campground and in the winter, we basically have the place to ourselves. Everyone behaves. We cook hot dogs and tell ghost stories. Super fun and safe."

Mom chuckles. "Wasn't born yesterday. I know you're giving me the G-rated version."

Sidney's face burns bright red. "I, uh, I…"

"It's okay," Mom assures her. "My son is eighteen. It's good to see him going out and meeting new people. I trust you all to take care of him." Her eyes settle on Roan, who's now come to stand beside me, our shoulders brushing.

"I won't be there." His voice is gritty and raw. "I have to get back to Roux."

Mom's eyes light up. "About that. I was just coming over here to ask you if it would be okay for Roux to spend the night with us. She tells me you're staying at the nice fireman's house and that he lives close by. I promise we'll take good care of her." She reaches up and ruffles Roan's hair. "I'll take care of yours if you take care of mine."

He's stiff but when he catches sight of Roux and Charlotte talking nearby, his shoulders sag in defeat. "Okay."

Jordy growls from behind me, but my mother doesn't notice his rage.

"Wonderful. How about we all meet up at The Mushroom Hut? My treat. Everyone loves pizza, right?" Mom beams at us. "You boys better shower first, though."

"We'll totally be there, Mrs. English," Sidney says, reaching over to take my hand. "Thanks for inviting us."

"Right. Meet you there," Roan grunts, pushing between Sidney and me, breaking our hands apart.

Mom tosses me a knowing wink, which I pretend I didn't see. She has no idea how much this guy hates me. And she just invited all the Hornets for dinner. Fucking great.

"We're almost there," Sidney assures me and points. "Turn here."

I'd wanted to drive alone, but Sidney hopped in my car when everyone left the pizza restaurant. The Hornets surprisingly hung out with Roux and Charlotte, ignoring us, while Sidney and Gio chattered my mom's ear off. No fights broke out, so I consider dinner a success.

Even if I couldn't stomach a single bite of the pizza.

I pull up to a snow-covered camp area, nestled in the woods, and shut off the car. Vehicles are parked already. It appears we've arrived later than most everyone. I'm about to open my door when Sidney runs her palm over my jean-clad thigh.

"I like your mom," she says softly. "Much nicer than mine."

"Thanks."

Her palm slides higher. "We could be good together, you know. Really good." She palms my cock through my jeans, making me hiss out.

Gripping her wrist, I pull it gently away. "No."

Shock morphs her pretty features. Apparently Sidney isn't used to being told no. For a brief moment, she seems tired. Used and abused and worn out. When she's not smiling, she looks pretty fucking sad.

I hold her hand, threading my fingers with hers. "It's not that kind of no. Not how you're thinking. More like the fact that I couldn't ever reciprocate."

"I give good head," she whispers. "I don't need anything in return."

"You should, Sidney," I say firmly, pinning her with a hard stare. "You're sweet and funny and fucking beautiful."

Her lashes bat hard at her cheeks, but it's because her eyes are watering and she's trying desperately to hold back tears. "Why are you saying these things?" A tear leaks down her cheek.

I reach up and swipe it away. "Because they're true. You'll make some guy really happy. Just not this guy. And, for the love of God, stay away from the Hornets."

"If I'm so funny and pretty, why doesn't anyone want me?" Her bottom lip wobbles. "Not you. Not the Hornets."

"I can't speak for those assholes, though I'm almost positive it's because they're self-centered dickheads who only love themselves, but I can speak for me." I give her a genuine smile. "Sid, I'm gay."

She blinks at me as my words settle in. "What?"

"Gay. Not bi. Just gay. I like guys."

"Oh."

Leaning in, I kiss her wet cheek. "But if I were straight, you'd be my type. The serious girlfriend with marriage potential type. I hope you find someone who sees that because you deserve it."

She hugs me and then cries softly into my neck. I stroke her silky hair, almost wishing I could be that person for her. I can barely be the person I need to be for me. Someone bangs on the window, making Sidney scream in surprise.

"Hey, lovebirds, save some kisses for me," Gio says, pressing his mouth against the glass.

We both laugh at his antics.

"Yeah, yeah, we're coming," I grumble.

He walks off chuckling. I grab her hand and squeeze it.

"Listen," I say with a sigh. "Since you're my friend and all, I want to confide in you. While I'm gay, and I already came out in my old hometown, I'm not ready for that here. Not with the Hornets breathing down my neck and just getting on the basketball team. Can we keep it between us?"

"Can I at least tell Wendy? Gio? I need to tell someone. Please," she begs. "You can't give a girl such juicy information and tell her to zip her lips."

"You can tell Gio," I relent with a smile. "If you let him ask you out."

She snorts. "Good one."

"I'm being serious."

"Have you seen him? He drives a van."

"So?"

Her lips press together before she lets out a huff. "He's Gio. I don't know. I'm not attracted to him."

"Because you're attracted to assholes like the Hornets? How's that working out for you?"

She rolls her eyes. "Ugh. They're such dicks. Gio does make me laugh and he doesn't ever try to stick his tongue down my throat or cop a feel." Then, she stiffens. "What if he doesn't want to ask me out?"

At this, I laugh. "Are you serious? That boy is obsessed with you. Show one ounce of interest and he'll ask you out in a heartbeat."

"Obsessed? Why? What did he say about me?"

I try to mimic Gio, which makes Sidney giggle. "She's so sassy, Hollis. Her lips. Look at them. She's running her head about the craziest shit and I can't look away."

"That asshole," she shrieks, swatting at me. "I do not run my head."

"You totally do, but it's endearing."

She lets out an exaggerated huff. "Fine."

"Fine?"

"I won't tell anyone but Gio and I'll let him take me out *if* he asks."

"He'll ask."

Chapter Fourteen

Roan

It's cold as fuck tonight, but I love it. Something about the way it numbs me to my soul, I can't get enough of. Lately, everything hurts inside, and the bone-chilling is a preferable ache. People are everywhere. Each Friday night, probably half—the cool half—of the seniors show up. Everyone piles around one of the main cabins sleeping in tents and vehicles. Cal usually builds a big-ass bonfire that somehow reaches higher than the cabin and still manages not to burn the forest down.

Tonight feels different.

Rather than relaxed and happy in one of my few retreats in my world, I'm anxious. Unnerved. Jumpy. It has everything to do with the fact Hollis is planted on a log beside Sidney and Gio. While Sidney is a Campfire Chaos regular, Gio and Hollis are not. It's as though the freaks have infiltrated our fun.

I could have said no.

I could have looked Kelsey in the eye and told her he wasn't invited.

But she was so happy he was included. She wanted to keep Roux for the night. I just couldn't do that to her. I may be an asshole to a lot of people, but unfortunately it seems as though Kelsey isn't one of them.

Jordy bumps my shoulder with his and hands me a beer. I sip it, my stare never leaving Hollis. Snow flutters down but melts as it nears the heat of the fire. Even wearing my coat, heavy jeans, and boots, I'm still not warm.

"He needs to go," Jordy mutters under his breath that reeks of someone hitting the bottle a little too hard tonight. "After everything he did…" He trails off, an angry silence finishing his statement.

After everything he did to me and Roux.

Problem is, he didn't really do anything. Not directly. If anyone is to blame, it's his mother. And I've already established how I feel about getting pissy with her. Hollis is just an easier target for blame. He practically begs for it. Like he's a goddamn martyr.

"How is Roux?" Jordy asks before chugging his beer. "Is she sad?"

His question pokes a hole right in my heart. Jordy may be a lot of things—unhinged, psycho, mean—but he's nothing but loving when it comes to me and my sister.

"She likes Mike's place. Has a good view of some ducks."

We both laugh.

Our laughter earns Hollis's stare. I hold his eyes with mine as I continue to talk to Jordy. The heat of the gaze from the porcelain boy is hotter than the bonfire flames.

"It's safe. One full night there and I could tell a difference, man. She's not so tense. The haunted look in her eyes isn't fully there." I break Hollis's heated stare to look at my best friend. "If a day away from that fuckface Alexander and my mom makes her feel that good, imagine what a lifetime will do."

His eyes darken into demonic orbs that would scare the fuck out of anyone but me. I understand Jordy's intensity. He loves violently. "You think they'll ever pull some shit and try to get her back?"

I shrug. "She's her mom. Right now, no. Mom is a skanky addict. So, legally, no. Now I wouldn't put it past them to do some shady shit, especially Alexander."

Jordy grips the back of my neck and pulls me to him, our foreheads pressed together. "He can fucking try," Jordy growls. "But I promise you he'd die trying."

Someone whistles, pulling us from our deep conversation.

"Carson got some roman candles," Cal calls out. "Who wants to shoot shit off the bridge?"

He's drunk as shit already.

Trey nods at me, understanding my concerned look. He'll watch over him. That's always been the deal. I look out for Jordy and he looks out for Cal. Someone has to keep those two assholes in line.

"Come on. Let's go watch these dickheads blow their hands off."

By the time we reach the pedestrian bridge that crosses the Horn River from the campground to a park area, the wind is howling and spitting hard pellets of snow and ice at us. The alcohol is no longer keeping me warm. I'll need to somehow convince Sidney to get out of her Gio and Hollis sandwich so she can warm my sleeping bag up tonight.

Thoughts of Sidney riding my dick with her pert tits bouncing normally sends a spike of fire burning through me. Tonight, I feel nothing. I glance at her friend Wendy. The girl isn't as giving sexually as Sid, but I know she's given head to a few guys on the team. I bet I could get her in bed.

Sidney giggles, earning my attention. Gio is fucking with her. Flirting maybe. Whatever it is, she's into it, grinning in a silly way I've never seen. Hollis watches with satisfaction. He's dressed in his substitute teacher coat, but he's wearing jeans and Docs. A scarf is wrapped around his neck and a beanie is pulled down over his head.

He looks warm.

I shudder against the wind, forcing my feet to remain glued on the bridge over the river rather than carrying me over to him, seeking his warmth. Despite the freezing temperatures, the river rushes by beneath us. Cal, the fucking idiot, shoots off several roman candles, not mindful of everyone around him.

One of the drunk guys named Tim, who almost took a firework to the face, pushes Cal. He and Cal get into a shoving match until Trey tackles him against the railing. The wood snaps off with the weight of their bodies. Both Cal and Tim land on the snowy wooden floor of the bridge, but don't fall off. I start toward Trey as he grips the handle tight, but more parts of the bridge railing snap. He nearly goes over into the icy waters when Hollis flies out of nowhere, grabbing his coat before it's too late. I freeze, shocked that he got him in time.

No way.

My heart hammers in my chest as Trey shakes Hollis off him and storms away from the edge. Tim stumbles away as Cal rises to his feet. Jordy and I approach Hollis.

Hollis's gaze finds mine, seeking approval. Fuck if I don't want to give it to him. He just saved my friend. He deserves something. A smile of thanks tugs at my lips. One his eyes drop down to admire. I lick my cold lips, loving the heat that races straight to my dick when his eyes widen.

I start forward, unsure what I want to do. Maybe I'll tell him thank you. Maybe I'll just hug him. My mind drifts to the fire station. How he ran his fingers through my hair. What if I pressed my cold lips to his? My dick is halfway to hard.

We're so focused on each other that we don't notice Jordy.

Swift. Angry. A storm.

"This is for Roux," Jordy snarls.

I watch, horrified, as my best friend shoves Hollis off the bridge. The collective gasp from the group nearly rumbles the earth. I catch Hollis's eyes before he falls over.

Not afraid.

Fucking terrified.

It haunts me to my goddamn soul.

I charge over to the edge seconds too late. I heard the splash but didn't see it.

"What did you do?" I yell to Jordy. "What the fuck did you do?"

"Holy shit," Cal gasp.

"I, uh," Jordy stammers.

We all stare at the icy, churning waters, waiting for Hollis to come back up.

A hand.

One desperate grab for the surface, but an utter failure. It reminds me of when Roux fell in the public pool one summer when we were younger. Thrashed wildly before she sunk to the bottom and had to be fished out by a lifeguard.

Oh my fucking God.

"He can't swim."

My words barely leave my mouth before I dive off the bridge, dreading every second before my body hits the cold-ass water.

Icy hell.

That's the only way to describe the way it feels the moment I become fully submerged in the river. My muscles all scream in agony at once, my bones stiffen in protest. It's my lungs, though, that feel as though they'll collapse in on themselves. I burst to the surface, searching for where he might have gone.

"There!" Cal bellows, pointing to something splashing nearby.

I swim blindly toward it, my body seizing from the cold. Fifteen feet away maybe. *Swim faster, goddammit.* I throw every ounce of power I have into swimming his way. The current is carrying us at a steady rate. If I don't catch up to him soon, the waters will quicken and then dump us into the Columbia River. We may as well be dead then. The currents are much too strong in that river.

My fingers, stiff and aching, make purchase. A coat. I grab for it, but pull too hard. The coat yanks off into my arms. I sink under the water with the weight of it until I release it. Under the icy surface, I see a pale limb. Swimming hard, ignoring all my pains, I snatch the cold arm. I manage to get my arms around him and kick to the surface.

"Hollis," I croak, my voice hoarse from the exertion and cold. "Hollis!"

No response.

Fuck.

Fuck.

Think, Roan.

I start for the shore, my mind reeling. He needs CPR. I remember the basics from what we learned in eighth grade gym class. It'll have to do. My feet hit gravel and I drag us onto the banks. People can be heard hollering a distance back. I'm not worried about them. Just him.

Hot tears burn down my cheeks as I try to focus on reviving him. Fuck. I need to revive him. I don't know that he's breathing. My mind goes into autopilot, remembering Mr. Lancaster's lessons. Pinch the nose. Tilt the head back. Breathe. Chest compressions. If he pukes, turn his head to the side.

Though my heart is frantic inside my chest, I focus on helping him. Remembering every lesson learned. I repeat my actions until he chokes.

Oh fuck.

He's alive.

A garbled cry escapes me as I move his head to the side. River water rushes from his lips, followed by the most beautiful whine in the world. Music to my ears.

I'm so tired.

He starts shuddering, choked sobs coming from him, and all I can do is fall against him, desperate for warmth now that the chill from the air on my wet body is making me colder. Sleepiness hits fast. My eyes flutter closed until a bunch of voices surround us.

Gio.

He's so loud.

Barking out orders left and right.

I'm lifted by Trey and Cal. Two other guys come for Hollis. I try to open my mouth to speak, but my teeth are chattering too hard. Sidney and Wendy both are sobbing hard nearby.

What the fuck just happened?

Where's Jordy?

I grow dizzy and dazed on our journey. We're led to someone's Tahoe and then pushed inside. They drive like bats out of hell until we're back at the cabin. Once more, we're led inside.

"We should call an ambulance."

"We can't call this in."

"Holy shit, we're going to be in so much trouble."

"What the fuck is wrong with Jordy?"

"Stop talking and get their clothes off?"

All the voices are talking at once. It's confusing and maddening. I'm blinking hard trying to stay awake as Cal and Trey practically rip all my clothes off. Why are they getting me naked? It's fucking cold. I glance over to see some guys from the team doing the same for Hollis.

His ribs.

I can see his ribs.

Why is he so blue?

"Don't touch him," I snarl, my voice but a whisper.

"We're touching you because we have to get you warm," Cal says, lowering me onto the cabin bed.

Not me.

Him.

Hollis.

"Get him in here too," Cal instructs.

The guys lower Hollis into the bed beside me. It's weird as fuck that we're all naked. Cal's body is warm though as he curls around my body. The other guy, Gage, is coming in behind Hollis. Trey and Gio are throwing blankets on us. It's like some fucked up, warped wannabe orgy.

But no one is having sex.

Gage's arm brushes against mine and I bristle. I don't like the fact he's in his fucking boxers, rutting against Hollis.

I don't care if it's for warmth, I don't like it. My arm slides around Hollis's cold, limp body and I pull him to me.

His head turns toward mine. Blue eyes the same color as his lips now are glassy, but they assess me in a way that makes me think he's okay. I try to get closer to him. I need to feel him—to know he's alive. His cold hands find mine, clutching weakly. Cal is a wriggly fucker behind me but damn if I'm not enjoying every second of his warmth.

"Who ever knew we'd end up spooning and I'd be the big spoon?" Cal's drunk ass breathes against my hair. "I know I'm taller, but you've always been the big spoon type. Wanna switch places?" He pinches my frozen nipple, making me growl in warning. "I'll take that as a no, big boy." The drunk fucker tries to bite my shoulder.

I manage to pull myself closer to Hollis. Our noses are cold as they touch, but I need to be able to feel his breath on me. To remind myself he didn't drown. Everyone is loud around us—hell, even the two idiots in this little naked blanket fort—but it all kind of becomes muted as I focus on Hollis's ragged breathing.

In and out.

In and out.

Alive.

So fucking alive.

Chapter Fifteen

Hollis

I blink awake when someone shakes me. Roan's golden-brown eyes blaze with fire as he stares me down.

"Don't go to sleep," he orders, his words gravelly.

Funny how just a couple of days ago, I said the same thing to him. I'm not sure how much time has passed, but Cal and another guy are no longer in the bed with us. The cabin has been darkened and the fire from the fireplace glows brightly. People are hooting and laughing beyond the cabin doors. It's then I realize I'm alone with Roan.

Naked.

Heat burns up my spine, warming my still chilled flesh. My lungs hurt from sucking in so much water and my extremities still tingle. As though in tune to my thoughts, Roan rubs his cold feet against mine.

"I can't swim." I don't know why I need to say the words, but I do. "My, uh, my dad tried to teach me, but I always panicked. When I would panic, he'd get pissed off. I knew it would happen, so I started coming up with excuses not to go in the first place. I wasn't a disappointment if I never gave him anything to be disappointed about."

I squeeze my eyes shut, hating that I see my dad's scowl as we stand in the middle of our pool. Him yelling at me to "fucking try." Me trying and failing. The crying. The pain in my stomach, which is always worse when he's angry.

"Fuck your dad."

I'm jerked from the past and pop my eyes open. Roan's stare heats me to my bones. His face is so close to mine. I like the way his body is touching mine. A truce. I'm tired of being at war.

"I thought I was going to die," I croak, my body trembling.

Roan inches closer, his nose rubbing along my cheek as though he's inhaling me. His lips are on my skin when he says, "But you didn't. I saved you."

Turning toward his hot mouth, I chase down what I desperately need. Him. My lips—cold and chapped—brush along his. He sucks in a breath as we pause. I want to kiss him, but something holds me back. I want him to want it too. His hand finds my bare hip and I'm ready for him to push me away.

He does.

He does.

He fucking does.

But he goes with me, pushing his naked thigh between mine as his tongue plunges into my mouth. We both groan, surprised at the kiss, but then we become ravenous. I'm weak and aching and dizzy. His kiss is invigorating, though.

Rough and gentle.

How?

Sweet and bitter.

Why?

His tongue slides against mine, waking my dick as though it's stroking it instead. I moan into his mouth. This seems to set him off because he slides all the way on top of me. Our dicks are stone sandwiched between us. His mouth parts as a sexy growl tumbles out. He grinds his hips against mine, sending currents of pleasure exploding through me.

"Roan." My breathy plea is heard because he kisses me harder. Needier. Frantic. He ruts against me, every bit as eager for this feeling as I am. My fingers find his damp, messy hair and I tug on the strands. He hisses, nipping my bottom lip.

"Fuck, Hollis. What the fuck?"

I want to kiss him everywhere.

Taste every inch.

Feel him inside me.

The thoughts stampeding through my mind are too quick and chaotic to sort out. It's madness. Roan is a crazy addiction. I need this. I need him.

"Why do I want this?" he asks, pulling away slightly, his amber eyes flickering with confusion. "Why do I want you?"

"What is your type?"

"Not her."

"Are you bi?"

"I'm nothing."

"I want it too," I tell him, shoving the memory of our previous conversation away. He's not nothing. He's so much more than nothing. A million times more than nothing.

"But you're gay," he growls. "I'm..."

"Don't fucking say it."

Our eyes snap to each other. The word was on the tip of his tongue. I kiss him, stealing it from his lips and devouring it.

"You're Roan," I murmur. "You're not nothing."

He kisses me harder, his hips rocking wildly against me. Our breathing becomes ragged as he takes us closer to the edge. The moment I start to come, I grip his hair and arch my back, aching for every movement against me. His mouth finds my neck. He bites me and then sucks with enough vigor, he'll leave a mark. My cum jets out hot and thick, soaking our bellies between us. It's slick and he groans against my neck.

"I'm checking on them, dipshit," Trey bellows as he stumbles into the cabin.

Roan tenses up and his heart pounds through his chest to dance with mine. His cock pulses against my slick skin, throbbing with the need for release.

"We're fine," Roan says, his voice tight. "He's still alive."

Trey lets out a sharp breath before falling onto the covers behind Roan. Roan is stiff, his face still against my neck. Within seconds, Trey is breathing deeply with sleep. I slide my hand between us, wetting my hand in my cum, and then wrap my hand around Roan's dick. Long, thick, hot. He chokes on a moan.

"Shh," I murmur as I stroke him. "Don't wake him."

Roan's lips press to my flesh and his hips flex slightly, meeting my hand at each stroke. I use my cum like lube and give him the best damn hand job considering our shitty situation. It only takes a few expert tugs before his dick swells and throbs out his release. He soaks us even more, but I love it. I greedily steal these moments with him because who the fuck knows what tomorrow will look like.

"Fuck," Roan whispers.

"Yeah, fuck."

I feel his smile on my neck and damn if that doesn't feel better than blowing my load all over the hottest mean boy I've ever met.

He's going to kill me.

And not in the way Jordy's psycho ass nearly did.

Roan has stuck his hand inside my chest and plucked my heart from its cage. It beats like crazy in his fist. He can keep it, or he can crush it. No matter what he does, it won't matter. I've given it to him, and it scares the shit out of me, because I know I'll never get it back.

"Still alive?"

I blink open my eyes, instantly feeling aches in every muscle, as I seek out the sound of the sweet, feminine voice.

"Define alive."

Sidney laughs. "You're talking, so you lived. I thought having to spend the night with the Hornets, you'd for sure be dead meat."

I sit up and survey the cabin. Everyone's gone. "Where'd everybody go?"

"No one sticks around past noon on Saturdays after Campfire Chaos. We're some of the last few. You're my ride, so..."

"Oh, shit. Sorry. I was completely out of it."

"Someone had a good dream," Sidney says, darting her eyes to my bare abs that are crusted with a fuck ton of cum.

Well, that's awkward.

"Um..." I rake my fingers through my hair and give her a frantic look. "It's..."

"It happens," she says with a laugh. "I'll pretend it was me you were thinking about."

I grin at her. "Because that doesn't make it any less uncomfortable."

She stands and walks into the kitchen area. I'm still

scanning the cabin, looking for clothes, when she returns with a wet rag.

"Where's my bag?"

"Still in the car," she says, tossing the rag at me. "I'll go grab it. Wanted to make sure you were alive first. It would have been wasted efforts to go grab clothes for a corpse." She smiles sweetly.

I shake my head at her as I scrub off my mess, trying not to give this girl too much of a show. "Nice, Sid."

"Not to mention, I didn't want to miss a naked shot." She shrugs her shoulders. Her words are meant to be playful, though. Something's different with her.

"Where's Gio?"

Her face blushes bright red. "He went home."

"Is he okay?"

"Of course he's okay," she says grumpily. "Why wouldn't he be?"

"It was just a question. I didn't see him after all that shit that happened."

She crosses her arms over her chest and frowns. "Sorry. I'm feeling…"

"Defensive?"

"Yeah."

"And why's that?"

"You were right."

My brows hike up. "With Gio?"

"Yeah. He's…I don't know how to explain him. He just sees a me not many people do."

"Did you two…"

"Fuck? Because that's what I'm known for?" Her cheeks burn bright red again and her bottom lip trembles.

"I was going to say kiss."

"Oh." She huffs. "Sorry. I suck at this." Her finger toys at a strand of her brown hair as she frowns. "I was upset after what Jordy did. They had you taken care of, but I was shaken up. Gio came over to me and hugged me. Asked if I wanted to talk about it. So we went for a walk. It got colder, so we decided to talk more in his tent." She swallows hard. "I feel like such a whore, Hollis."

"What? Why?"

"He kissed me. It was sweet. Nice. I really liked it. Too much. I just threw myself at him and started getting naked." A tear races down her cheek. "He kissed me again. Softly. Then told me to put my shirt back on." Another tear. "I was devastated at having been rejected. I bawled my eyes out. He just held me. Cuddled me to him. Kept kissing my tears away. When I calmed down, he said he wants to get to know me first. Asked if we could go out on a date. He wants to take me to dinner. Maybe meet his mom. I felt like such a skank."

"You're not a skank, Sid."

"But I am. I've been freely giving it up to anyone who'll give me the time of day. It's just sex. Empty sex. They never stick around for the after. I didn't realize I wanted an after." She chuckles. "Gio isn't even my type, but he just sees me. I've never been seen like that before. I'm excited to go out with him tonight. Not because I think we'll have sex, but because I want to spend more time with him and argue with him about all the dumb stuff he says. He's funny and a smartass, but he's sweet." Her lips turn up. "He's a great kisser too."

"Gio's a great guy and you're a great girl. You two need to make a go at it. I'm happy you're giving him a chance."

She stands and fishes out my keys from my soaked jeans pocket. "Now that I'm taken care of, we just need to find you a boyfriend."

I don't want a boyfriend.

I want a Hornet.

"How about we start with my clothes first, Cupid."

Chapter Sixteen

Roan

Jordy paces the living room of our garage apartment, looking more broken than ever before. I didn't realize my best friend was going through some mental shit. Enough that he'd try to kill Hollis over it. It's fucked up, and I'm going to get to the bottom of it.

"Talk to me, man," I urge, crossing my arms over my chest. "Tell me what's going through your head."

I don't blame him. He's my brother. In that moment, he probably felt like he was trying to protect us. But normally, he wouldn't make such a life-changing decision. I don't need him going to prison for me. I need him here with me.

"Jordy…"

"I just," he grits out, rubbing his palms over his buzzed head. "I get so fucking angry sometimes." He drags his hands over his face, his fingers spread wide, and peeks his dark eyes at me, before letting his hands fall at his side. "You're family. He's a threat to my family."

"Hollis isn't a threat," I tell him. "Sure, he's stirring shit up when it comes to me and Roux, but it's not like that. He doesn't intentionally mean to harm us." I take a step closer to him and grip his shoulder. "He's just the tip of the iceberg. What's going on?"

He cracks his neck and walks away from me to continue his pacing. "Just some shit with Juno."

His brother Juno who owns the garage can be a mega dick. At one time, he used to whip up on Jordy. Then, Jordy bulked up so he could return the ass kicking. Ever since, Juno has left him alone. They get along enough for Jordy to work there with him. Their parents are older and oblivious to their sons' troubles. His mom is clueless and thinks her boys do no wrong. Their father is a workaholic who works long hours at the tire factory.

"Is he being an asshole again?"

"Juno's always being an asshole. This is..." He lets out a heavy sigh. "He's mixed up with some people."

"What kind of people?"

"Fucking criminal lowlifes."

"Juno? Since when?"

"Since he's been struggling at the shop. Did some jobs for a guy named Rex. Mostly just chopping some stolen cars."

I frown, rubbing the tension from the back of my neck. "You can't get involved in that shit, man."

He scowls at me. "I already am, Roan. I've been helping him because what choice do I have? But it's never ending. Rex pays him good for this crap, so the jobs keep coming. But so do his asshole friends."

"Are they giving you trouble?"

"Nothing I can't handle."

"Do we need to kick anyone's asses?"

Jordy snorts. "And risk you losing Roux? Fuck no, man. Why do you think I've left you out of it? You have enough to deal with just trying to keep food in her mouth. And now with you two staying here, it's too much. I'm not getting you involved."

"I can help," I mutter, though we both know I can't.

"I don't want you to." He levels me with a firm glare. "You take care of Roux. She's the most important thing to me. To us. I'd do whatever the fuck I had to in order to make sure she's far away from this crap. She needs you. I've got this."

But he doesn't.

He's barely hanging on by a thread here.

"What if you just quit working there?" I ask. "Maybe we could find a job together someplace else. The tire factory with your dad maybe? I need to figure out a way to pay Mike back for all this."

Jordy's anger melts away and he just stares at me. Like a father would his son who doesn't understand the complicated ways of the world. "I can't untangle myself. But you haven't been to the shop in ages. Just stay away, okay? Keep doing what you have to do for Roux."

"I don't like this," I growl, irritated that he's going to take on this burden himself. "It's fucked up." It's driving him to places I never thought Jordy was capable of. Like pushing some kid into a frozen river, hoping he would die.

A shiver runs down my spine as I remember how fucking cold that river was.

"I don't like it either," Jordy mumbles. "But I'll figure it out. It's what we do. We're Hornets. We don't let life fuck us. We get on our feet and fuck life."

I pull him to me and hug him. "Don't push me away. If you need help, you know where to find me. I have Mike and the station. He has connections. If we need to get the police—"

"Don't. Don't ever say that." His voice is fierce and hard. "They'll fucking kill you. Just don't."

And as much as I hate to, I know I'll never mention it again.

"I can't keep Roux safe if I'm worrying about you," I tell him. "Take care of yourself. We need you."

"Like I said," he growls. "I've got this. Now let's go pick up Little Hornet and grab lunch. I'm fucking starving."

Conversation officially over.

But no matter what he says, I know he doesn't have it. He's barely holding it together. Just another goddamn thing to stress out over.

"Who the hell is Kayden?" I demand, tossing my sister's notebook onto her bed.

She pushes her glasses up her nose and rolls her eyes. "A boy."

"No boys. Ever."

"Why not?" she demands, her brows furling angrily.

"I don't know. Because you're thirteen."

"Almost fourteen."

"Big fucking whoop. Fourteen is still too young for boys."

"You're not my dad." She grabs her notebook and shoves it into her backpack, tears welling in her honey-brown eyes that match mine.

Guilt nearly knocks me the hell over. I've been a mess this weekend. I'm worried about Jordy. Stressed over Roux's and my living situation. And then there's Hollis.

Fuck.

I've been trying to push what happened far into the back of my mind. But the last two nights, it's all I can think about. I lie awake thinking about how terrified I felt when I saw him go into the water, which makes no sense since I barely know him. Mostly, I think about kissing him. His hot, urgent tongue. The way our bodies rubbed together. How he came all over me and then used his fucking cum to jack me off.

Two nights in a row, I jerked off to that image.

Why?

I don't even like guys.

Except him.

Hell, I'm not sure if I even like him.

But I like the way he felt. The way he tasted. Each sound that rumbled up his throat. It's maddening and addictive. I want more, yet I want to run away. Today, at school, I'll have to face him. He didn't try to message me all weekend, or if he did, I don't know because my phone was ruined in the river. I don't know what the fuck to even say to him.

"I didn't mean it," Roux says, throwing her arms around me. "I'm sorry."

"Hey," I murmur, rubbing her back. "I'm not mad. Just lost in thought. Promise it's not about you."

She pulls away and smiles. "About a girl? Sidney?"

"Not Sidney."

"Oh good. Sidney's a hoochie."

I snort. "What's a hoochie?"

"A girl who makes out with all the guys and wears shirts that let her boobs hang out."

"If you ever turn into a hoochie, I'll beat your ass,"

I tease, ruffling her hair. "No boys need to see that shit. Especially Kayden."

Her face falls. "Kayden is so hot. He doesn't like me, though. The only reason he talks to me now is because of Charlotte."

"Oh yeah?"

"You've seen her," she mumbles, rolling her eyes. "She's so beautiful with her blond hair and fancy clothes. I'm..." She waves at her outfit. Guilt swarms up inside me that I can't buy her nice clothes like Charlotte wears. "I'm just me."

"You're not just anything, Roux. You're everything. To me, you're the best damn person on the planet."

She beams at me. "Now if you could only convince the boys at my school."

"Maybe the boys at your school don't deserve you. Maybe you'll find someone better when you go to high school next year." I'll still whip anyone's ass who looks at her wrong, but at least she can have something to look forward to.

"So if a boy asks me out, you're going to let me go?" she taunts.

"You're pushing it, kid. I might let him think about dating you, but I doubt I'll let him actually do it."

"Punk."

"Just protecting you."

Someone honks and I peek out the window. Jordy is out front in his Ford Explorer. We lock up and head downstairs.

"Hey, Little Hornet," Jordy says when we get in his car. "Liking your new place?"

"It's super nice, Jordy. You gotta come over and hang

out one day. There's even food in our fridge. Roan says he's going to teach me to cook some stuff."

Jordy grins at her in the mirror. "He only knows how to make grilled cheese."

"The best grilled cheese," I argue. It is the best. I butter it just right and watch it like a hawk so it gets toasty but not burned.

"I make tacos that will make you cry," Jordy brags. "Your brother's grilled cheese pales in comparison."

"Hey, I can make tacos," I grumble.

"Not generic-ass tacos." Jordy shakes his head. "Flap meat seasoned with lime salt and pepper. Sautéed onions to throw in there. Heat up some soft corn tortillas. Heaven in your mouth, Little Hornet."

"Yum," she groans.

"I'm not done yet," he teases. "I make a homemade salsa too. Tomatoes and tomatillos with chiles de árbol. Garlic, salt, clove, onions, a little cilantro. Your mouth will be spoiled, niñita."

"You can move in with us. Be our own personal chef," Roux tells him.

He laughs and fuck if it isn't a great sound to hear. "And I didn't even tell you about my homemade guac."

"Dude," I groan. "We get it. Your culinary prowess outshines mine every day of the week."

He ignores me, continuing to taunt. "Ripe avocados, tomatoes, green jalapeno chilies, cilantro, lime juice. Just mix it all in and serve it up. You've never had good food until you've had my food."

Roux giggles in the back. "You're conceited."

"It's not being conceited when it's the truth," he volleys back.

We continue our banter until we pull up to the middle school. Roux jumps out and gives us a little wave before walking toward the doors. When a lanky boy with dark hair that hangs in his eyes walks up to her, Jordy and I glare.

"Who the fuck is that?" Jordy demands.

"If I had to guess, it's Kayden."

The boy in question shoots us a panicked look. I guess he can feel the intensity of our stares.

Roux turns to look at us and mouths, "Please stop."

"Just go," I grumble.

Jordy drives up slowly, turning his neck to give this kid the stare down. Finally we leave the parking lot with a squeal of tires.

"You know we're going to have to kill him," Jordy says. Normally, I'd think he's joking, but after the Hollis shit, I'm not so sure.

"She likes him. It's the first boy who's ever talked to her. This shit is hard," I complain. Sometimes being more of a father to your sister than a brother is confusing.

"It's not hard," Jordy bites out. "She doesn't get to talk to boys. She's a kid."

"Try telling her that."

"I will."

Stubborn ass.

"And your role as her favorite will soon be downgraded. I made her cry earlier when I threw a fit over this boy. Trust me, leave it alone if you don't want her to hate you."

He doesn't confirm nor deny he will as we pull into the parking lot of our school. Of course Jordy parks right next to Hollis's purple Mustang.

Before we get out, I grab Jordy's arm and level him with a firm look. "Leave him alone."

His face grows stormy.

"I'm serious, Jordy. I need you to just back off when it comes to Hollis."

"You think he's going to tell what I did?" His eyes darken.

"No. I just don't want to see him get hurt."

"Why not? He's just a fucking gay rat. No one gives a shit about him."

I pop my knuckles and shrug. "Someone does."

"Someone, huh?"

"Yeah. And someone cares about you too. So don't fuck shit up because Juno is a dick and pissing you off. I need you. You feel me?"

"I still think he's a little bitch," Jordy tells me. "But I won't fucking touch him."

I let out a heavy sigh of relief.

"But that doesn't mean I won't tell him what a little bitch he is." He climbs out of the vehicle and starts stalking toward a group of people.

Hollis, wearing another substitute teacher coat, turns just in time to lock eyes with Jordy. His eyes widen, a flash of fear glimmering in them. I'm out of the car and rushing to catch up to Jordy in my next breath. I manage to grab his backpack right before he reaches Hollis. All the kids around him seem to slink away. Sidney and Gio step forward like their scrawny asses will do shit.

"Watch yourself, rat," Jordy sneers at Hollis. "Wouldn't want you to misstep again and fall. Like last time."

Jesus fucking Christ.

Hollis's blue eyes dart to mine, hurt and accusing. "Not a problem, man," he says to Jordy, but glares at me. "I'll stay away."

I shoot Hollis an apologetic look, but he's already turning his back on us. A bold move considering Jordy is unpredictable as fuck. I grab my best friend and manhandle him toward the door. This whole situation is bullshit.

Chapter Seventeen

Hollis

I lay my cheek against the cool gray-painted cinderblock wall. I'm not going to puke. I'm not going to puke. I'm not going to puke. My stomach recoils and burns, but nothing comes up. It's a good thing I passed up bacon and eggs this morning. That shit would be sick coming back up. Another wave of nausea hits me. Thinking of food is not wise.

Instead, I think about Dad's text, which isn't much better.

Dad: We need to talk.

I don't want to talk to him. Not after everything he did. The way he went on a fucking rampage because he found out I like guys. Big deal. Apparently to him, it's the biggest deal. I've never seen a grown man throw such a temper tantrum in all my life.

I should have known he would have flipped.

I'm an embarrassment to his name.

Don't I even know what this could do to his reputation at the hospital?

In other countries, people are killed for this bullshit.

The last part is what sent Mom into a rare momma bear rage. She got into a screaming match with my father and told him I was his son. That he wasn't allowed to treat me that way. He told her I was worthless and since I was eighteen, I needed to go. She said that if I go, we all go. He'd be left all alone. My father said it was better than living with a freak.

And here we are.

Mom yanked her kids up so fast and left his ass, he didn't have much time to react. He was pissed. Blamed me. Blamed her. But too much of an asshole to fight to try and at least get her and the girls to stay. Instead, the stubborn dick let us leave.

And now he wants to talk.

Too little, too late.

What does he even want to talk about? Does he want them back? Does he want to make amends? Is he trying to get our cars back?

The not knowing makes my head spin. But I also don't want to talk to him, so I guess I'll never know.

I pull out the other phone in my pocket. I'd bought it Saturday after I dropped Sidney off. For Roan. But then he avoided me like the plague and now has sided with his psycho bestie.

I expected more from him.

That kiss…it just felt like more than a simple night of pleasure.

As soon as I feel better, I stand and shove the phones into my pocket. I'm shaky as I make my way over to the sink. After a quick splash of water on my face, I stare at my reflection. I'm paler than usual. The bags under my eyes are dark and pronounced. My cheeks seem hollowed out. Frankly, I look like shit. I feel like it too.

I should go back into the lunchroom where I abandoned my untouched lunch tray. Gio and Sidney are probably worried about me if they're not still making out. It's weird to see geeky Gio with someone like Sidney, but they somehow seem to work. Everyone else is totally freaked out by them. Even her friend Wendy has taken to hanging out with some other girls.

The door to the bathroom opens and I close my eyes, not wanting to make eye contact with anyone when I feel like this. Footsteps squeak across the linoleum. But when I don't hear one of the stalls open, I open my eyes.

Oh, fuck.

Roan stares at me in the mirror, just a couple feet beside me. His bronze eyes are intense and assessing. They could almost be confused with worry. I know better, though. He's not worried. If anything, he's worried I'll tell everyone he had a weak gay moment.

Whatever.

"What?" I rasp out, hating that my voice is shaky.

He steps closer. "You okay?"

"Yep."

"Liar."

"What do you want?" I demand, turning to glower at him. "Your friends are waiting. Jordy is waiting."

He lets out a heavy sigh and runs his fingers through his hair, his eyes darting in an almost frantic way. "Listen…"

"I get it," I hiss. "It was an accident. You were drunk. Whatever. I'm fine."

Scowling, he shakes his head. "I wasn't drunk. It wasn't a fucking accident, Hollis."

Hollis. Not rat.

My heart cracks down the middle.

God, I hate this guy.

"Just not good enough to acknowledge or talk about," I state bitterly. "Could have fooled me when you came all over—"

He grabs the front of my sweatshirt and pulls me closer. "Lower your voice."

"Right," I sneer. "Wouldn't want it to get out that you kissed a guy and fucking liked it."

His eyes dart to my lips and it makes my heart flop inside my chest. "I didn't like it."

I flinch at his words.

"I didn't like it," he mutters, leaning closer. "Because I loved it." His breath is hot, just inches from my mouth. "Confusing as fuck, but I loved it."

"I loved it too," I say with a sigh. "But that's because I'm gay. Gays like kissing guys. It's the way of our rainbow-colored world."

"I loved the other stuff too." Roan's lips inch closer to mine. So close. "It felt good."

This guy makes no sense. I don't understand him one bit.

"But," I whisper.

His lips press to mine, urgent and desperate. It ignites the anger inside me, turning it into a blazing inferno of need. Our mouths part and I slide my tongue against his, eager for another taste. Strong fingers bite into my hip as he walks me back toward a wall. He kisses me hungrily and wildly. The moment his hips press against mine, I feel just how aroused he is. His dick is every bit as hard as mine. We both want this.

I slide my fingers into his hair, tugging, pulling him closer to me. I'm starved for more of him. He blew me off after that night, hasn't apologized, and I just forgive him. The guy doesn't deserve my forgiveness, but I gift it anyway.

"I'm sorry." His words come out as a breathy surprise against my wet, swollen lips. He trails a line of wet kisses to my earlobe. "Everything's just so fucked up." His teeth tug at my earlobe and I nearly nut in my pants.

Holy fuck.

"Roan," I groan, greedily touching him wherever I can.

His lips find the side of my neck and he licks the skin there. Then, he sucks me into his mouth. Hard. Urgent. As though he wants to leave a memory of his mouth for all to see. I moan, tugging at his hair.

Someone laughs just outside the door and Roan practically jumps three feet in the air. He retreats away from me, his eyes wide with panic. With his disheveled hair and boner, there's no hiding he was just making out with me. No one comes inside, so he broke away for nothing.

"Fuck," he groans. "I, uh, I kind of lost control."

I lick my lips, craving another kiss, but knowing I won't get another one now that he's been spooked. "I liked it."

A grin tugs at his lips. "I liked it too." His smile falls. "But…"

"You're not gay. Got it."

He rolls his eyes. "It's not that, rat."

"Oh, look, the pretty boy can rhyme."

His eyes darken. "Don't be a dick."

"You literally just called me a rat. You're the dick, not me."

"Stop talking about dicks or mine won't calm the fuck down." He smirks. "We can talk about dicks later."

Later?

I frown at him. "What do you want?"

"You."

Not the answer I was expecting.

"I'm right here." I fling my arms in the air. "Come get me."

He looks over his shoulder and flinches. "I can't."

This is my last school all over again with Lucas.

"Because it's okay to fuck around with me behind closed doors, but not where anyone can see." My words drip with bitter venom.

Slowly, he approaches me and raises a hand to run his knuckle along my jaw. "I don't give a shit what those assholes think."

My eyes lift to meet his. "So what's your deal?"

"Roux."

"Roux won't care who you date. She's cool."

He smiles, but then it fades. "Yeah, but how do I know this won't somehow hurt her? What if the social worker freaks if she finds out about my…relationship?"

Now I feel like an asshole. He's afraid they'll take her away from him for good if he slips up.

"Relationship, huh?" I arch a brow at him. "You don't even like me."

"You're growing on me," he says, leaning in to steal a quick kiss. "Like a fungus."

"You should get a job writing inscriptions on Hallmark cards," I deadpan.

He snorts. "Seems like a cool job."

"The last guy I dated…" I sigh. "We had to hide."

Shame burns in his eyes. "That's fucked up."

"Yeah." I kiss him again. "But it's fine. I came out once before and it nearly ruined my life. Not exactly eager to do that again."

"So what is this then? Some kind of truce?"

"More than a truce. A pact."

"A pact for what?"

"To see where this goes. In secret."

"What if it goes nowhere?"

"Then nobody has to know about our fuck up."

He smiles. "And what if it goes somewhere?"

"You have to admit you like me then."

"I don't think I'll ever like you," he teases. "Not you. You're too perfect, porcelain boy. Makes me want to break you."

"Wow," I say with a whistle. "Put that in a proposal and I'll marry you tomorrow."

He laughs, playfully shoving me away. "You're such a smartass. Am I the only one who gets to see this wonderful side of you?"

"It's one of my secrets. You're my secret. It's fitting you know all the shitty sides of me too."

His eyes narrow. "Speaking of…what's the deal with not eating?"

My stomach clenches violently at his words.

"Sometimes food makes me sick. The end." I shove my hand in my pocket and hand him a phone. "Here, secret lover."

"Don't call me that," he grumbles as he eyes the phone warily. "What's that?"

"Don't make me say it."

He clenches his jaw.

"It's a phone," I say slowly like I'm teaching a caveman my language. "You put it to your ear—"

"No shit, Sherlock," he snaps, his shoulders going rigid. "Why are you handing it to me?"

I shove it into his jeans pocket and leave my hand inside his pocket. "Because you're my secret lover and I need to get a hold of you."

"I'm not some fucking girlfriend you have to impress, rat."

"And I'm not an asshole, rat lover."

A muscle ticks in his jaw. "Don't call me that."

"Dude, you have no room to talk." I slowly pull my hand from his jeans, letting my fingers brush against his dick along the way. "Yours got ruined when you had to rescue my ass. It's called returning a favor. Just use the phone and forget all this proud crap you do. Okay? It can be another damn secret. I…" I let out a heavy sigh. "I got another one at the house for Roux."

He blinks several times in shock, his jaw clenching.

"So she can talk to Charlotte. I overheard her talking about how kids were teasing her and since I was already replacing ours, it cost like ten bucks more to add another one."

It wasn't ten bucks.

It was over a grand that I took from my savings—money that should have gone to help Mom out but didn't—to replace my phone and buy two more, but I'm sure as hell not telling him that.

"Ten bucks, huh?"

"Yep."

"When you lie, your cheek twitches."

"When you're being an asshole, your mouth moves and words come out."

He barks out a laugh. "I hate you."

"Now you can call me on your phone and tell me how much. Just make sure you breathe heavily into the phone. For reasons."

His smirk is hot. He quirks up his brow, making his barbell piercing glint in the bathroom light. "What reasons?"

"Do it and you'll find out."

He bites on the inside of his bottom lip, his amber eyes dancing with humor. "I'll find out tonight. When you're all cozy and half asleep, I'll call you. Breathe heavily to piss you off."

"It's hard to be pissed off when you're naked and your secret lover is breathing heavily on the other line." I give him my best smoldering look. It works because his eyes drift to my lips, lingering there.

"Are you always this much of a brat?"

"Guess you'll have to spend more time with me to find out."

He smiles. "See you after practice. We can spend time together cleaning your aunt's attic. I'll put you to work. That'll teach your mouthy ass."

"Never speak the words 'mouth' and 'ass' to a gay man and not expect him to get turned right the fuck on." I lift a brow. "You're poking a bear."

He walks right up to me, lips nearly on mine, and boldly rubs my dick through my jeans. "I'd rather stroke a rat."

Fucker.

I groan, my lips parting with need.

He gifts me with a wild grin and then he's gone. I'm left with a boner and a thrill buzzing through my veins.

I'm not sure what sort of shit I've tangled myself into with Roan.

I just know I'm not ready to get out.

I'm in.

One hundred percent in.

Chapter Eighteen

Roan

Jordy shoots me a sour look on the way to the parking lot, but doesn't fight me. I told him I was hitching a ride with Hollis since we're going to the same place. He didn't want to give in. I could tell. But then Juno called.

I wanted to ask him what Juno wanted.

Instead, I gave him a look that said, "Be careful."

Charlotte and Roux are sitting on the hood of Hollis's Mustang talking to that damn boy again. As soon as Jordy sees him, he starts stalking toward him rather than his Explorer. The kid—Kayden—freezes when he sees all that wrath directed at him.

Jordy is like trying to tame a pissed off bull.

Impossible.

"Hey, Roux," Jordy says, his voice a growl. "I'm leaving."

Roux frowns, looking over at me before nodding at Jordy. "Okay. Bye."

Kayden takes a few steps back, wise to put space between him and the bull.

"See you in the morning." Jordy pulls her to him for a side hug. "You call me if anyone's a dick to you." He makes a point at glowering at Kayden. "Got it, Little Hornet?"

Her face is red from embarrassment. She likes this kid

and Jordy is even more overbearing than me. "Yeah, fine. See ya."

Jordy smirks at the kid and then fist bumps me on the way to his car. Hollis comes up behind me, hitting the fob on his Mustang.

"My car's not a bench," Hollis gripes.

Charlotte rolls her eyes at her brother. "Don't be lame."

Kayden snorts, but all it takes is a venomous look from me to have the kid retreating. "See you guys tomorrow." He waves and then turns to take off trotting. Dumbass lanky motherfucker.

The girls pile into the backseat and I sit shotgun. Hollis fires up the engine. He fumbles with the music before turning on something I don't recognize. It's catchy, though. I like it. The girls must know it because they start singing along.

For so long I've been wound up so tight I sometimes think I might snap. But right here, in this moment, I feel relaxed. Freed. Like a teenager enjoying himself, not worrying about adult shit like custody of his sister or where his next meal will come from. I wish I were free enough to reach over the console and give Hollis's muscular thigh a squeeze. To thank him for showing up and fucking shit up.

He shoots me a curious glance. I smile and wink at him. His pallid cheeks flood with color. I like when I turn the porcelain boy a pretty pink. It looks good on him. Makes him look alive. I especially like the purple hickey visible on his neck.

I gave him that mark.

Me.

A possessive part of me gets a thrill at seeing it. All through basketball practice, I kept staring at it. It took everything in me not to get a fucking hard-on. Coach was already annoyed with my playing. The last thing I needed was to give him something else to lose his head about.

When the girls start whispering about Kayden, I turn up the music to feign disinterest when really I'm listening hard.

"He likes you," Charlotte murmurs.

"No," Roux hisses. "He likes you."

"No, dummy, he likes you. Have you seen how he smiles at you?"

Roux giggles. "I don't think so."

"I know so," Charlotte argues.

"Shh," Roux gripes.

They lower their voices. Even though I don't care for this dipshit boy, I'm thankful for Charlotte. She's the best thing to happen to Roux. My sister is coming out of her shell and laughs a whole lot more.

When I glance over at Hollis, a warm feeling washes over me. Maybe it's not just Charlotte changing things around here. Maybe it's her brother too.

He flashes me a wicked grin that sends heat burning straight down to my dick.

Fuck if I don't feel thankful for him too.

This is torture.

I thought I'd get Hollis up in the attic alone with me and I don't know…suck his face off. But his aunt has decided to come up here and nose around in the boxes. He keeps smirking at me, which only serves to make my dick even harder.

My life is chaos at the moment, and I don't even care because this thing with Hollis is addictive. I want to explore it and see where it goes. It sucks I have to be careful, though. With Roux, I always have to be careful. I don't ever want to do anything to fuck things up for us.

"I think that's enough for one night, boys," Ms. Frazier says. "The meatloaf should almost be done. Wash up and come on down."

I'm already prowling Hollis's way before she even makes it down the ladder. What stops me, though, is the sour look on his face. My hands grip his hips because I need to touch him, but I don't kiss him like I want to.

"What's wrong? Are you sick?" I demand, my eyes roaming over his features, looking for tells.

Dark bags under his eyes.

Pasty skin.

Trembling.

"Sit down," I instruct, pulling him down to the attic floor.

We sit cross-legged and facing each other. His hands are shaking. I take them both in mine. He has smaller hands than me, but they're still masculine. If you told me two weeks ago I'd be holding hands with a guy, I would've fucking laughed. Now, it just feels right.

"What's going on with you?" My words crack with emotion.

He scowls. I don't know why he's so damn defensive about this shit.

"Nothing."

"If you tell me nothing one more time, I'm going to drag you out back and beat you." I give him a wide, wicked smile.

He rolls his eyes. "It's fine. I just…certain foods make me sick."

"Like?"

"Meatloaf," he snaps angrily.

"So why do you eat it?"

"I don't."

"Why don't you eat something else?"

He shrugs. "I don't like to make waves. Mom and Aunt Karen are doing the best they can."

"What foods don't hurt?"

"Blander ones. It's not a big deal."

"Hollis, it is a big deal. You barely fucking eat. I've known you a little over a week and I've seen you consume less than I do in a day. It's not healthy. Have you seen a doctor?"

"My dad is a doctor. I'm fine."

God, he's so damn stubborn.

"Come on." I rise and help him to his feet. Our lips meet for a frenzied kiss, but someone hollering from downstairs has us reluctantly breaking apart. I go first down the ladder so I can catch his woozy ass if he passes out. Thankfully, it doesn't come to that.

We head downstairs and I watch Hollis. He nearly turns green when he looks at the meatloaf. It's a little chaotic as everyone loads food on their plates. Hollis piles on the mashed potatoes and green beans and then takes the thinnest slice of meatloaf known to man.

No one notices.

He hides his issues in plain sight.

The girls—Roux and Charlotte—are too into each other while Penny is obsessed with her iPad. Karen and Kelsey are busy with asking everyone about their day. No one notices Hollis. No one but me.

I sit beside him and squeeze his thigh under the table. When no one's looking, I steal his tiny slab of meatloaf because he makes a face every time he looks at it. Once it's on my plate, his shoulders relax and he mutters out a thanks.

"How are you liking work?" Hollis asks Kelsey. "Your boss still annoying?"

"Yes. Totally. But I made a friend named Beth. She's like my chosen mom. Not by blood, but she's just good people. Even lets me call her Momma Beth." Kelsey chuckles. "Everyone needs a mom like her."

"So she's old?" Hollis teases.

"Hush you," Kelsey says with a smile. "She's a grandma. Has like nine grandkids and one on the way. Some of them are the girls' ages."

Penny perks up. "Can they come over?"

"Maybe one day. I don't want to seem like a freak latching onto this woman, but I swear if she wasn't there, I would've quit already. She keeps me sane and hooks me up with good romances. We've even gone to lunch a couple of times."

"You look happy, Mom," Hollis says. "I'm glad."

They share a long, heavy look filled with love and I'm jealous. I've never had anyone look at me like that before.

And then it happens.

Her gaze turns my way and it's still filled with pride and affection. "What about you, honey? Things better with Mike? Are you guys happy?"

"I, uh, yeah. We're good."

Her blond brow hikes up. "I can tell when I'm being avoided. Is he good to you? He doesn't hurt you, does he?"

"Nah," I say with a chuckle. "I could take Mike. He's great."

This relaxes Kelsey and she nods. "Good. Maybe we

ought to invite him to supper on Wednesday. If there's anything we can do to help make the transition easier, I want to help."

"We don't need help," I bite out sharply.

Roux glowers at me. "Roan!"

Kelsey simply shakes her head. "Tough luck, kiddo. In this family, you don't get a choice. We help whether you like it or not. Right, Hollis?"

He smirks at me. "Yep."

It's then I realize where he got his annoying do-gooder attitude. Hell, even Ms. Frazier is that way, offering to let me do jobs here to get tutoring for Roux. They're all so nice. It's a little jarring considering I haven't been exposed to anything good in regard to family.

Roux is once again all smiles as she tells Kelsey about a test she aced. Kelsey and Karen both praise her. It warms me to my fucking soul to see Roux getting the attention she deserves.

It's gonna hurt when all this goes away.

Good things always go away.

At least in Roux's and my life they do.

"Hop in the shower. You smell like a barnyard animal," I instruct Roux once we walk into our living room of our garage apartment.

"Punk," Roux says with a huff. She obeys, though, and bounds off toward her room.

Fuck, she has a room.

I'm still blown away by that fact.

"I guess I'll go," Hollis murmurs from behind me. His

mom asked if he'd run us home and he happily obliged. I was glad when she told Charlotte she couldn't come along. I'd wanted a second alone with Hollis.

"I thought you were going to help me study," I blurt out. "I mean, I don't want to study, but you said I should."

He chuckles, the sound deep and throaty. It makes my dick twitch. "You don't want to study. But, yes, I think you should." He kicks off his shoes and then plops down on the couch.

I find my backpack and pull out my homework assignment. Rather than make out, like I'd rather do, Hollis jumps right in and starts explaining the assignment to me. I like his voice, so I get lost in what he says. We've worked through nearly all the problems by the time Roux gets her ass out of the shower and comes to say good night. The last three problems are torture, but I pay extra attention so we can get finished and move on to other things.

"See, not so diffic—"

His words are cut off when I attack him with a kiss. He smiles against my lips and allows me to ease him down onto the sofa. I kiss him hard and eagerly, making sure to grind my hard dick against his. It escalates until we're both breathy and stifling moans.

"Want to continue this in the bedroom?" I whisper against his lips.

His fingers slide into my hair. "You can't fuck me tonight."

I guess I hadn't thought about fucking, but now that he's suggested it, I want it. I'd just wanted to undress more and not worry about Roux coming in.

"Why not?" I challenge, because I live to fuck with him.

"Because it's been a while since Lucas. And he was my first and only. We just need to…prepare."

"Just fuck me then," I offer, though I'm pretty sure that will hurt like hell.

His blue eyes flash with barely contained hungry lust. "You're definitely not ready. Maybe one day we'll get there." He rewards me with an evil grin that makes my dick pulse. "I could suck you off, though."

Holy fuck.

I've had my dick sucked plenty of times, but never by a guy. And never by someone who looks like they'd blow their load just for a taste. It's a temptation I can't ignore.

"Let's go," I growl out as I stand, pulling him up with me.

He bites back a laugh as I haul him to my room with me. As soon as I get the door closed and locked, I'm on him. I start tugging at his clothes, eager to see him naked. He's just as greedy, ripping off my hoodie and shirt all at once. His fingertips slide down my abs, making me shiver, and then he's frantically working at my belt. The moment his hands shove down my boxers, I lose all sense of reality.

I want him.

I want him so fucking bad.

"Lie down." His voice is commanding and deep. Fuck if I don't want to obey.

Dropping onto the bed on my back, I stare up at him, my dick weeping for attention and hard as stone. He pushes down his own boxers and fists his impressive cock. The sight of him is such a fucking turn on. Sure, he's lean because he never eats a goddamn thing, but he's also muscular from basketball. His chest hair is sparing and golden. It's darker blond around his dick. I want to bury my nose there and inhale him.

What the hell has gotten into me?

Have I been into guys all along?

Is that why girls are just fucking meh to me?

All this time I thought I was broken inside. That I couldn't love properly or be interested in another person. Truth is, I've been looking at the wrong sex. Because when I look at Hollis, I crave him like nothing I've ever wanted before. My mouth waters and my dick throbs. For him. Just a taste. To feel his skin on mine. Whatever he gives me.

"I like the reversal of power," he says with a wicked glint in his blue eyes as he kneels on the bed.

"You're the one who's gonna suck my dick," I tease back.

His smile becomes predatory. "You have a lot to learn, man. When your dick is in my mouth, I'm in charge."

He spreads my thighs, making me feel ridiculously exposed. His eyes take in my twitching dick, heavy balls, and now my ass. A smile tugs at one side of his lips.

"You just going to look at it all day or do something about it?" I challenge, hating the bout of nerves that have suddenly consumed me.

His gaze softens as he grips my dick. "If you don't like it or want to stop, just tell me. I won't force you."

Now I feel like an asshole.

I reach forward and run my thumb over his mouth. "I want it. I'm just…fuck, I'm nervous, okay?"

He bends, his blue eyes locking on mine. "I'll take care of you." With those words, he flicks out his pink tongue and licks the tip of my dick. I suck in a sharp breath of air.

"Holy fuck."

He grins before taking me into his mouth. I'm staring down at a guy as he bobs up and down my length with better skills than any girl I've been with. My fingers latch onto his hair and I try desperately not to fuck his mouth. When he massages my balls, I nearly lose it.

"Jesus, Hollis," I hiss out. "You're going to kill me."

He pops off and then sucks on his middle finger. "I'm about to. This shit will blow your mind."

Chapter Nineteen

Hollis

I've only ever been with one guy. Lucas. And he never looked at me the way Roan is looking at me right now.

His eyes are wide and trusting.

I can tell he's nervous by the way he bites on one corner of his bottom lip, but he's also aroused. The red blush on his cheeks and groans coming from him are evident of that. His taste is exactly how I'd imagined. Salty. Masculine. Unique. I'm going to suck him dry. Make him realize just what he's been missing until he met me.

Taking him deeper in my throat, I make sure to keep my eyes locked on his golden-brown ones. With my wet fingertip, I tease at the puckered hole of his ass. He clenches, fear shining in his eyes.

I pull off his dick and smile. "I'm going to put my finger inside you."

"Well, do it already."

He's grumpy because he's afraid.

"Demanding," I tease, licking at his tip. "I'm in charge right now. So lie there and hush."

His scowl is somewhat playful until I take him deep into my throat. As soon as his hips thrust up, I push into his body. He lets out a string of strangled curse words, his ass tight around my finger. Slowly, I ease into him, seeking out his prostate. I know the moment I touch it because he cries out. Such a sweet, vulnerable sound from a hard, often mean boy.

My name is whimpered on his lips as his salty cum shoots abruptly into my mouth. I keep massaging his prostate until his dick ceases twitching, swallowing down each jet of cum. His hips stop flexing up and he lets out a ragged breath. I slip off his dick and grin.

"What do you think?" I waggle my brows at him.

He grabs my biceps and hauls me up to his mouth. His tongue is curious and probing as he kisses me, tasting his remnants on my tongue. We grind together as we kiss. He grows hard again, which feels good against my dick.

"Hollis," he murmurs, fingers biting into my hips to urge me to move against him. "I like this. I like you."

I nip at his bottom lip. "Me too."

His dick is hot and still slick from my mouth, so it feels really damn good rubbing against it. The sounds coming from him are erotic and ones I want on repeat in my head. It only takes a few moments of our desperate kissing and rubbing for us both to come. We soak Roan's chest, which makes him laugh.

"What sort of fucked up shit have you pulled me into?" he teases, his eyes hooded and smile lazy.

I relax against him, not at all concerned about the cum that's slick between our chests. "You started it."

"Me?" he scoffs. "I was fine until you rolled up being all peppy and shit."

"Someone has to be the happy to your grumpy. Jordy sure as hell isn't."

His brows furl. "He's going through some shit. Friday

was…it won't happen again." His fingers stroke through my sweaty hair.

"I sure as hell hope not," I mutter. "That river was fucking cold."

"He's stressed and overprotective of Roux and me. His lines got blurred." His amber eyes sear into mine. "It's not an excuse, just a reason. I'll do a better job of keeping him in check."

"He still hates me. You saw how he was at school today."

"Jordy hates everyone pretty much."

"Well, he's going to have to get over his hate toward me," I tell him with a grumble. "You're mine now and he's bound to learn that sooner or later."

"Yours?" Roan laughs. "I barely know you and now you're claiming me?"

"That's my cum all over your stomach and I did just suck you dry." I smirk at him. "By definition, I think I've claimed you properly."

My phone starts ringing in my jeans, effectively killing the moment. He frowns as he watches me bolt to answer it.

"Hello?"

"Did you get lost?" Mom asks.

"Studying. Roan and I had an assignment due and he didn't finish his."

"Hey now," he groans, tossing a pillow at me.

Mom, having heard him, chuckles. "Glad you're having fun, but you should probably let them get to bed. It is a school night."

I roll my eyes. "Sure thing. I'll be home in a few."

After hanging up, I let my eyes rake over Roan's naked, muscular form. He looks like a Roman god sprawled out on his bed. A statue sculpted from granite painted to look real. His dick is flaccid but still fucking beautiful as it lies on his lower stomach that's still wet from our cum. His bicep muscle bulges when he bends his arm and lays his head on it. I want to lick him. I want to crawl up his body and lick every salty inch. Even his armpit. The dark hair there is masculine, and I bet smells uniquely him.

He's an addiction I'll never break.

My stomach tightens with nerves and I tear my eyes from his. It's going to kill me. Wanting him. Caring for him. Being with him. I feel it in my bones. The bed squeaks and then he pads over to me, a towel in his hand. He cleans me off and then himself before tossing it to the floor. It's still damp, probably from his morning shower.

"You okay?" His voice is gritty and rough. Worried.

I tilt my head up to look at him. "Yeah."

He grips my jaw and kisses me softly. "Just because I don't want to talk about this thing between us to the school and everyone else for Roux's sake doesn't mean I don't enjoy every second of it."

"I get it." And I do. I really do. It still stings, especially after Lucas and everything with my dad.

He pulls me to him for a hug. Being naked in his arms feels so damn right. "I'll make it up to you."

"How's that?"

"I'll take you out."

My head snaps up to look at him. "Like on a date?"

"Don't guys date?" he asks, frowning.

"I guess. I mean, I'd like that." I chew on my bottom lip for a second. "Lucas and I never went on a date."

His eyes flash with anger. "Lucas is a dumbass. I'm taking you out like he should have."

"How come you never took Sidney out?"

He steps back and glowers at me before tossing my clothes at me. Pain stabs inside my stomach at his sudden mood change.

Why did I ask him that?

Because we're in a relationship that involves dates. I thought we could talk about everything. Quickly, I dress while he puts on a pair of gray sweats and nothing else. If I weren't feeling unwanted at the moment, I'd most definitely attack him with my mouth for looking like such a goddamn snack.

"Right, so bye," I grit out, turning my back on him.

He stalks over to me, his arms going around my middle. I'm pulled against his chest as he nuzzles his nose in my hair.

"I don't date. The girls I've been with were just for a night of fun. I didn't like them. Not like I like you."

Oh.

So I'm special to him.

That most certainly takes away the sting.

"I wasn't trying to piss you off," I tell him, my hands resting on his that are holding on to me. "She's my friend and she's got some self-esteem issues. I was just wondering."

"I know." He sighs. "I'm not used to this. Opening up to people. Jordy and the guys know me best, but even then, we don't just openly talk about our feelings often. I feel… exposed."

"Whatever we talk about is ours," I murmur. "I'm safe to talk to."

He twists me around and pins me to the door with his hips. In way of apology, he kisses me until I'm dizzy. It takes another worried phone call from Mom to tear us apart for good.

"Call me," he growls. "When you get home. So I know you made it safe."

I smirk at him. "You still owe me a breathy phone call. You couldn't get out of that, even if you tried."

"Go before I drag you back to my bed."

"Don't threaten me with a good time."

His warning glare sends me on my way with a chuckle.

"What are you doing?"

Roan lets out a heavy sigh over the phone that goes straight to my dick. "Trying to figure out what to make besides grilled cheese. I've been told I'm a lame ass cook."

"I know it's not tutoring day with my aunt, but you could always come over here."

"I wish," he murmurs, "but I already promised the guys we'd hang out tonight. I need to check in on Jordy."

It's been three days since I blew him in his bed, and it's been strained ever since. Not between us. The hiding. I can tell, at school, he wants to haul me to him, but he always refrains from doing what we both want. Plus, he's worried about his best friend. Jordy hates me, so it's not like I can even chill with them. So, for the time being, Roan and I have to keep our relationship a secret, even hiding it from his friends.

"I miss you," I state, hating the whine in my voice. We've stolen kisses in the bathroom at school, and at my house on Wednesday when he and Roux were there. But other than that, we haven't had another opportunity alone.

"Are you coming to Campfire Chaos tomorrow night?"

"I don't want to."

"I won't let him hurt you. I swear, Hollis."

I believe him. I would just rather have him to myself. If we go there, we'll be separated. I'll go off with Sidney and Gio while he and the Hornets hang together. It'll be torture watching him all night and not getting to touch him.

"I know. We'll see."

"I can already tell when you're pouting," he teases.

"To be honest, I don't want to see you all night and not get to touch you."

"Who says you couldn't touch me?"

"You'll be with the Hornets."

"So? You don't think I'm going to tuck in early and drag you back to my tent?"

"How romantic."

He laughs and the sound warms my heart. "Of course the first guy I decide to hook up with is high-maintenance as fuck."

"Ha. Ha. Ha," I deadpan. "And maybe I'll be the *only* guy you ever decide to hook up with. I'm kind of a big deal. You won't ever find anyone like me again."

He's quiet for a moment, which makes my nerves go haywire. My stomach aches something fierce until he gives me a reprieve, gifting me with a gravelly response.

"The *only* guy," he confirms. "Come Friday night and then Saturday night we'll go out just the two of us."

"You play dirty."

"The only way to play. Dirty is fun."

"Fiiiiiiine," I drawl out. "I'll go, but if I end up in the river again, you owe me more than a date."

"Hollis," he growls. "You're not going back in that river

and Jordy won't touch a hair on your goddamn head. I swear to you."

I'm about to throw back a teasing remark when my phone beeps. Incoming call. From Dad.

"Fuck," I mutter.

"What?"

"My dad is trying to reach me."

"Your dad's a real asshole, huh?"

"Yep."

"So's mine."

He doesn't give up much on his personal life, so when he does, I'm like a kid on Christmas morning, eager to open the present to learn more about him.

"I don't know if your aunt told you, but my dad's in prison." His voice grows cold. "At least when he was around, Mom gave a shit."

"I'm sorry."

"It is what it is. We were given shitty dads. It's our duty in life not to turn out like them."

My dad may not be in prison, but he destroyed his son with his cruel, callous words and ability to cut me off based on my sexuality.

"My dad hates my being gay so much, he didn't just give me up," I say with a ragged sigh. "He gave them up. How could he do that to them?"

"And to you. To all of you, Hollis. Not just them."

Tears burn at my eyes. I feel like I'm going to throw up, just like I always do when I think about my dad and what he did because of me. "I hate him." And I hate how my voice cracks with emotion. That Dad still hurts me every day and he's not even here.

"I hate mine too. At least your mom's cool as shit."

"Your mom is a bitch. You and Roux deserve someone who cares."

"I'm okay," he murmurs, his voice devoid of emotion. "It's Roux I worry about."

"Roux has you," I remind him. "Better than your shitty parents combined."

The line grows quiet, both of us lost in thought.

"You'll have fun tonight with the guys," I say. "They probably miss you."

"I wish it were you coming over instead." Big, mean Roan is pouting and I love it.

"Me too."

"This weekend is all about us," he tells me in a fierce tone. "I'm going to suck on your neck until it's nice and purple, so no other fuck faces like Tyler Cuntingham will even think about flirting with you."

Cunningham was flirting with me?

I think back to basketball practice this afternoon. He was being extra friendly, but I didn't think he'd been flirting.

"Someone's jealous," I taunt, laughing at him.

"I'm not jealous."

"You totally are. This is hilarious. Is he going to be at Campfire Chaos?"

"It'll be his ass that ends up in the river," Roan grumbles.

Liar.

He's not like his psycho best friend.

"It's cute you're jealous." I love poking this bear.

"Not jealous, rat."

"Totally are, rat lover."

"Don't call me that." His voice is filled with amusement

and then it fades. "Dammit. They're here. Tomorrow night. And if Cuntingham so much as looks at you at the game tomorrow, I'm tripping him. He can fall on his fucking face for all I care. Coach can kick me out of the game."

"You're so precious," I tease. "Defending my honor."

"Bye, fucker."

"Bye, hero."

He mumbles out a "fuck you" before hanging up.

My heart skips several times.

Roan Hirsch is jealous. Because he likes me. Really likes me. He's possessive and doesn't want other guys looking my way. I haven't felt so overjoyed in as far back as I can remember. I'm still grinning when my phone rings.

Dad.

He sucks the joy right from me.

Chapter Twenty

Roan

"Ah, Jesus," Trey complains. "Who invited him?"

I squint in the snowy darkness, trying to make out who's walking toward us. As soon as I see three familiar faces, I tense up. It's Sidney, Gio, and Hollis.

"Sidney," Cal tattles. "She invites everyone to Campfire Chaos. It was much better when it was just the four of us. Fucking girls."

"She's fucking that nerd." Trey nods toward Gio. "Her own clan of bitches have left her high and dry. So I think we should just tell her she's not cool to come anymore."

"I mean, she's not sucking any of our dicks lately, so she's kind of useless." Cal's cold words hit me right in the chest. Before I can respond, Jordy pipes up.

"She never sucked *my* dick," Jordy growls. "And you know it makes you sound like total cunts right now. Discussing like a couple of bitches how you won't invite some chick anymore because she's no longer sucking your dick."

I smirk because it's true. Trey and Cal are cool most days, but sometimes they act like such douchebags.

"You gotta pay to play," Cal says, grinning wolfishly at us.

"I think she's paid plenty," I grind out as I rise to my feet. "Sidney's cool. Leave her alone." After the last time we slept together, around New Year's, I swore to myself I'd stop using her for sex, because it's true. Sidney deserves more than that.

Jordy throws a handful of snow at Cal. When they get into it, slinging it back and forth, I trudge over to where the three of them—Gio, Sidney, and Hollis—are erecting a tent. Gio pauses every few minutes to steal kisses from Sidney. I've never heard her laugh before. Not like this—carefree and happy. Her giggles from before were flirty and forced. She's fucking snorting right now.

Hollis gives me a knowing look. One that says he knows I'd like to be stealing kisses right now, but I won't. He's mistaken.

"Yo," I call out to him. "Want to help me grab wood for the fire?"

No one pays attention as we walk away from the camp area and into the woods. I find a thick tree and push him up against it. My gloved palms find his neck and I kiss his cold lips. He grips my coat, pulling me closer. Our tongues lash playfully until hunger and need take over. I want him. Naked and pressed against me. I want him to fuck me or me to fuck him. I don't care as long as we're doing it together.

"Better calm down before someone sees," he reminds me.

I don't care if anyone sees.

I just want him.

My lips trail kisses to his neck and I suck on his skin, loving the groans coming from him. I'm marking the porcelain boy's flesh so that it's purple and blue and angry looking. Maybe it'll tell Cuntingham to look away.

Hollis is mine.

I bite his neck playfully. His reaction turns me the hell

on. He grips me tighter and thrusts his hips against mine, a needy moan climbing up his throat.

"I can't wait to get you in my tent tonight," I growl against the shell of his ear. "I'm going to—"

My words are cut short by the thumping of loud bass. A black SUV rounds the curve, blinding us in its headlights. We break apart and I squint, trying to figure out who the fuck is crashing our party. I know everyone who comes here and no one has a car like that. It passes us, heading for the campfire.

"Come on," I say, taking Hollis's hand and squeezing it.

We walk hand in hand back toward the group and I reluctantly let go at the last second. Some guys hop out of the black SUV and walk right over to Jordy. I don't like the way they've crowded him.

"Stay here," I order, trudging around the campfire to my friends.

Cal and Trey are standing behind Jordy, their eyes narrowed and bodies tense. Hatred gleams in Jordy's eyes. When he sees me approaching, fear flashes in his eyes. Fucking fear. Oh hell no.

"Can we help you?" I snap, coming to stand beside my best friend.

The motherfucker clearly in charge who wears a red bandana laughs at me. "What are you? The fucking butler?"

I fist my hands, but Jordy grips my bicep, stopping me from pummeling this asshole.

"What do you want, Rex?"

Rex.

"Just checking up on you, buddy." Rex grins. "You haven't been to work in a few days. Juno's swamped. I told him I'd pay you a visit to see what's up."

"School. Basketball," Jordy bites out. "I'm in high school in case you forgot."

"I didn't forget," Rex says. "I also didn't forget you have a job helping your brother with cars at his shop. My cars. They're piling up, which means I can't sell that shit. You know what happens when I don't sell that shit?" He sneers at Jordy. "I don't make money. The way I see it, you're keeping me from getting paid. Want to explain to me why you've got beef with me, kid?"

"I'll help him," I blurt out. "Get caught up."

"Hey," one of Rex's friends says. "Aren't you that fucker who beat the shit out of my buddy?"

I freeze, turning my attention on the guy. I've seen him plenty of times before at the apartment. He runs in Alexander's crew. Fuck.

"You're a goddamn idiot if you think we're rehiring you," Jordy sneers my way, ignoring the guy. "You fucked everything up. Trey will help me. We'll get your shit caught up, Rex."

"Yep," Trey agrees, though I don't know he realizes exactly what he's agreeing to.

Jordy shoots me a fiery glare that tells me to back the fuck away now. I refuse to leave him, but I keep my mouth shut.

"Good," Rex says. "Very good. See you tomorrow."

They all turn to leave except Alexander's friend. I glower at him, warning him with my hate-filled stare to leave before I bust him in his fucking teeth. He spits in the snow before leaving without another word.

As soon as the vehicle is gone, kids start laughing and cutting up again, no longer interested in what the Hornets are up to. I can tell Hollis is worried, but he stays back with his friends.

"You," Jordy snarls. "In the cabin with me. Right the fuck now."

Feeling like a scolded child, I follow him inside. As soon as the door slams shut behind me, he rages.

"What the fuck were you thinking?" he bellows. "I need you to stay the fuck away so you don't get involved!"

I shove him. "You're my best goddamn friend. If you're into shit, I'm there with you."

"No," he snaps, gripping my coat and slamming me into the wall. "You don't get to because you have a motherfucking job. Roux. Don't ever forget."

All the fire is snuffed out as I take in his words.

He's right.

I was so careless.

"I didn't think," I mutter. "I just...I didn't like how he was talking to you. I wanted to help you."

"You will help me," he says in a softer tone, "if you and Roux just stay out of it."

"That guy was Alexander's friend."

He releases me and scowls. "I know. I'll take care of it."

"How? He knows we're friends."

"I'm good at what I do for them. Rex likes me, hence the fucking visit. If Franco starts sniffing around, I'll say something to Rex to get him to back off."

"What if he doesn't back off?"

"He will."

"And if he doesn't?"

"I'll fucking make him."

It's cold as fuck, but now that Hollis has joined me in my sleeping bag, I'm quickly warming up. Rather than let me fuck his brains out, he runs his thumb along my bottom lip. I can't see him in the dark, but I can feel his frown.

"What?" I grumble.

"Is everything okay?"

"I'm just worried about Jordy. He's gotten himself into some messy shit."

His lips brush against mine. "He seemed hell-bent on keeping you away from it."

"If I want to protect Roux, then I need to."

"But..."

"But I hate leaving Jordy to deal with it alone."

"He has Trey."

"Trey's mouthy ass will get himself shot."

I'm no longer interested in talking about stressful shit. I roll onto Hollis, kissing him deeply. He moans loudly and fuck if I don't hope that Cuntingham hears it.

"I brought lube," Hollis murmurs. "I've been fingering my ass to get ready."

Fuck.

My dick jolts, pre-cum already leaking from the tip.

"You're going to let me fuck you?"

"We don't exactly get much time alone," he whispers. "I will take what I can get from you when I can get it." He nips at my bottom lip. "Take your clothes off, Roan. Let me feel you."

Goddamn him.

He gets so confident and bossy in the bedroom. It makes

me want to obey every fucking word. He's dangerous, but I don't care. I want to devour every wicked drop of him.

Undressing inside a sleeping bag proves to be difficult, but I manage to remove the lower half of my clothes. Once he's halfway naked too, I rub my cold skin against his. It feels good with his solid muscles twitching and flexing beneath mine.

He fumbles in the dark and I hear something unzip.

"Here. Condom. Lube."

I paw at him in the dark until I find them. As much as I want to sheathe my dick, slap some lube on it, and shove it inside him, I don't. I've missed him this week. So I take my time kissing him. Our kisses grow more fervent and soon I'm rubbing my dick against his. I love every hiss and sharp breath of pleasure he takes. Gripping my dick, I slide it along his ass crack.

"I've never done anal before," I tell him. "I'm, uh, experienced sexually, but not there. Can we do it like this?"

"We can do it however you want," Hollis murmurs. "This first time, I want to be able to kiss you. I'd like it this way."

Face to face.

I'd assumed gays just fuck doggie style, but I guess with the right maneuvering it, you could do it at any angle.

"We'll do it this way then. I want to kiss you too."

He takes the lube from me and I can hear the cap pop open. I busy myself with rolling a condom on. His hand finds my dick as he strokes lube onto it. Then, he moves his hand between us.

"What are you doing?"

"Fingering my ass to get ready for you."

"Fuck, Hollis. You kill me."

"You kill me too," he says, a smile in his voice. "My fingers feel good, but you're going to feel so much better."

My dick aches to be inside him. I reach between us, my hand covering his as he fucks his own asshole. Since my fingers are still lubed up, I slide my finger between his two, joining him. He groans and slides them out. His body tightens around my finger. Fuck, he's going to feel so good.

"Stretch me, Roan," he orders. "Your one little finger isn't doing shit. Have you seen how big your dick is?"

I groan and ease another finger inside him. His body stretches to accommodate me. Then, I push another one inside, despite the hiss he makes.

"Does that feel good?" I murmur. "When I fuck you with my fingers?"

"Hell yeah."

"You want my dick, though, don't you?"

"God yes."

"Beg for it."

"Please, Roan."

Jesus, he's so fucking hot.

Sliding my fingers out, I grip my dick and then press the tip against his hole. We both moan when I push into him. Slowly. So fucking torturous.

"You may think I'm made of glass, but I won't break," he taunts. "Fuck me like you've missed me."

I seek out his mouth and buck my hips, loving how his body clenches around my dick so tightly I see stars. He feels good. Really fucking good. I nip at his lip and thrust again. Hard enough to make him yelp.

"Mine," I murmur against his mouth. "So fucking mine."

It's the truth.

I've never felt so goddamn possessive over anyone in my life. Like if I fuck him hard enough, I'll get to claim him forever. How is it a boy I barely know has stolen every part of my soul?

"Yes," Hollis breathes. "Fuck. You feel so fucking good." He groans. "Roan, touch my dick. I want to come with you in my ass."

His words are dizzying, and I greedily yank at his dick. We're frantic and messy, both of us eagerly racing to the finish line. I know when he's close because his ass tightens around me and he lets out a small cry of pleasure. It sends me over the edge, forcing my orgasm out of me without warning. I groan against his mouth as my dick pumps into him. It makes me hate the condom, wishing I could fill him up without a barrier. His heat soaks my hand as I jack him off. The thought of him inside my ass, doing the same, is both terrifying and exciting.

I fall against him, my mouth latching onto his neck. It's bruised from the last time I sucked him here, and I don't relent. I bite and nip on my now favorite part of him because it's a silent claim to the world. Mine.

"You just going to keep your dick in there forever?" he teases, his breaths coming out in pants.

"Yep. I'll just get hard and fuck you again."

"You wear me out."

"I'm just getting started, rat. Can't wuss out on me now."

He laughs. "You have to let me catch my breath, rat lover."

My dick twitches inside him. "Nah, I kind of like you breathless."

His moan is loud when I drive my hardening dick deep into him.

"I want to fuck you bare. One day will you let me?"

"I've only ever been with Lucas. You could do it now if you wanted."

As much as I want to, I refrain. Barely. "Let me get tested. I want to make sure I'm clean. I used condoms, but I fucked too many people to not be safe."

I hate myself right now.

If I'd kept my dick in my pants rather than fucking my way through half the girls in our senior class, I'd be able to fill Hollis's ass up with my cum.

"I can wait," he tells me, his voice soft. "It's fine. Don't do whatever you're doing right now."

"Fucking you?"

"No, dumbass, blaming yourself."

Our mouths meet again, this time in a sweeter kiss. I don't know how Hollis wrecked my life so easily, but he did. It's been messy ever since that very first day. I wouldn't change one second of it, though.

In all honesty, I want him to wreck me some more.

I want him to decimate me.

Chapter Twenty-One

Hollis

Saturdays are officially date nights. For the past three weeks, Roux stays the night with Charlotte while Roan and I run off together. Mom knows. I know she knows based on the sly smiles she gives me. But since we haven't come out to anyone, she doesn't say a word about it. It makes me love her even more.

"You're not listening to me," Roan says, jerking me from my thoughts.

"I'm just tired." Not a lie. I feel off. I blame it on my dad's incessant calling.

He studies me from his position on his couch. All sprawled out and relaxed. Looking hot as ever. On his bare stomach is a plate of cheeses and crackers and grapes. Ever since I told him heavy foods make me sick, he keeps stuff I can eat on hand. I've probably eaten more in the last three weeks than I did the three months prior combined.

"Want to go to bed?" he asks, frowning.

"And miss this amazing movie," I joke. "Not a chance."

He picks up a cracker and a slice of cheese, assembling it before handing it to me. "I'm being serious. You're pale as fuck and spaced out."

Irritation prickles at me. "I'm fine."

"Oh, and add grumpy to that list too."

I chomp on my snack, rolling my eyes at him. My phone buzzes and it's my dad. Again. I throw it across the room. It hits the wall with a loud thump before falling to the carpet.

"Definitely grumpy," Roan mutters.

I flip him off. "I have nothing to say to him."

He sets the plate on the coffee table and sits up. His coppery orbs assess me. I can never escape his scrutiny. The man sees right inside me. Most days, I love it. Other days, it's annoying.

"I know how to cheer you up," he says, a wolfish grin turning his lips up. His eyebrow lifts, drawing my attention to his piercing.

"You're going to fuck me?" My body warms at his words. I can't get enough of him, especially when he's inside me, which is as often as we can manage the past three weeks.

He grabs the back of my neck to pull me to him for a kiss. "I was thinking you could fuck me."

My dick wakes right the fuck up, straining in my jeans. "You're not ready."

"Bullshit," he argues. "I've let you finger my ass nearly every time we're alone. We're ready for this."

Not me.

Not him.

We are. Us. I love that there's an us. Might be a secret us, but it's better than no us.

"It's going to hurt," I taunt. "I'll make you cry, little Roan."

"I'm not little and you fucking know it, rat."

"All I hear is 'wha-wha-wha,' rat lover."

"Fucking asshole."

"That's where I'll be in ten minutes," I bite back at him. "Deep inside your ass."

His lips turn up on one side. "Make sure you go bare. If you're going to be inside me, you can come inside me, babe. I want you to."

Babe.

All I heard was babe.

This guy owns my heart and I don't want it back. He can keep it. It belongs to him.

"I thought you were worried, *babe,*" I say, teasing him with the endearment.

"I'm negative. Finally got word back."

"Holy shit. We're really going to do this."

"We really are. Now take off your clothes and suck my dick, pretty boy. I want to come at least once before you fuck me up with that big dick of yours."

His words are tough because he likes being a hardass, but I don't mistake the fear laced in them. Not letting him overthink, I start tugging down his sweatpants. He lifts his ass, to help in my efforts to undress him. His hard dick springs free, slapping against his stomach as I pull the pants off his body. I shed my shirt, loving how he devours me with his hot stare.

"You once called me high-maintenance, but you're the needy boyfriend. Always needing your big dick sucked on," I tease, kissing his lips before trailing my tongue down his chest. "I bet you want my fingers in your ass when I suck you off too. Greedy boy."

He grunts, hunger flashing in his gaze. "Stop talking and start sucking."

"Suck on these first," I tell him, pushing my fingers into his mouth. "Get them nice and wet so I can stretch your asshole. My dick is big, man. You're probably going to scream like a little girl."

He bites on my fingers, a warning sparking in his eyes.

Not heeding his threatening looks, I grip his dick with one hand and then lick the tip. His hips buck up, desperate for more. I rub at his asshole with my wet fingertip and then push into him. He hisses at the intrusion.

"More," he rasps out.

I suck on his dick as I offer him another finger. And then another. His body is putty in my hands as I fuck him with three fingers. It only takes a couple of rubs against his prostate before he's crying out with his release. Hot, salty cum jets into my mouth and I swallow it down. I ease my fingers from his ass and then stand abruptly, eager for round two.

The room spins and I lose my footing. If it weren't for Roan's hands suddenly gripping my hips to keep me steady, I would've toppled over.

"You okay?"

"I'll be better when I'm inside you."

He stands and slings his arm over my shoulders, pulling me to his side as he guides me to his bedroom. Once we're fully naked, he kneels on the bed.

"I want you to fuck me like this," he says as he drops to his hands, offering his ass to me. "Claim me like I always claim you."

"God," I groan as I snatch up the bottle of lube from the bedside table. "You're going to kill me with that ass. I won't last long. Just so we're clear. I've been dreaming about this for weeks, so I'm going to nut the second I'm inside you."

He laughs. "Too much talk and not enough action."

I lubricate my naked dick and then climb on the bed behind him. He shudders when I slap my length along the crack of his ass. Then, I slide the tip down the crevasse to his puckered hole. I keep my dick steady with one hand and grab onto his hip with the other.

"I'll go slow," I breathe. "Tell me if I need to quit."

"Don't quit."

I smile as I breach the first rings of muscle with my crown. His body tries to force me out at first, but then I'm easily sucked into him thanks to the lube. Inch by inch, I bury my dick inside this beautiful, complicated man. Pleasure threatens to detonate inside me, ending this as quickly as it started, but I manage to keep hold on everything.

Don't come.

Not yet.

Just a few more moments.

"Can I move?" My words are gruff and needy.

"Yes, please," he rasps out.

Slowly, I ease out of him and then thrust back. We both groan. Dizziness washes over me. I thrust again, this time harder. My balls slap against his, sending chills running through me. His ass squeezes around my dick and he meets my next thrust when he pushes back against me.

Fuck.

Fuck.

God, this feels good.

I drive into him again, probably too hard, but his groans are the pleasure filled kind.

"Mine," I murmur. "Mine."

"Yes," he hisses out. "Fuck, Hollis, you're fucking me."

I smile as I piston my hips again. Waves of delicious ecstasy crash over me. I hit him again and again with my thrusts. When he starts stroking his dick, it's such a turn on that I lose control. I fuck him hard and quick, needing to claim him.

"Oh, fuck," I cry out the second my nuts seize up. My dick throbs as jets of hot cum shoot inside him. No barrier. He gets every drop.

"Holy shit," he groans. His ass milks me as the sound of him stroking himself makes juicy wet noises, indicating he's found release again as well.

I slide out of him, staring in awe as my cum oozes from his red, battered hole. I want to run my tongue along the sore flesh and press my cum back into him, but the beautiful sight is stolen from me.

Black.

Black.

Oomph.

I blink away the heavy darkness to find Roan crouched over me. On the floor. How'd we end up here?

"What the fuck, Hollis?" he hisses. "What just happened?"

I squeeze my eyes shut as a wave of nausea strikes. "I'm going to puke."

It takes everything in me to scramble toward the bathroom. I've barely made it to the toilet before I'm retching. First comes the cheese and crackers. Then, fuck, not again.

"Is that blood?"

My stomach clenches again, splattering more blood against the bowl. "Just go," I croak out between gags. "Please."

The sink runs and then a cold rag gets pressed to the back of my neck. Hot tears of embarrassment and self-loathing have more puke coming up. I can't look at the blood. Not with him also seeing it. It's one thing for it to happen when I'm alone, but with witnesses, it makes it all too real.

When I've emptied my stomach, Roan strokes my back

with his fingertips and murmurs, "What the fuck is wrong with you?"

"Nothing," I snap, hating the bitterness in my mouth.

"It's not nothing."

"It just happens sometimes. I'm fine."

"You're not fucking fine," Roan snarls, rising to his feet. "Something's wrong."

I roll my eyes as I yank the cold rag off my neck to wipe my face off. My overnight bag is already on the counter, so I rise on shaky feet, flush the toilet, and then begin brushing my teeth. Roan starts the shower and before I can escape when I'm done with my teeth, he guides me under the hot spray.

"It's not fine or normal," he grits out, taking my face in his hands. "Why are you puking blood?"

"I don't fucking know, okay? Just drop it."

He shakes his head. "I won't fucking drop it. You're sick. You need a doctor."

Rage swarms up inside me. I had a doctor. My dad. He fucked us up and now I have nothing. I don't want a doctor. I just want to be left alone.

"Stop," I bellow, shoving at him. "Just stop." Tears well in my eyes before spilling down my cheeks. "Mom has enough to worry about. This will just be one more thing."

Roan's gaze softens and he pulls me to him, hugging me tight. His fingers run through my hair and he kisses my head as I cry under the spray of the shower. I don't know what's wrong with me and I don't want to know. I just want it to go away. I just want my mom to be happy. I just want to be with Roan and not have this other shit get in the way.

"Please go to a doctor," he begs. "For me. Please."

I nod and bury my face against his neck. He hugs me

tighter. Truth is, every day feels worse on me. Whatever is wrong isn't just going away. He's right. I do need to get to the bottom of it.

We make it through the shower and manage to dress in our underwear before crawling back into his bed. He holds me in the dark like he has the power to fix me. I wish that were true.

"I have like two really good things in my life, Hollis, and you're one of them. Please don't take that away from me."

His words hollow out my aching gut.

I'll go to the doctor. Figure this shit out. If not for me, for Roan. He's begging me and I won't let him down. Too many people in his life have already done that. I'll be damned if I'm another one on that list.

Chapter Twenty-Two

Roan

I love watching him sleep. It feels creepy and stalkerish, but I don't give a fuck. He's mine. If I want to stare, I'll stare, goddammit. Before he wakes, his pale face is so serene. Like an angel. I feel like the devil who's somehow managed to capture something he's not supposed to have. Hollis is too good for me. I know this, but I don't care. I'm greedy and selfish enough to keep him anyway.

His pink lips are parted and plump. It makes me want to kiss him. Morning breath and all. I drag my gaze from his pouty lips down his chest to his stomach. A shudder ripples through me. Last night was scary as fuck.

Blood.

He was puking up blood.

What does it mean?

A million horrible things flit through my mind, every single one of them resulting in them taking him away from me.

I can't lose him.

I've never been so fully obsessed with another person like I am with Hollis. I want him to consume me. It's the most fulfilling thing I've ever experienced in my life.

I'm considering waking him with my mouth on his dick when someone bangs on the front door.

What the fuck?

"Stay here," I grit out when Hollis's blue eyes pop open.

I climb out of bed and walk into the living room. After I throw my sweats on, I answer the door, ready to kick Jordy's ass if he's busting down my door before noon on a Sunday.

It's not Jordy.

Jesus fuck.

"Mom?"

She looks better than I saw her last, which means she's trying. Sometimes she tries. Her long, dark brown hair has been straightened and glimmers with some glitter shit she's sprayed in. Amber eyes that match mine and Roux's have been done up with smoky eye shadow, black cat eyeliner, and thick black mascara. Her lips are painted a glossy pink. She's obviously headed to work because she's dressed like a typical stripper in tight-ass spandex shit. No kid wants to see his mom dressed like this.

"Hey, Roany," she purrs, eyeing my living room with interest. "Did I interrupt you with your girl?"

It's obvious with clothes littered in the living room, the two glasses on the table, and all the half-eaten snacks that I'm not alone.

Crossing my arms over my bare chest, I block the doorway. "You interrupted my morning. Yes. Now what do you want?"

She purses her lips and waves a manicured hand in the air. "I'm here for Roux, sugar."

"No."

Her eyes flash with fury. "You don't get to 'no' me. You're my son, and while you may be eighteen now, Roux is not. It's time for her to come home."

"Fuck no," I growl. "How did you find us?"

She rolls her eyes. "Please. I know you two have been playing daddy with Mike for years. It's the first place I came to be honest."

"Leave."

"Not until I have my daughter." She narrows her eyes at me.

"She's not here, Mom. Spending the night with a friend."

Mom laughs. "Roux doesn't have friends. Is she here?"

"She has friends," I snap. "You'd know this if you weren't fucking high all the time."

"Look at me," she bites back. "I'm fine. I'd fallen off the wagon, sure, but I'm fine now. I want my baby girl back home. You're welcome to come back too, you know."

"No, Mom. She's not safe there."

"Oh, please. She's fine."

"Alexander—"

"Just looks after you two like you're his. Better than your worthless daddy who left me high and dry. Better than fireman Mike who thought he was too good taking on a woman with baggage. Joke's on Mikey, though. Look where you two ended up anyway."

I start to shut the door in her face, but she sticks her heeled foot inside before I can close it. "I want you to call her and get her here. I'll wait."

"No. She's not going with you."

Her face turns red with fury. "She is not your child, dammit. She's mine. You've always acted like you were better than me. You're not, you piece of shit. I'm the one who kept food in your ungrateful mouths. I've had to shake my naked ass for years to keep a roof over your damn heads. And this is the thanks I get? Screw you, Roan. You're just like your fucking father. I want my little girl right now. Find her."

"No, Mom," I spit out at her.

"I'll call the police."

I stiffen, watching her features for any tell she's bluffing. Fire blazes in her eyes. She's not. Fuck.

"They'll know you're a fucking tweaker," I threaten. "I'll tell them."

"They've known for years," she says in a sickly sweet voice. "But they always let me keep you two. They know children belong with their mother."

"Leave."

"I will because I'll be late for work if I don't, but this isn't over, Roan. Tell Roux to pack her shit because I'll be back. I'll bring the cops if I have to. You've been warned. Don't make a fucking scene."

She stomps down the stairs and over to Alexander's beat to shit Maxima where he waits in the driver's seat. How dare she bring that trash to my home? He watches me through the windshield, as he blows out a billow of smoke that clouds the car. Mom bitches to herself the whole way to his car. Thankfully, they drive away.

This isn't the end, though.

I feel it in my gut.

Fuck.

"Are you okay?"

I swivel around to find Hollis dressed and sitting on the arm of the couch. A worried expression twists up his handsome features.

"No," I rasp out. "I…she's going to…I don't know what

the fuck to do." I run my fingers through my hair and tug at the strands. "Fuck, Hollis. What do I do?"

"You can't do this alone," he says, standing and pulling me to him for a hug.

"What can you do?"

"Not just me. We'll talk to my mom and Aunt Karen and Mike. We'll figure something out together."

My chest warms knowing I have other sane adults on my side.

"Okay," I croak. "Let's go."

I've buried my face in my palms, overwhelmed as fuck. If it weren't for Hollis's gentle pats on my back, I'd go into a full-on panic attack. His touches are soothing. It's enough to have me pulling my hands away to regard everyone allowed in this "family meeting" as Kelsey called it. She sits on the sofa, Roux cuddled up next to her. Mike sits on the other side of Kelsey, trembling with rage. Penny and Charlotte were sent to their rooms. Ms. Frazier sits in her chair while Hollis and I share the loveseat.

"I say we call her bluff and let the cops get involved," Mike grumbles. "I don't think they'll side with her."

Ms. Frazier leans forward in her recliner. "As long as there aren't drugs in the house or visible signs of her using, they'll make Roux go back."

Kelsey's lips thin out and she hugs my sister tighter. "Maybe we could talk some sense into her. Let her know Roux is safe and happy right now. Surely, as a mother, she knows she isn't providing a safe environment for her children."

I scoff and Roux shoots me a sour look. Our mother

is selfish and doesn't give a shit about our environment or well-being.

"You can't talk sense into Miranda," Mike says, voicing what both Roux and I are thinking. "I dated the woman in one of her rare 'good' moments and it was evident I couldn't do a thing to help her or those kids because she was stubborn and wouldn't allow it."

"Me and Roan will run away," Roux threatens. "If she tries."

Ms. Frazier shakes her head. "Bad idea, honey. They'll just find you and put you back. God only knows how unsafe that would be for the two of you. Always on the run. No food or money. Terrible idea."

Roux pouts. I'm irritated that it's no longer a viable option for us. When it was just Roux and me, I never thought twice about taking her. But Ms. Frazier is right. Not to mention, we'd be forced to leave everyone we care about.

I can't leave Hollis.

Not now.

There has to be a better solution.

"We could just wait for her to get fucked up again," I offer with a shrug. "It's only a matter of time. Then, maybe she'll back off."

Ms. Frazier doesn't chide me for my language. "And if she doesn't?"

"I don't know," I admit grumpily. "We can't leave, though. She's right about that, Roux."

Roux scowls at me. "Since when did that plan change?"

"Since we started connecting with people." I wave around the room. "Do you really want to leave them?"

"No," she admits sadly. "Kelsey and I were just planning my birthday party."

I hate my mom so fucking much right now.

If only she'd leave us the hell alone, Roux could continue on with planning her fourteenth birthday party and I could continue on with my relationship with Hollis.

Secret relationship.

As though he senses my thoughts, he draws his hand away from my back. He's respecting my wishes. I hate that we have to hide.

Do we, though?

Aren't these people we can trust?

"I have a boyfriend and I don't want to leave him," I tell Roux, ignoring the burning stares. I'm worried that Hollis will be pissed at me for blurting that shit out. Instead, he takes my hand and threads our fingers together.

"No one is going to make you leave your boyfriend," Kelsey assures me in her sweet, motherly voice. I believe her.

"Oh, my," Ms. Frazier says. "I didn't realize...I thought you two were friends..."

"Boyfriend?" Mike's voice comes out gritty and confused. "What?"

I turn and meet his eyes. "Hollis is my boyfriend. We didn't want to say anything, because I was worried about how that might impact my getting to keep Roux with me."

Hollis's thumb swipes over mine, comforting me with such a simple touch. "Everything he does is for Roux. I respect that."

"But it shouldn't be held against me," I bite out. "So, fuck it, that's the truth. No more hiding."

Ms. Frazier nails me this time. "Language."

"Sorry," I grumble.

"Your relationship with my son has nothing to do with Roux's well-being," Kelsey assures me, squashing any self-doubt I have. "You're allowed to be happy, Roan. And so is Roux. All we can do is strive to make that happen and pray for the best."

Mike nods and pats Kelsey's thigh. "She's right. Just keep being kids and stay away. If she comes to the door, don't answer. I don't know that she'll go to the cops, but there's no way we can stop her. Our best bet is to hope she doesn't."

Kelsey invites Mike to stay for an early supper and Roux runs off to go see Charlotte. Ms. Frazier heads to the kitchen to start dinner. It's freeing to hug Hollis to me and no one look at us funny. I was sure Mike would, but he didn't seem to be bothered, just surprised.

"You okay?" Hollis asks, his hand squeezing mine.

"Not really." I notice he's trembling. "Are you okay?"

"Feeling dizzy."

"Come on. You need to go lie down until dinner. I'll walk you up."

He doesn't argue and clings to me as we go up the stairs. It's another thing to worry about. Not only is my mom being a bitch, but my boyfriend is sick. As soon as he flops onto the bed, he passes out. I curl up next to him and pull out my phone to text Jordy.

Me: Mom came by trying to get Roux. Everything is fucked up right now.

He responds immediately.

Jordy: She can't go back there!

Me: I know this, asshole.

Jordy: It won't happen.

Me: I hope not.

Jordy: It. Won't. Happen.

I wish I believed his words.

Chapter Twenty-Three

Hollis

"Wake up, English!" Coach roars, his booming voice echoing in the gym.

Jordy steals the ball and tears down the court with it. He shoots and makes the basket, which sends Coach into a frenzy. I know he's yelling at me, but I can't focus on his words. The gym spins around me. My heart is racing in my chest and I feel like I'm going to puke.

"Hollis!"

I black out, still fully aware of what's around me but unable to do anything about it, and stumble. My shoulder hits the gym floor hard as I crash to it. Strong hands grip my arms and roll me to my back. Squinting my eyes, I'm happy to see Roan.

Worried.

Freaked out.

Panicking Roan.

Our teammates crowd around us, including Coach.

"Hollis," Coach says, his voice calm and soothing. "Look at me. How many fingers am I holding up?"

"Three," I croak out.

"What happened, kid?" he asks, frowning.

"I, uh, I blacked out."

"He needs to go to the nurse," Roan grinds out. "Someone help me."

"Nurse Jones isn't there after school," Coach says. "Why don't you take him on home?"

Roan nods as he helps me to my feet. Cunningham is right there at my side, offering to help but gets shoved out of the way by Jordy.

"Got this, Cuntingham," Jordy practically snarls at him.

They walk me to the locker room and I'm starting to feel better. Neither of them lets me go. When we get inside, they sit me on a bench and Roan kneels in front of me, taking both my hands.

"We need to go to the doctor," he says, his voice urgent.

Jordy hovers nearby like a fucking vulture, just waiting for me to die so he can feast on my bones.

"I'll be fine," I mutter.

"Dude," Jordy grunts out, "you look like you're about to die."

"I'm not about to die." I shoot him a nasty look. "Try not to look sad about that."

Jordy smirks at me. "My boy likes you for some dumbass reason. So you don't get to die, rat. Sorry."

"This fucking guy," I grumble, rolling my eyes. "How do you put up with him?"

Roan laughs. "You're both about evenly matched on stressing me the hell out. Maybe you two should start a 'How Can We give Roan a Heart Attack Today' club?" He rises to his feet. "Come on, babe, let's go."

Babe.

I dart my eyes over to Jordy to gauge his reaction. He

cocks his head to the side, studying his best friend with intensity. Roan pulls me to my feet and hugs me to him.

"I guess you've probably guessed it by now," Roan says to Jordy.

"You're fucking the rat." Jordy's nostrils flare.

"He's my boyfriend, and we're fucking each other."

Jordy's eyes widen slightly. "Since when, dude? You fuck girls."

"And when have I ever really liked one?" Roan demands. "You gave me shit about fucking anything that walked. Even you thought it was weird."

"But him?" Jordy asks.

"I can't explain it," Roan says. "It just is. I like it. I like him. You're my best friend. It shouldn't matter who I date."

Jordy eyes me warily before shrugging his shoulders. "Whatever, man. I always have your back, even if you're slumming it in the gutters with a rat."

"*My* rat," Roan says, kissing the top of my head.

"Rat lover," I joke back, poking him in the ribs.

Jordy eyes us back and forth before shaking his head. "Fucking weirdos. Text me later, Roan."

I wake up sweaty and confused. A heavy boy is draped over me in my small ass bed and he's snoring. I'd smile, savoring the moment, if I didn't feel like I was going to combust from heat. I kiss his head and then ease out from beneath him. From down the hall, I can hear BTS playing on Charlotte's stereo and Roux laughing at whatever antics my sister is pulling. I'm thirsty as hell, so I go on a hunt for water. I've just stepped off the bottom stair to head for the kitchen when I overhear Mom in the living room.

"I understand that, Garrett," she hisses. "But it's not that easy."

I should walk toward the kitchen and make myself known. Instead, I eavesdrop on her conversation with my dad.

"Stop." A huff. "Listen to yourself." Pause. "He's not answering because you killed him with your hateful words!" Her voice breaks and so does my heart. "He'll speak to you when he's ready." Pause. "If you just show up, you're going to upset him more."

A sharp pain lances through my stomach.

Dad? Coming here? Fuck no.

"Yes, Garrett, you've made it perfectly clear that you're a surgeon as if I weren't the one to raise your children while you built your career." Another pause. "Your sorries come too late."

I sit down on the bottom step, my hands shaking profusely.

"I'll get him to the doctor. And if he wants you to know, he'll take your call." A pause. "Yes, I know you're worried. We all are. Yes, I believe he's anemic among other things." A heavy sigh. "I've told you all the symptoms. He doesn't eat. I hear him throwing up. No, I don't think it's an eating disorder."

My stomach roils as I listen to my parents discuss what's wrong with me. I feel betrayed by Mom, which is unfair to her. I can't stop the feeling, however.

"Yes, I'll let you know if the symptoms worsen." She lowers her voice. "The girls miss you, but I don't, Garrett. No matter what you say, it's over. It has been since you slept with Serena."

What?

"Goodbye, Garrett. We're done talking tonight. I'm hanging up now. Bye, Garrett." She lets out an annoyed sigh and then tosses her cell phone loudly on the table.

I stand and walk into the living room. Mom seems tired. As soon as she sees me, she brightens.

"Hey, honey. Feeling better?" She beams her fake ass smile at me.

"Yeah. You want to report back to Dad now?"

Her smile falters. "You heard."

"Who the hell is Serena, Mom?"

"Come here," she says, patting the sofa beside her.

I shake my head. "Just tell me."

"Please, honey."

With a frustrated sigh, I stalk over to her and plop down. She takes my clammy hand, kissing the back of it like she used to when I was small.

"Serena is a barista."

"Dad slept with a Starbucks chick?" I ask in disbelief. "When?"

"Apparently often last year." She sighs heavily. "I found out about it last summer. It came out when we were vacationing in Barbados. I'd picked up his phone and seen a text from her."

I remember our last family vacation. I'd been so obsessed with Lucas that I wasn't paying much attention to my parents. Dad seemed to be groveling. Mom was cold and standoffish. I'd thought they were just bickering.

"He said he'd break it off. He did," she tells me. "He'd already broken us, though. I closed my heart off to him. He's gone so much with work, the trust couldn't be repaired. I worried about every female he came in contact with. It was headed for divorce and then…"

"And then I conveniently gave you an out," I snarl, jerking my hand out of hers.

"No," she says fiercely. "Your dad lost his damn mind and I did what I had to do to protect you. Our prior relationship had no bearing on the way he was treating my son."

A strangled cry escapes me. "Mom, you let me think I was the reason you left him."

"What was I supposed to tell you, Hollis?" she asks tearfully. "Oh, I know your father just broke your spirit and your heart, but let me also tell you what a shitty husband he was to me by sleeping with some college coffee girl." She swipes a rogue tear from my cheek. "Honey, you were hurting, and I couldn't add to it. It was all too much. I just had to get you and the girls away from him. He was spiraling and I didn't want you all to get hurt anymore."

"You should have told me," I accuse, hating how pained my voice is.

"You're right. I should have. I'm sorry." She pulls me to her, and I go. I let my mom hug away the pain inside me. "I tried to protect you and it didn't work. You're hurting and you're sick and there's nothing I can do to fix that." She kisses my hair. "I love you, baby, and you know that."

I do.

I just need…

"We're going to walk home," Roan says from the stairway.

I look over my shoulder to see him and Roux standing there. They both wear guilty expressions like they overheard our conversation.

"I'll take you home," I grit out, rising to my feet. "I think I'm going to stay the night, Mom. I need some space right now."

She nods and stands, giving me a sad look. Then, to Roan she says, "Please take care of him."

"Yes, ma'am."

It's been over a week since my blowout with Mom. Roan and I are both on edge for different reasons. He's waiting for the shoe to drop with his mom. I'm worried my dad is going to show up at any moment.

"I got an A on our algebra test," Roan says, grinning at me as we leave the school and head toward my Mustang.

"Seriously?" I nudge him with my shoulder. "I guess we'll be celebrating tonight."

His smile widens. "Someone looks like he wants to suck dick when we get to my place."

"I was thinking in the 'Stang," I say, waggling my brows. "While you drive us home."

I toss him the keys and he catches them, laughing. We're so focused on one another that we almost miss the squeal of tires. I'm suddenly shoved behind Roan.

"Stay back," he warns.

A piece of shit Maxima rolls to a stop and some big, scary looking dude jumps out. He charges right for Roan, swinging at him. The guy misses him the first time, but his knuckles crack against Roan's face, making his head swing back. It takes a second for me to leap into action. I jump on the dude's back, putting his thick neck in a headlock. I'm able to distract him enough he focuses on me and not Roan. We fall back and his weight just about knocks the air out of me. He shakes me off and is back on his feet. Roan's ready for him and punches him hard in the gut.

"What the fuck are you doing here, Alexander?" Roan demands, dodging another hit.

Oh shit.

The dude who put a gun to Roan's head.

This guy is dangerous.

"I've come to kick your ass," Alexander roars, throwing punch after punch at Roan. Several hit him, sending a dazed Roan falling back.

Alexander reaches for the back of his pants when Roan hits the pavement on his ass. I don't wait, I tackle this motherfucker again. His gun falls out of his pocket, clattering to the ground. He punches me hard in the stomach, making everything turn black. I'm yanked off him, but it's by Roan. He's protecting me.

I hear guys yelling. The Hornets. They're charging for us like fucking gladiators with Jordy leading the charge.

"Fuck," Alexander grunts. He scrambles up and runs to his car. In seconds, he peels out and hauls ass out of the parking lot.

"Get him," Jordy yells to Cal and Trey.

Those two bolt for Cal's truck and tear out of the lot after him. I turn in Roan's arms and hug him tight. Our hearts are pounding hard in our chests in tandem. He squeezes me until I can barely breathe.

"What the hell happened, man?" Jordy demands, pacing beside us like an angry bull.

"I don't know," Roan grumbles. "Just showed up and stared beating the shit out of me." He pulls away and takes my face in his hands. "I told you to stay back."

"And let you get your ass beat all by yourself?" I volley back. "Fat chance."

"Dumbass," he mutters not unkindly. His lips press to mine. "That was so stupid, but kind of hot too."

"Seriously, man? I'm right here," Jordy grunts.

"It was hot?" I ask, astonished.

"Seeing you try to beat that prick's ass to defend me. Hell yeah."

We kiss, uncaring that we have Jordy as an audience. He mutters about us being freaks, but that's the extent of his displeasure.

"Oh, look," Jordy says, "the fucker left me a present."

I pull away from Roan to look at Jordy. He holds Alexander's gun in the palm of his hand.

"Maybe we should go to the river and dump it," I suggest. "You're great at tossing things into the river."

Jordy snorts. "Careful, rat. You keep that smartass attitude up and I might actually start to like you."

Roan winks at me.

Holy shit.

I think I just somehow earned points with my boyfriend's psycho best friend who tried to kill me.

Chapter Twenty-Four

Roan

"He's so hot," Roux says loudly on her phone, talking to Charlotte. "So hot. Oh my God, I think I'm going to die."

Girls.

They're so annoying sometimes.

As she babbles about Kayden—because that's all she talks about—I try to decipher Jordy's instructions he texted to me on how to make his "real" tacos. I'm not even sure if I bought all the right ingredients. My phone buzzes and it's from the asshole himself.

Jordy: Any word?

Me: Nope.

Jordy: I have Rex on it.

I don't like Jordy owing Rex shit, especially because of me.

Me: What's Rex going to do?

Jordy: Tell him to back the fuck off.

Me: At what cost?

Jordy: Does it matter? Anything for you and Roux.

It's been days since the Alexander shit, but I'm still

completely unnerved by it all. Tonight is date night for me and Hollis. I'd hoped to cook Roux a nice meal before taking her over to hang out with Charlotte. Looks like we'll be having grilled cheese. The one—and only—good thing about having a boyfriend who won't fucking eat is I don't have to take him to dinner. He isn't interested. We go to a lot of movies instead.

Someone knocks on the door. I frown, wondering if Hollis decided to come early to pick us up. Shoving my phone in my pocket, I head for the front door. I peek through the window and see a familiar face.

"Carol?" I open the door to Roux's social worker. "What are you…" I trail off when I see two cops with her. "What's this?"

She gives me a gentle smile. "We've come to take Roux home."

I'm already shaking my head. "W-What? No. She lives here."

"Her mother—"

"Fuck Mom!" I bellow. "She's an addict who has an abusive boyfriend who wants to kill me!" Are these people fucking insane?

"Son, I'm going to have to ask you to calm down," the cop with blond hair instructs, his hand awfully close to his gun.

"Calm down? You're about to take my sister from her happy home and toss her back to the wolves!"

"You don't have custody," Carol tries to explain. "This living arrangement was temporary."

"She can't go back there," I cry out. "They'll hurt her!"

"We've inspected Mrs. Hirsch's apartment and find it suitable—"

"This is wrong," I roar. "No!"

"What's going on?" Mike's voice carries up the stairs outside.

"Oh, good. You're here," Carol says. "We're taking Roux back home."

"Fuck," Mike curses.

"You know the rules," Carol states. "My hands are tied."

"What's going on?" Roux asks from behind me.

"Go to your room," I plead to my sister, like that might somehow keep her safe. "Please."

"Sweetheart," Carol says in her nicest social worker voice. "I'm here to take you back to your mom."

"No!" Roux yells. "I don't want to go back!"

I try to slam the door in their faces, but the blond cop pushes inside. Before I can swing at him, Mike is on me. I struggle against him. "Let me fucking go!"

"No," he snarls. "You let them do their job. This isn't the way to stop it. We'll find a way, but this will only get you in trouble."

My eyes blur with tears as the cops have to physically restrain my sister, who tries to run. I'm no match for Mike's brute strength, though I fucking try. Our screams are like wild animals being captured and beaten.

"Roux!" I bellow. "Roux!"

"Roan! Help!"

I'm in a rage and I'm lost. I can't save her. I can't fix this. I don't know what to do. They haul her out of the living room, just past me. My fingers brush along hers as she's dragged away. We're both fucking crying.

How do I fix this?

How do I save her?

"Please," I beg anyone who'll listen. "Please. They'll hurt her. Please don't let them hurt my baby sister."

Mike hugs me to him tight. Like he can hold all the breaking pieces of me together. He can't, though. There's too many. If I don't have Roux, I have nothing. Alexander will hurt her. He'll hurt her just to fuck with me. They send her back and it's inevitable.

I cry and plead and struggle to no avail. Carol packs up Roux's stuff and then they're gone. I've given up my fight when it's just Mike and me.

"Roan, I'm so sorry," he mutters, his voice cracking.

I break away from him and run into her bedroom like she might still be there. It smells like her perfume she wears now. Sweet and innocent. They'll break her. Fuck, they'll break my sister. I fall face first onto her bed and scream into the mattress. The tears don't stop as I try to figure out how I'm going to fix this.

I have to fix this.

I'm not sure how long I've lain here losing my fucking mind, but it's long enough that Hollis has arrived and I never even knew when he showed up. He's just here. Holding me. Kissing me. Whispering assurances that make my heart squeeze. I hug him to me, inhaling his scent and hoping this is all a bad dream. His phone keeps buzzing in his pocket, but he ignores it to look after me.

"I'm here," he murmurs, his fingers stroking through my hair, soothing me. "I'm here."

I manage to crack my eyes open so I can look at him. He's

not my pale porcelain boy today. No, he's gray. Why the fuck is my boyfriend gray?

"Is this a nightmare?" I croak.

"Yeah. Feels like one."

It's not a nightmare, though.

Roux has been taken from me and my boyfriend looks like death.

"I'm going to steal her back," I tell him, violence thrumming in my voice. "Then I'm taking you to the motherfucking hospital."

His lips that once were pink but are nearly as gray as his skin press together. "You can't steal her, Roan. You have to be smart." I don't miss that he ignores my comment about the hospital.

"I'm tired of being smart," I growl. "It has gotten me absolutely fucking nowhere."

Hollis whines and I think he's going to argue with me, but he's hurting. Like really fucking hurting. He rolls away from me, curling into a fetal position, his arms clutching his stomach.

"Hollis," I bark out, sitting up. "What's wrong?"

He shudders. "I'm going to be sick."

I jolt into action, helping him to his feet and taking him to the bathroom. He's barely on his knees before he starts puking.

Oh fuck.

Blood.

He's puking up blood and not a little like last time.

"No, no, no," I beg, yanking my phone out of my pocket. "Hollis, babe, it's going to be okay."

He groans, his head lolling forward. I stroke his hair with one hand while dialing Kelsey with the other.

"Roan," she answers. "Are you—"

"It's Hollis. He's puking up a lot of blood. Help!"

"I'll be right there. I'm calling nine-one-one."

We hang up and I text Mike.

Me: Hollis is puking blood. Upstairs. Help!

I don't wait for his reply. I'm too busy making sure Hollis doesn't fucking die on me. Within minutes, Mike rushes into the bathroom. He squats down beside Hollis and starts trying to ask him questions. Hollis is completely fucking passed out.

Oh God.

"Hollis," I say, shaking him. "Wake up."

"Paramedics are on the way," Mike assures me. "We just need to keep him from hurting himself before they get here."

He's passed the hell out, so I don't know how he'd hurt himself. I'm panicking when Kelsey blasts into the bathroom.

"My baby," she cries out. "Hollis, baby, it's Mom. What's going on, honey?"

We're a mess, trying to rouse him, when the paramedics arrive. They gently push the three of us out of the way so they can get him on a stretcher. I'm damn near ripping at my hair when Mike tells us he'll drive us to the hospital.

"He's going to be okay," Mike assures me from the front seat of his truck. "He's in good hands."

Kelsey is on the phone, speaking rapidly and answering questions to someone on the other end. I'm nearly catatonic by the time we reach the hospital. Mike parks out front, letting me and Kelsey climb out while he goes to park the truck. She has her phone pressed to her ear as she guides us inside.

"I don't know, Garrett. Just get here when you can. It's the only hospital here. You can't miss it." She hangs up only to call someone else. "Oh, God, Karen. I'm freaking out."

She continues to talk as she walks over to a front desk. The person motions for us to wait in the lobby area with a million other people. Kelsey finds a chair, but I can't sit. I pace in front of the vending machine, worry eating me from the inside out. Someone vacates a chair and I fall into it, suddenly exhausted. My life is a mess and I don't know how to fix any of it.

I wake when someone tosses a package of muffins at me. With the heel of my hand, I rub at my eye. The waiting room has thinned out some. Mike settles in the seat beside me with a package of muffins for himself.

A man strides over to us. Muscular. Handsome. Confident. Familiar. He sits beside Kelsey and for a moment, I think he's the doctor. I perk up, listening to what he has to say.

"It's a perforation on the stomach. A pretty good-sized tear from an untreated ulcer," he tells her. "They're prepping him for emergency surgery."

Doctor.

Definitely the doctor.

"I told you to get my son to the doctor. I knew something was wrong," he hisses, his voice turning nasty.

I'm already on my feet stalking over to him, crushing the muffins in my fist. "Do not blame this shit on her when all she's ever done is take care of your fucking kids."

The guy's eyes—blue and just like Hollis's widen—and he gapes at me. "And who the hell do you think you are, young man?"

"I'm your son's boyfriend," I spit out at him. "And if you have a problem, you can take it up with me."

Mike grips my shoulder. "Enough, bud. That's enough."

"I'm going to have security take this brat out of here," Hollis's dad states, an air of superiority in his tone.

"Garrett," Kelsey says in exasperation. "Cut the kid some slack. Cut me some slack. We're all doing the best we can. He's worried about him. If you think you're going to go in there and act this way around Hollis, he'll never forgive you."

Garrett's shoulders hunch. "It's just a serious condition, Kels. If he were to go septic, his organs could fail. We could lose our son. I feel like had I been around, I would've seen…" He trails off, fisting his hands. "This is all my fault."

The idea of losing Hollis makes me suck in a sharp, horrified breath. Both Garrett and Kelsey wince. They must feel that pain every bit as much as I do.

Mike gives my shoulder a squeeze. "Want to grab a coffee?"

Kelsey gives me a small smile and a nod. "We'll be right here. I'll let you know if anything changes."

I allow Mike to guide me down to a Starbucks kiosk. I'm numb as he walks over to take our order. My phone buzzes in my pocket. As soon as I pull it out, my heart stutters.

Roux.

I fucking forgot she had a phone.

"Roux," I grind out.

Sobs.

All I hear are sobs.

I lose my fucking mind.

Chapter Twenty-Five

Hollis

"There you are," an unfamiliar voice says. "How are you feeling?"

I blink in confusion. I'm in the hospital. "What's going on?"

"You, sir, are getting ready for surgery. I'm your nurse, Fran. Dr. Edmond will be in soon to go over what he'll be doing." She smiles. "Your parents are here to see you."

Parents?

Dread washes over me, making the heart rate monitor beep like crazy. I don't have a second to process her words before Mom rushes in. Her eyes are red from crying or fatigue, I'm not sure.

"Oh, baby," she croons, grabbing my hand. "I'm so sorry. I didn't realize you were so sick."

"I'm fine," I tell her in the brightest tone I can muster.

"You're not fine," a deep voice booms. "Your stomach is bleeding, son. That hole is only going to get bigger left untreated."

I cringe, closing my eyes. "Why is he here?"

"I'm sorry," Mom whispers. "I am."

"I'm here because you're my son," Dad says with such arrogance I want to slap him.

"You kicked us out," I mutter, lacking the energy I crave to yell at him.

"I'm not here to fight." Dad regards me with a haggard expression. "I'm worried about you."

Hot tears burn in my eyes. I blink them away. I hate my father. I hate that he's here. I especially hate that a tiny part of me misses him. That same little boy always seeking impossible approval.

"The CT scan showed no signs of peritonitis, which is fantastic news because if you were septic, that'd change the ballgame, son." He places his hands on his hips. "The hole is decent and will only grow if they don't repair it. If we were back home, I'd do it myself, but luckily I'm here and I'll be able to advise the surgeons here on what to do."

Oh, God.

Mom rolls her eyes at him. "Perhaps you should go discuss it with the doctor now."

"Dr. Edmond is on his way," Fran chimes in. "You might find him in the hall. You should hurry." She winks at me.

Dad smiles, patting the top of my head. "We'll talk after, Hollis. I love you."

I look away from him, tears brimming in my eyes.

"I thought we'd never get him out of here," Mom grumbles. "How you doing, baby?"

"I'm tired. I want to see Roan."

Mom's smile is weak. "After surgery, okay?"

"Is he okay? Is he wrecked?" Guilt swarms inside me as I worry about how he feels. He was destroyed about them taking Roux and then I got sent to the hospital. There's no telling that boy's state of mind right now.

"He's been better," Mom says. "He had to leave."

"Mom…"

"He took Mike's truck." She frowns. "Roan's a big boy. He can handle himself. Right now, we need to focus on you."

"Mom, he's going to do something dumb. He's messed up right now. Why didn't you try to stop him?"

She takes my hand. "Because you need me more than he does right now."

"You almost ready?" Fran asks as she checks my vitals.

No.

I'm not ready.

I need to make sure Roan's okay.

"Where's my phone?" I demand. "I need it."

Mom digs through a bag at her feet. "Here you go."

I dial Roan's number and it goes to voicemail.

Fuck.

"Make it quick," Fran warns. "I can hear Dr. Edmond outside that door. He's no nonsense. When he comes in, he'll want to take you right back to surgery."

Ignoring her, I flip through my numbers until I find Jordy's. Roan gave it to me once for emergencies. I'd laughed it off, assuming I'd never have to call him, but here we are having a goddamn emergency.

"What?" he snaps.

"It's me. Hollis."

"Rat? Where's Roan?" The instant fear in his voice sets me on edge.

"Not here. I'm afraid he's going to do something stupid."

"What do you mean? Why aren't you with him?" he demands.

"I'm about to go in for emergency stomach surgery." I close my eyes. "They, uh…they took Roux back to her mom's."

"They did fucking what?" he roars.

"Roan was here and now he's not. For him to leave me, something bad is going to happen. Please help him, Jordy. Please."

He curses. "Right. Okay. I'm on it."

"Thank you," I breathe.

"Rat..."

"Yeah?"

"Stay alive. For Roan."

"I'll do my best, man."

"Still want to be a firefighter?" I ask, running my fingertip along the grooves between his abs.

"Yeah."

"I always wanted to bone a firefighter."

"Freak." Roan chuckles, his stomach muscles tensing in a delicious way that makes me want to lick them. "What are you gonna be? Not a doctor, which sucks because I need a sugar daddy."

I swat his stomach. "Maybe Mike will be your sugar daddy."

"Gross," he says with a laugh. "I think Mike wants to be your mom's sugar daddy."

"What? No fucking way."

"Dude, have you seen the way he eyes your mom's ass?"

No. I'm going to kill him.

"Aww, little Hollis is getting mad because someone likes his mom."

"Fuck off."

"Only if you're fucking off with me."

I tilt my head up to look at him. He rolls his body onto mine and kisses me. Sometimes his kisses are vulnerable and sweet.

Those kisses imbed their way into my heart. It's times like this that I realize I'm going to do whatever it takes to keep Roan Hirsch as mine. Whatever it takes.

"So no doctor. What then? Substitute teacher?"

"You have a fetish for substitute teachers," I grumble.

"It's your fault. You showed up in your spiffy coat and your expensive car. I can't help it I fell for the whole gig."

"Fell, huh?"

Instead of responding, he playfully bites my jaw. "Tell me."

"I like the idea of helping people, but I refuse to give my soul to a hospital. Dad lost us when he married medicine."

Roan kisses me again, softer. Gently. Like he can kiss away the pain inside me—pain Dad is responsible for.

"Maybe a paramedic," I say thoughtfully. "I don't think I'm tough like you to want to run into burning buildings. But helping them once you bring them out to me, I can do."

"Oh," Roan teases, "I like the idea of you looking hot in your suit and standing in front of an ambulance. Definitely going to jack off to this image later."

I grab his ass and squeeze. "Make sure you call me when you do because I'll be doing the same thing thinking about you in all that heavy fireman's gear."

"I might have already jacked off to fantasies of you as my teacher."

We both laugh.

"You want a lesson, huh?" I tease. "You're nice and clean after your shower. Maybe I'll give you a lesson in rimming."

"Eating ass?"

"Pay attention," I say in a firm, authoritative tone, "and you're to not speak crudely in my classroom, young man."

His smile is deviant, and his eyes light up with wickedness. "Yes, Mr. English."

Damn, when this bad boy is obedient, he really gets my dick hard.

"Good boy."

"Hollis."

"Hollis."

"Hollis."

I wake from my dreams, confused and unaware of where I'm at. All I know is it's warm. It's quiet. I'm on a cloud.

"You're coming off the anesthesia," a man says. "The surgery went well. While the perforation wasn't too big, it was surrounded by some abscesses that needed to be drained. We've closed up the hole and fixed you right up."

My eyelids are too heavy.

I drift off.

All I see is amber.

Eyes.

Eyes.

His eyes.

Roan.

Chapter Twenty-Six

Roan

I have no plan.

Just get Roux.

Everything else, I'll figure out along the way. Getting a ride was easy enough. Mike was distracted when I asked to borrow his truck. Kelsey's primary concern was making sure Hollis was okay. And while everything screamed in me to stay at the hospital with Hollis, I couldn't ignore my sister's terrified sobs.

"Please come get me. I'm scared. I don't feel safe."

The roads are slick tonight, but I still drive like a bat out of hell. My veins are buzzing with energy. Adrenaline is fueling me. Within ten minutes, I'm pulling into Mom's trashy apartment complex. I see Alexander's shitty Maxima, so I know he's home.

Fuck.

I'm going to have to come to blows with this motherfucker.

Anything for Roux.

After I whip into a parking spot, I climb out of the big truck and run into the building. People laugh at me as I run like my ass is on fire, but I don't give a shit. It feels like an eternity until I get to Mom's floor.

Loud music thumps from her door, which means Alexander is having one of his parties. I turn the knob and peek my head in. The apartment is a cloud of smoke. My eyes burn from the smell of pot. It pisses me off that Roux has to be exposed to this shit. There's a black light on and people are dancing. I skate down the entryway and veer off down the hallway undetected. Mom's bedroom door stands wide-open and the light is on.

Unreliable bitch.

Mom lies sprawled out on the bed, half naked and blissed out on heroin based on the needle sticking out of her arm. One of Alexander's friends has his hand between her legs, rubbing. Fucking gross. I hate them all. I'm about to tell him to get the fuck off her considering she's passed out, but then I hear it.

A squeal.

Roux.

I bolt toward her room. When I go to shove the door open, it only opens about six inches. Something heavy is blocking it. The dresser.

"Roux!" I call out. "It's me! Let me in!"

"Roan!"

She runs to the door, sticking her skinny arm out, tears running down her cheeks. She's safe. I just need to get her out.

"Help me," she pleads.

"Help me," Alexander mimics, stepping behind her and chilling my blood.

Another voice laughs from inside the room.

They're in there with her. Oh my fucking God.

"You so much as—" I start but am cut off when he slaps a hand over her mouth and drags her away. "No!"

I start slamming my shoulder hard against the door, hoping to move the dresser far enough so I can get in. I'll push my way in there even if I have to destroy the whole goddamn door. Her screams only have me shoving harder and harder. From my vantage point, they only seem to be terrorizing her but not hurting her. They push her around and are laughing like fucking lunatics. They're obviously high on something.

Franco grabs her, pulling her to him despite her squirming. "Oh, look. Little Roux's getting tits now." When he rubs on her chest, I lose my mind, roaring and snarling like an animal.

She claws at his face and slips out of his grip. Alexander yanks her to him by her hair. With his eyes on me, he starts yanking at her pajama pants.

No.

No.

No.

I step several feet back and then run, pushing hard against the door with all my might. I'm able to make my way inside. I stumble over some shit on the floor and then swing at Alexander. He ducks, tossing Roux into the floor, and then puts his fists up. I swing for him again, but someone kicks me hard in the back.

Franco.

"Roux, go," I order, just as Alexander clocks me in the jaw.

I sway on my feet and aim a hard punch at his stomach. He groans but recovers quickly, pushing me toward Franco. Franco kicks the back of my knee, causing me to fall to the ground. They both start kicking me hard. Every blow is harder than the last. All I can think about is Roux.

Run, Roux, run.

She lets out a rage-filled cry as she throws her bedside lamp at Alexander. It hits him in the arm. Doesn't hurt him, just pisses him off. He chases after her. I manage to kick up at Franco, nailing him in the nuts. He howls, distracted, and I crawl after Alexander. That fucker has her trapped in the closet. He strikes her, but I tackle him as he does it, making it lose some of its impact. We scuffle in the bottom of the closet, mostly wrestling to get the upper hand.

"Roux, get the hell out of here," I hiss out, as I punch Alexander in his ribs.

"Not without you!"

Franco shows up and grabs my sister by the hair, dragging her back into the bedroom. Her screams are maddening. I manage to untangle myself from Alexander to go after them. Franco is undressing my sister. My thirteen-year-old sister. When I see her naked ass, I lose my mind with fury. I tackle him and start pummeling his face. Blind rage takes over. I'm about to slam my fist into him again when someone kicks me in the head from behind. I fall over, blacking out. I come to with a knee pressed into my back.

No.

No.

No.

Alexander is finishing what Franco started. He has her pants and panties off, his hand pawing at her. Tears of hate and sorrow blind me. Why are they doing this? She's just a kid.

"You fuck with me," Alexander bellows, glaring down at me, "I fuck with you."

He starts to unbuckle his belt and I dry heave. I can't do this. I can't see this. God, fucking help us.

All I hear is their maniacal laughter.

It's fucking haunting.

Alexander pulls his dick out. His big fucking dick. And I am helpless. I squeeze my eyes shut. Please, God. Please.

Pop!

I open my eyes, trying to understand how Alexander is now on the ground in front of me, a big hole in his forehead. Blood is pooling around him.

Pop!

Franco falls heavily on top of me. My voice is hoarse from screaming for Roux, yet I continue to call out her name. Continue to reach for her. A man comes into the room, stalking straight over to my sister.

"Please don't hurt her," I beg. "Please."

I manage to roll Franco's body off me and crawl my weak and battered body toward the man who's touching my sister.

"What the fuck—" someone says from the doorway.

Pop!

The man shoots this guy too. Is he going to shoot my sister? No, he seems to be helping her pull her pants back up. He's vibrating with wrath. I grab onto his jeans and look up at him.

Jordy.

Jordy.

It's fucking Jordy.

He falls to the ground with Roux in his arms. Her entire body trembles as she sobs. I manage to reach over and grab her shaking hand. She and I cry, clinging to one another as Jordy stays deathly still and completely silent.

He's hurt.

Is he hurt?

Why won't he say anything?

"J-Jordy," I chatter out, my entire body overcome with chills.

He doesn't answer. Doesn't move.

"What the hell did you do to my—" another guy exclaims from the doorway.

Pop!

I gape in shock as Jordy puts a bullet through this guy too. This is bad. This is really bad. My hands are shaking as I try to take the gun from him.

"Don't," he growls. "I need to get any others who come in here. For Roux."

I nod, tears leaking down my cheeks. "O-Okay."

His eyes leave mine and remain affixed on the doorway. I try to hug them both, but Jordy shakes me off. I don't like this. I don't like how he's acting. It scares the fuck out of me.

"J-Jordy, b-bro, we g-gotta g-get outta here." My voice keeps cracking and breaking. I can't stop fucking trembling.

"It's not safe," Jordy says in an icy tone.

I can hear sirens close by and I pray to God this will all be over soon.

"I want to leave," Roux begs, practically crawling up Jordy's torso. "Please, Jordy. Take me away from here."

He tries to push her off him, but she clings tighter. I grip her leg, fearful she'll run away and I'll never see her again. The three of us are a fucking mess.

"Please, Jordy," she wails. "Please."

"It's not safe, Little Hornet." His tone is colder than anything I've ever heard before.

A loud voice booms from a speaker. "Come out of the bedroom with your hands up."

Roux screams, clawing at Jordy, trying to hide her face in his neck. I cling to them both, terrified as fuck. Jordy keeps his gun pointed at the doorway like more bad guys are going to walk right through it.

The music that was playing has long since been turned off. I can hear men whispering to each other and heavy footsteps thudding. Someone tells someone else to get a paramedic. There's an unresponsive female in one of the rooms. I also hear the words, "Suspect is armed and has hostages."

That's not right.

He's the hero, not the suspect.

"Roan," Roux sobs. "I'm scared."

"M-Me t-too." Why the fuck is my voice shaking so bad?

"Sir," the voice booms again. "Lower your weapon so no one else gets hurt."

"They deserved it," Jordy barks out. "They tried to rape a thirteen-year-old girl!"

"I'm Captain Fitzgerald. Let's talk this out, son. What's your name?"

"Jordy Martin."

"Listen, Jordy, I know you're scared. Who do you have with you?"

"Roan and Roux. I'm protecting them."

I squeeze my best friend and my sister as though I can protect them with an embrace.

"I can see that. We'll get all that sorted out at the station," Fitzgerald assures him. "You have to put the gun down, though. We don't want you to accidentally get someone shot."

"Please don't shoot Jordy," Roux begs them.

"Sweetheart," Fitzgerald says. "We're going to do our best not to let that happen. I have to protect my officers and the both of you, though. If Jordy does exactly as we say, no one will get hurt."

I try to sit up but everything hurts too fucking bad. All I can do is stay in the fetal position beside them.

"Jordy," Fitzgerald says in a calm voice. "Can you let Roux come out through the door?"

"No!" Jordy yells. "Alexander's friends are out there! Look what they already did to her and Roan!"

"I can assure you, son, the only people out here are officers and paramedics. We only want to help."

"Let me see your badge," Jordy growls. "So I know you're not one of them."

"Lower your weapon and I'll be glad to show you."

Jordy relaxes his arm, letting his hand that's holding the gun rest on my shoulder. "Show me."

Fitzgerald holds up a badge, the metal glinting in the light. "See. I'm the captain of the Horn River police department. I'm safe. Can you set the gun on the floor where I can see it?"

"Do you have any women?" Jordy asks. "For Roux?"

"Officer Kline is here."

"You can call me Jessica," Officer Kline says from nearby. "I'll be able to help Roux. Can she come to me, Jordy?"

Jordy hugs Roux and kisses her head. "Go, Roux. It's safe."

"I'm scared," Roux whines.

"We're right b-behind you," I mutter, my teeth still chattering.

"Okay," she whispers.

She stands up on shaky legs and walks around the bed, stepping over two bodies. When she nears the door, a blond female officer bravely reaches for her, pulling her over the other two dead men. There is commotion and relieved voices on the other side.

"Great job, Jordy," Fitzgerald says. "You did a good job. Now we just need to help Roan. Is he hurt?"

"I…I…I don't know." Jordy sounds tired and confused. "I hope he's okay."

I try to nod, but my head is killing me. "I'll be all right."

"Maybe you should go hang out at the hospital with your rat," Jordy offers, snorting with inappropriate laughter. "Fuck. Fuck, Roan. What the fuck did I do?"

"Listen," Fitzgerald says in his calming voice. "We're not going to worry about all that right now. If we do, then everyone will get upset. We need you to make good decisions right now, Jordy. And a good decision would be to set that gun down. Then, shove it away."

"Am I going to die?" Jordy asks, his voice cracking. "I don't want to die."

I start to cry because I've seen the movies. They always shoot the guy trying to help. Jordy is only trying to help.

"Don't cry, pussy," Jordy jokes, but there's unmistakable fear in his voice.

"P-Please d-don't shoot him," I beg Fitzgerald. "Please."

"Boys," Fitzgerald says in a fatherly tone. "No one is getting shot as long as everyone cooperates. Roan, can you move? Can you come out like Roux did?"

I try to lift my head, but the headache only intensifies. Bile rises up my throat and I dry heave. "I d-don't think s-so. I f-feel like I'm g-going to p-puke."

Jordy looks down at me. "His head is bleeding."

"Okay," Fitzgerald coos. "It's okay. We have paramedics here to help Roan."

I think about Hollis in his paramedic clothes.

God, I miss him.

"Since Roan can't get up, Jordy, we're really going to need your help so we can get him the aid he needs," Fitzgerald says in a stern voice. "That means tossing the gun away and putting your hands in the air. It's just procedure. To keep everyone safe."

"You won't shoot me?" Jordy asks. "They still need me. You can't shoot me."

"No one is going to shoot you," Fitzgerald tells him. "Please, son. Let's get Roan checked out. This will be all over soon. You two boys could use a good night's sleep."

"I'm tired," Jordy agrees in a childlike voice. "Really tired."

He yawns and pushes the gun away. His fingers brush over my head on a sore spot and I wince.

"Good job," Fitzgerald praises. "Now put your arms up. I'm going to walk into the room. You'll see both my hands. Officer Young is going to come behind me with his weapon, but that's just to keep us all safe. No one is getting shot, okay?"

Jordy lifts his arms. "Okay."

Everyone moves in slow motion. An older man with salt and pepper hair walks in just as he said. He's smiling grimly at us, his eyes raking over me, assessing me for damage. Young creeps in behind him.

"Now, Jordy, I'm going to have to handcuff you until we sort all this out at the station, okay? So don't fight me on this. It's to keep everyone safe."

Fitzgerald steps over me and then comes behind Jordy. Young pounces on me, scooping me up like I don't weigh just over two hundred pounds. I can hear Fitzgerald reading Jordy his rights as he cuffs him. The room spins and I turn my head to throw up. Everything is a blur.

Voices.

Lights.

Managed chaos.

"Jordy," I whine. "Roux."

"Roux is going to the hospital too. To get checked out," a male paramedic tells me. "Everything is going to be okay."

My eyes meet Jordy's dark ones as they lead him out of the apartment. Fitzgerald said everything would be sorted out at the station. Everything is going to be okay.

As the stretcher rolls out of the apartment, I close my eyes and let relief settle in my bones.

We did it.

We're safe.

No one got shot.

Chapter Twenty-Seven

Hollis

"Where am I?" I ask a woman with white hair.

She smiles kindly at me. "You're in surgery recovery. Dr. Edmond said he already spoke to you. The surgery was successful. Now we're just waiting for you to wake up before we put you in a room." She pats my hand. "How are you feeling?"

"Fine."

Her laughter reminds me of my grandma's. "Wonderful. Would you like to see your parents now?"

I nod, though I don't especially want to see my father. She disappears and I fall back asleep. When I wake again, both Mom and Dad are at my bedside.

Dad is normally aloof and impassive, but right now, he looks relieved, which is confusing because I figured he'd want his gay son to die off in surgery. He takes my hand and squeezes it.

"Glad to see you awake, little buddy."

My heart clenches at the name he called me when I was little.

"They fixed it," Mom tells me, her eyes brimming with tears. "Everything's going to be okay."

"Roan?"

Mom stiffens. "You'll see him soon."

"Where is he?" I croak.

"Here. Both he and Roux are."

I frown, trying to make sense of her words. "In the waiting room?"

"They're being checked out."

"What? Why?" Alarm has me wanting to sit up, but everything feels heavy and achy. The pain meds have me feeling as though I'm in a fog. "I want to see them."

"We can talk about it later," Mom says in a gentle voice. "They're okay, though. That's all that matters."

Oh, fuck this hurts.

I hit the nurse button, needing her to show up with my pain meds already. This action has both Mom and Dad waking up. We've since been moved to a room and I can see the sunrise from my vantage point.

"What's wrong?" Dad asks, walking over to me and assessing me. "What's your pain level?"

"I hurt," I groan. "It hurts."

"You had stomach surgery. There will be pain. I'll go find a nurse." He pats my hand before leaving.

Mom's phone rings and she speaks lowly to someone. Then, she hangs up. Her eyes lift to mine, guilt swarming in them.

"Who was that?"

"Mike."

"What did he want?"

She sighs before standing. "To give me an update on the kids. Roux has been discharged and has been released to him. Roan is still here."

"Where? Why?"

"Just getting CT scans and some other things. Those men beat him up pretty badly." Her eyes water. "He was lucky Jordy came when he did."

Jordy?

"How is Jordy? Did he get hurt too? Is he okay?"

Mom frowns. "They arrested him."

"Why?"

"He shot and killed four men, Hollis."

I gape at her. "He did?"

"Roan and Roux both say it was to protect them, but it's a mess right now. Nothing you need to worry about, though. We need you to focus on you."

Oh God.

Poor Roan.

His best friend killed four men for them.

This will eat him alive with guilt.

"I want to see him," I beg. "Take me to Roan."

She walks over to me and takes my hand. "As soon as we can, we'll make it happen."

I wake to whispered voices.

Mike and Mom.

"Perhaps you two should take this conversation elsewhere," a pissed off voice snarls. Dad. "He's trying to rest."

I crack my eyes open. Mike has his arm around Mom, hugging her as she cries. Dad is pacing, eyeing Mike like he's carrying the plague.

"Where's Roan?" I ask, my voice hoarse.

Dad rushes over to me and pours me a glass of ice water. "Here. Drink this."

I take his offered glass and gulp down the cold drink. Mom and Mike both stand and walk over to me.

"How you feeling, kid?" Mike asks me.

"I'll feel better when I see my boyfriend."

Mike smiles. "You're just as annoying as Roan is. I'm here because his bossy ass made me come check on you."

I relax my body, happy as hell. "Is he okay?"

"Another concussion. Some internal bleeding, but they've got all that under control. They're keeping him for monitoring."

"Where's Roux?"

"Aunt Karen came and got her," Mom replies. "Poor thing was exhausted."

"Jordy still at the station?" I ask, frowning.

Mom's lips purse together. "It doesn't look good for him. His parents and brother are there. They've hired an attorney. We don't know much yet."

Mike clutches Mom's shoulder, which makes my dad snort with disgust.

"Why do you all seem like there's more bad news?" I hate that they're both looking at me sadly.

"Miranda woke up. She's claiming someone drugged her. Keeps asking about her baby girl." Mom's face reddens with anger. "She told the police Roan was there to kidnap Roux."

Oh shit.

"I told Roan to keep his mouth shut," Mike grunts. "I don't want him incriminating himself. The police already have record of having to take Roux from Roan, so kidnapping isn't a far stretch."

"This is bullshit," I mutter. "She's an incompetent druggie."

"It's all a mess right now," Mom agrees. "For now, worry about getting better."

Feeling helpless to do anything but sleep, I close my eyes and dream of Roan.

Soft flutters on my hand wake me from my slumber. I've slept off and on for the last couple of days since I had surgery. None of those days have I seen or spoken to Roan.

Yet, here he is.

Sitting in a chair beside my bed, rubbing his thumb along the back of my hand.

"Roan," I whisper.

He lifts his head and I cringe. His face is black and blue. One eye is swollen almost all the way shut and he has stitches on his cheek. His bottom lip is busted in two spots.

"Hey," he mumbles. "Long time no see."

"What happened to you?"

He closes his eyes and a tear leaks out. My heart breaks at seeing him so destroyed. His entire body trembles as he loses it. All I can do to comfort him is squeeze his hand.

"Roan..."

"Everything's so fucked up, Hollis. Everything."

"Talk to me, babe. Tell me."

He coughs, clearly trying to compose himself, but he fails. His words come out as sobs. "S-She told them I was there to k-kidnap Roux. D-Defended that fucker Alexander." He sniffles and lets out a sharp sigh. "Jordy lied t-too. To p-protect me."

"Oh no."

"If I c-contradict what he says, I'll go to j-jail t-too. I don't know what the f-fuck to do." He trembles as he cries. His free hand tugs at his hair in frustration while his other hand clings to me like I'm a lifeline.

"What did Jordy tell them?"

"Said he used m-me to get inside. Lied and s-said he's in a rival gang as Alexander."

"But that's bullshit," I snap. "Why can't it just be a slam dunk case? Your sister was in danger and you saved her. Jordy did what he did to protect you both."

He swipes at his tears. "B-Because it's n-not that simple. Either way, he's in deep s-shit for killing four men. This way, I stay clean."

"What are you going to do?"

"J-Juno and Mike and your mom all told me I need to just let Jordy do what he wants. Then I'm still out here f-for Roux."

"Oh, fuck, Roan. I'm so sorry."

He rests his forehead on our conjoined hands. "I just need t-to think. I just need to sleep."

"Sleep," I murmur, squeezing his hand. "Sleep. Then we'll figure it out together."

His breathing comes out soft and rhythmic a moment later. It lulls me into my own nap. At least when we're sleeping, we don't have to deal with all the unfair bullshit.

We're going to figure this out.

We have to.

Chapter Twenty-Eight

Roan

Two months later…

His dark eyes are vacant. Jordy is no longer the kid playing basketball with me or fucking with me about my lack of cooking skills. No, he's dressed in a cheap suit that probably belongs to his dad awaiting his sentencing.

I hate how resigned he is to his future.

Hollis grips my hand so tightly, I think my bones will break. It would feel better than the shredding of my heart.

Roux fidgets from beside me. She's upset. We both are. But there's nothing we can do. Jordy was adamant about what really went down. Some fake ass story that the cops pretty much rolled their eyes over, but one they accepted, nonetheless.

Gang rivals.

I was some tool for him to get to Alexander.

He swore to them that I was just there to visit my sister, not kidnap her like Mom claimed. The dudes attacked me and Roux, and then Jordy killed those men. He told them it was convenient, because they needed to die anyway.

During the trial, they attempted to get answers from Jordy. The name of the supposed gang he was with. Why they had beef with Alexander. How come he told the cops during the standoff he was protecting us and never mentioned these alleged gangs. It was a shitshow and Jordy just sat there stone-faced and quiet. The one time he decided to speak was to plead guilty. Everyone was pissed off. The lawyers. The judge. Us. But what can you do when someone just willingly takes the heat for shit?

Nothing.

My mind drifts to the one time we spoke.

"My attorney says I'm going to prison no matter what I tell them," Jordy says, swallowing. "No need to have them drag you through the mud."

"It's not dragging me through the mud," I hiss. "It's being honest as to why we were there. She was being assaulted. I went there to save her. You were worried, so you came too. The four men were trying to hurt us. You killed them. The fucking end, Jordy. We all go home. Together."

He shakes his head, his dark eyes sad as they probe me. "We're not boys anymore, man. We're adults. Your mom's claim means you're looking at serious jail time for attempted kidnapping. Years, Roan. You have a future."

"Oh, give me a fucking break," I snap. "You have a future too and you're ruining it. Ruining everything."

"For Roux," he growls. "And you. Besides, I'm not ruining everything. I'm being smart. For once in my damn life, I'm being smart. You 'visiting' your sister and getting caught up in a gang beef keeps you both innocent and victims. I'm going to prison either way, so I may as well keep you clean."

"This is bullshit! You were defending us!"

"I think it's time for you to go. It's done, brother."

I hastily swipe at my tears. "It's not done. I'll tell them all this. That it's all just your way of protecting us. You'll get a lesser sentence. You can come back to us."

His features grow cold. "I'll deny it." He sneers. "I used you. To kill those motherfuckers."

"Stop, Jordy," I beg. "Please. The cops who responded already know you were protecting us. Come on, man, we can fix this."

"This takes the focus off why you were there," he snaps. "How many times do we need to go over this? They will toss your ass in jail just as quickly as they will me for what I did. Do you want Roux all alone with your mom and her next asshole boyfriend?" He cracks his neck. "I sure as hell don't. Who's to say the next one doesn't hurt her in ways that can't be undone? She needs you."

"She needs you too," I argue, choking on an angry sob. "We both do."

"You have the rat and she has his sister. Just…" He sighs. "Just let me take the fall for this and stay clean. Make me proud. Go fight fires like you always wanted. Go make babies with the rat for all I care. Just make sure Roux is right there with you and safe. Swear it to me, Roan. On our friendship, brother."

Defeated, I nod.

I'll do it for him.

I'll do it for Roux.

Because, honestly, I don't know what else to do.

As the memory fades, I stare at Jordy. He's so resigned to doing this. It kills me. But, after researching the laws, he was right. If they dug and could prove I had plans to kidnap Roux, which they easily could, I would get a few years if convicted. A few years that Roux cannot afford to lose of me. I'd read up on Oregon laws and his sentence would be reduced if he could prove extreme emotional distress, which was plausible considering he was trying to save us, but that would once again shine the spotlight on why I was there. We all know it wasn't for a friendly visit. I was there to take her.

I let out a heavy sigh of frustration. This fucking sucks. I'm shaking and barely able to hold it together. I'm thankful to have Hollis by my side. Cal and Trey are sitting on the other side of Roux, both just as upset as we are. Our friend is up there, in front of everyone, facing a horrible future. The lawyer warned us that if the judge is harsh, he could be spending life without parole. He thinks, though, with the holes in the case and Jordy's age, the judge might be more lenient. Only time will tell.

The sentencing trial goes quickly.

I'm numb through it all.

Until it's time for sentencing. The judge shakes his head in exasperation before speaking.

"I may be old, son, but I'm not dumb. And neither is anyone in this courtroom," the judge says, frowning at Jordy. "This wasn't premeditated. There's no proof of gang affiliation. We have several testimonies from law enforcement officers who arrived on the scene. You were protecting your friends." The judge pinches the bridge of his nose before sighing. "But I can't force you to tell the truth. You've plead guilty and that's out of my control."

The courtroom is nearly silent as we all wait with bated breath for the sentencing.

"What is under my control is your sentencing. My hands are tied where Oregon law is concerned, meaning you have to serve time. How much, though, is up to me. Considering your no priors and age, I don't think it's necessary for you to spend your life in jail. You're still young, therefore you're still thinking like a boy. I'm hoping you'll begin thinking like a man soon. The minimum sentence I can give you, son, is ten years at Oregon State Penitentiary with eligibility for parole after four."

The same goddamn prison my father's at.

Ten years.

And that's the best we could hope for.

"I suggest," the judge says in a firm tone, "that you get really familiar with the appeal laws of our state. I suggest you sit and think about how this impacts your life. Maybe one day we can revisit this case." The judge shakes his head again. "Try not to lose yourself in there, kid. You'll get out before you know it and still have a chance to do right by yourself."

As he mumbles on more of the court sentencing jargon, I shut down. I'm dying inside because I feel like this is all my fault. I don't know how to fix it. I don't know how to free my friend.

A loud whistle catches my attention over all the murmurs of voices.

Jordy.

Dark, penetrating eyes on me.

"Take care of Little Hornet." He mouths the words, but I hear them clear as day.

I nod sharply, which earns me a rare smile.

And then they take my best friend away.

"I don't want to go," Roux whines. "Not today. Not after seeing them take Jordy away."

I stroke Roux's hair and let out a heavy sigh. "I know.

But Mom will be here any minute to get you. We have to play this right. You have your phone, right?"

Roux nods.

"Good. Call me or text me if anything is weird. Captain Fitzgerald said he'd be the first to check on you if you needed anything. We'll do this the right way this time."

"I miss you, though. She stole all my birthday money, you know." She huffs. "For bills she said, but I don't believe it. I hate living with her."

Who the fuck takes their kid's birthday money?

"I know you do. I'm sorry."

"Don't worry," Hollis says, patting her foot. "Tomorrow is another school day. Roan and I will pick you up first thing in the morning. Charlotte will talk your ear off and all will be right in the world."

She laughs. "She does talk a lot in the mornings."

"More than you," I tease. "Seriously, though, everything is going to be okay."

Bang. Bang. Bang.

We all three groan in unison. Mom allowed Roux to attend the hearing, but only because she was at work. Now she'll take my sister back home. This fucking sucks.

I rise and stalk over to the front door. I swing it open and glare at my piece of shit mother. She reeks of cigarette smoke and her eyeliner is smeared. Her hand trembles when she waves for Roux to come with her.

"Are you high?" I demand. She hates when I ask her this.

"No, asshole, I'm tired as fuck. Been stripping to keep the electricity on because your stupid best friend killed my boyfriend. Now I have to pay for everything by myself."

Testy.

"Aww," I sneer. "Poor Mom. Actually having to be a fucking parent for once."

"Get your shit," Mom bellows to Roux. "I don't have time for this. I'm ready to go to bed."

It's three in the afternoon.

"I'm coming," Roux grumbles.

"See you tomorrow," Hollis tells her.

Roux hugs me and I kiss the top of her head. "Take care. Call me later."

Mom shoots me another nasty look before wobbling down the stairs in her stupid high heels. She and Roux climb into Alexander's Maxima. The bitch peels out, making a mess out of Mike's yard. I shake my head in frustration.

"Come on," Hollis says, taking my hand. "You need a nap."

I'm numb and broken and sad as fuck. Jordy is going to prison. Ten fucking years. My eyes are blurry by the time we make it to bed. Hollis is gentle as he strips me down to my underwear. He does the same and then we crawl into bed. My boyfriend holds me, allowing me to just blank out for God knows how long.

It's dark by the time I decide to speak.

"It's all my fault."

He runs his fingers through my hair. "Nope. You can't take this on your shoulders."

"If it weren't for me, he wouldn't have felt like he needed to rescue us."

"Jordy is a big boy. He knew what he was doing."

I sigh. "Maybe I should have been more adamant about

my reasons for going there. Maybe that would have somehow reduced his sentence. I don't fucking know."

"It was hard for them to prove he killed in defense when he killed four people," Hollis says gently. "So even if you told them you were there to take Roux, it doesn't change that. Either way, ten years was a good outcome for him."

"Nothing feels good about any of this."

"I know," he murmurs. "But there's nothing we can do about it. It's done."

We lie in silence for a while longer until his stomach growls.

"You need to eat," I state.

"Yeah. I can make us something."

It's weird seeing Hollis eat now. I guess if I had a bleeding hole in my stomach, I'd never be hungry either. I'm glad they fixed him. He's healthier looking than I've ever known him. It's one less thing to worry about.

Neither of us gets up.

"Roan," Hollis practically yells. "Phone."

I squint against the lamplight and take my phone from him. "Hello?"

"Roan, it's Carol."

My blood turns to ice. "Where's Roux?"

"I have her with me. She's safe," she assures me. But her voice is off. Something is wrong. "Roan, your mom…"

"What?"

"She overdosed on heroin tonight."

The line grows quiet.

"Hello? Roan, did we get disconnected?"

"Is she in the hospital?"

Carol sighs. "She passed away. I'm sorry."

I'm not.

I don't voice that. Barely.

"I'm bringing Roux to you," Carol says. "I'll stay as long as you two need me to."

We hang up and Hollis frowns at me.

"What happened?" he asks.

"Mom's dead. Roux's coming home."

He pounces on me, kissing me hard. "Thank fuck."

"Thank fuck," I murmur against his lips.

Finally, a win.

"Remember when Cal threw me in the pool fully clothed one summer?" Roux asks, a smile in her voice.

I chuckle. "Jordy broke his nose."

"He deserved it," she sasses.

"He did. If Jordy didn't punch his dumb ass, I would have."

"You were too busy rescuing me knowing full well I could swim," Roux tells me.

"Aww," Hollis teases. "Roan's a hero."

"I really did save your ass, brat," I say to him with a smirk.

We all laugh. Laughing feels good. It's been a few days since Roux came home and we're still in shock. With Mom. With Jordy. With all of it.

"I'm going to get a Coke. Want anything?" Roux asks as she stands from the sofa.

"I'm good," Hollis says and I nod.

She leaves to go into the kitchen. Hollis chooses the moment to crawl up my body and steal a kiss. Kelsey visits a lot lately because it's the only way she gets to see her son. He and I have been glued to each other after all that's gone on. It just feels good having someone to lean on.

"How are you doing?" he asks, his lips hovering over mine.

"Better now that Roux's here."

"Good."

He kisses me deeply again and doesn't pull away in time. Roux groans in exaggeration.

"Gross, Hollis. Stop mauling my brother."

Hollis slides off me and shrugs. "I can't help it he's so hot."

I laugh and Roux makes a sour face.

"Don't tell him he's hot. He'll act like he's the shit," Roux tells him.

"Hey now," I chide. "Don't say shit."

"Why not?" she demands.

"Because shit's a shitty word, you shithead."

She snorts. "I'm going to say shit only because you don't want me to. It's what you get for tonguing your boyfriend in front of me."

Hollis cracks up laughing. "Oh, man, you have your hands full, babe. This one is a major brat." He ruffles her hair, messing it up. "You've been hanging out with Charlotte too much. She's a bad influence."

Roux swats Hollis's hand away. "Whatever."

Hollis curls up against me and continues to pick at Roux by poking at her with his toes. She tries to mean mug him but ends up giggling. I almost feel happy. But in the back of my mind, I think about the cost my happiness came at.

Jordy.

Hollis, sensing my somber mood, stops fucking with Roux and threads his fingers with mine. "It's going to get better," he assures me. "I promise."

My heart lightens a little.

I believe him.

It has to.

Chapter Twenty-Nine

Hollis

Six months later…

I yawn, checking my phone for the millionth time. He's been gone for too long. The news is on, and I anxiously wait for some sort of coverage about tonight's fire.

Nothing.

Nothing is good. Means there were no fatalities. It's not breaking news, so they'll just mention it on the news at ten.

Still, I worry.

One of the not-so-wonderful things about dating a volunteer firefighter.

While I wait for my hot fireman to get his ass home so I'll stop worrying, I flip through the cable channels. Now that Roan works at the tire factory during the week, he's pulling in consistent paychecks and can afford things like cable and a car.

A smile tugs at my lips when I think about his truck. This summer, we took it to Horn River more times than I can count just to fuck under the stars. Pretty romantic if you ask me. When we weren't fucking, he taught me how to swim. I learned pretty damn quick considering the reward was him. Always him. Roux would die if she knew what sort of nefarious deeds we got up to when she was not around.

I wish she were around tonight. She's spending the night with Charlotte. It makes the garage apartment pretty damn lonely. Mom tells me if I ever came home, I wouldn't go stir-crazy when Roan was gone. I'm not interested, though. I like being here when he finally does drag in after putting out fires. I give him a proper hero's welcome.

A car door slams outside and I jolt up in bed, craning my head to listen. Heavy footsteps thud up the stairs and then keys jangle. I fling the blanket off the bed and pad down the hall to greet my man. His exhausted amber eyes seek me out the moment he steps inside.

"Thank God you're home," I grumble, rushing over to him.

He hugs me tight, inhaling me. "Easy fire tonight. They think a copy machine overheated at the real estate office and caught fire." He chuckles. "Mike used it as one of those finer teaching moments."

I pull away to kiss his mouth. "Did you learn lots?"

"To keep my mouth shut when he's on one of his tirades," he says with a snort. "Otherwise, you earn toilet duty at the station."

"Ew."

"Hey, I know Mike better than anyone. My lips were sealed. Now Frank, on the other hand…"

"Poor Frank."

"April didn't feel sorry for him when we got back. She said most of the piss is his anyway because his aim sucks."

We both laugh.

"You need a shower. Want me to make something to eat?"

"You could shower with me," he says with a sly grin. "Then I could eat you."

I grab his ass and squeeze. "You're bad."

"Only sometimes."

"Mostly always."

"How was class tonight?"

"Meh," I grumble. "My professor is an idiot. I hate English."

"Man, sucks to be you. Your last name is English and you hate English."

I shrug as I pull away. "You could always fix that."

"You can't con me into a proposal, rat. I'm on to your sneaky games."

"Dude, you literally asked me to check the drain last night in the shower so you could sneak attack me from behind. If anyone plays games, rat lover, it's you."

He smirks at me and starts shedding clothes on the way to the bathroom. "You like my games."

"That's debatable."

"Get naked, Hollis. I'm dying to fuck you in the shower."

I rip off my shirt and saunter into the bathroom after him. His eyes drag down to my scars on my stomach. I don't disgust him, though. He seems relieved each time he sees them.

"Maybe I'd rather suck your dick," I say with a wicked grin.

He turns on the water, bending his white ass over. I

don't miss the opportunity. Pouncing on him, I rub against him from behind.

"Or, I could just fuck you instead."

He straightens and leans against my chest. My hands roam over his naked torso that's all too ripped these days now that he's volunteering at the fire station on nights and weekends and slinging tires at the factory during the day. All that physical labor has left him cut as fuck, and me reaping the benefits.

"Mmm," I murmur, nipping at his ear. "Someone likes that idea." I grip his cock and stroke him in a teasing way that makes him groan.

"You play dirty," he complains.

I laugh when he shakes me off and steps into the shower. I finish shedding the rest of my clothes before joining him. We focus on cleaning each other and then our mouths fuse together. I'm always so relieved when he gets back from a fire.

"Did you take your medicine?" he asks, sensing my mood.

"Yes."

"Good boy."

"Brat."

After my stomach healed, I began seeing a therapist. He's helping me through the shit with my dad. We're nowhere close to being friends, but we are talking. Dad has apologized to me, but it's not enough. So, we talk on the phone and just try to regain our footing. I've learned since seeing my therapist, Daniel, that I've been suffering from anxiety. I take an anti-anxiety medication each day that helps me not obsess over things. It's nice to feel in control of my feelings and my stomach not eat itself away anymore.

"Touch your dick, Roan. I want you to jerk off, imagining you're inside my tight ass," I croon, kissing his shoulder.

"Goddamn you and your dirty ass talk that turns me on every time."

I bite back a laugh as he starts stroking his dick. Reaching down to the bottle of lube we keep in here when Roux's not around, I pop the cap and pour some onto my dick. I smear it all over my cock and then use the excess to finger his needy hole. When he's good and prepped, I grip his hip and push into him from behind. We groan in unison.

"Fuck," he hisses. "You kill me."

I nip at his shoulder. "You like it."

"Nah, I love it, Hollis."

"And I love you, Roan."

He stiffens and grows quiet. I'd normally have a spike of anxiety, worrying over his response, but I don't. Sure, it's the first time either of us have spoken this sentiment, but I won't regret it, even if he doesn't feel that same way about me yet. I do love him. I have for probably as long as I can remember. His ass pushes against me, his silent tell for me to fuck him harder. I dig my fingers into his hip and thrust wildly into him.

God, he feels so fucking amazing.

I fuck him until I'm crying out his name. My cum bursts out of me, filling his tight ass up and marking him as mine. I'll never get tired of the way that feels. Gently, I slide out and slap his hard ass.

"Your turn."

"I want to go lie down," he murmurs.

My body grows cold at his words, but I talk myself through my worries like Daniel taught me. It's usually in my head. My fears and stress. Just because someone is quiet or frustrated, doesn't mean I'm always at the root of it. So rather than obsessing, I also clean myself off. We dry off and then I follow him into the bedroom. He sets the bottle of lube on the end table and then climbs onto the bed. His features are stony, his body tense.

"Are we going to sleep?" I ask, needing him to offer me a branch so I know I'm not sinking alone over here. "Should I turn off all the lights and lock up?"

His expression softens. "Not yet, babe. I haven't been inside you yet."

"Okay," I mutter, exhaling a relieved breath.

"Grab the lube," he orders. "I want you right here where I can kiss you."

All anxiety floods away and desire creeps back in. "Bossy."

"We all know who the bossy one in the bedroom is," he says, rolling his eyes. "And it's not me."

I smirk as I hand him the lube and climb onto the bed to straddle his thighs. "I can't help it."

"When we started this, I thought I was in charge around here."

"We all make mistakes," I tease. "That was your first one."

He laughs as he lubricates his beautiful dick. "Rub your asshole on my cock, porcelain boy. I'm ready to fuck you."

I rock my hips along his shaft, loving the way he hisses in pleasure. When I'm good and slick, I lean forward to seek out his mouth. He positions his dick against my hole and I slide down, taking every hard inch of him. His mouth is ravenous as he kisses me like I might disappear any moment. We kiss hard and frantic as he fucks me from below. He breathes heavily against my mouth, his strong hands squeezing my ass cheeks.

"Fuck, Hollis," he groans. "I love you too."

His words catch me off guard. All I can do is kiss him with everything I have. It doesn't take much more thrusting and then he's coming deep inside me. His energy is depleted and he relaxes, gazing up at me with a lazy, sated smile.

He's the sexiest man I've ever seen.

Mine.

He's mine.

"Move in with me, rat."

"Most people don't invite rats in. You're confused," I tease.

He smacks my ass. "I'm not confused. I'm in love. Say you'll do it."

"Yeah, rat lover, I'll do it. I'll move in with you. But only because you're obsessed with me."

"I'm not obsessed," he grumbles.

"You so are. Ask literally anyone."

"And what about you?"

I grin and press a kiss to his lips. "I have been since the second I laid eyes on you."

He flashes me that arrogant smile of his that makes me want to flip him over and fuck it right off his face. This beautiful, mean, obnoxious boy consumes me. Owns my heart. Makes me crazy as hell.

I love him so goddamn much.

"No necking at the dinner table," Mike bellows as he passes me the salad bowl.

"Necking," Roan says with a snort. "You're showing your age there, old man."

Aunt Karen laughs. "Necking does date you." Then, she turns her faux fierce scowl my way. "Seriously, don't do that at my dinner table."

Charlotte pretends to gag herself. Roux giggles. Penny doesn't look up from her iPad. Typical family dinner night. The table just keeps growing with people. Especially now that Mike has starting seeing Mom. I'm not so sure I'm in love with the idea, but he treats her a helluva lot better than Dad ever did, even on their best days. Mike treats her like a beautiful woman he wants to impress and spoil. Mom eats up every second of it.

"How are Cal and Trey doing?" Aunt Karen asks Roan. "I haven't heard from them in a while. I know you guys were close."

Roan flinches slightly and I know it's because she doesn't ask about Jordy. There's not much to learn. He's in prison. Will be there for a long time. It hurts less not to talk about it, I guess.

"They both went to OSU," he tells her. "Corvallis never knew what hit 'em."

"I feel sorry for the dean," Aunt Karen agrees. "They're probably terrorizing that town."

"They've changed the name from Campfire Chaos to Corvallis Chaos," Roan says with a laugh. "They've recruited a bunch of kids to party it up every Friday night like old times."

"Damn Hornets," I joke, nudging Roan with my shoulder.

He flashes me a hot smile that burns its way straight to my dick. "You love us."

"Just you."

"It's not fair, Mom," Charlotte whines. "I can't have a boyfriend, but Hollis can make out with Roan every time we have a meal."

"This would be making out," I taunt, pulling him to me for a sloppy kiss.

"Hollis!" Mom scolds. She's smiling, though. Always smiling these days. The real kind of smile.

"Sorry," I say, though I'm not.

She winks at me.

Dinner goes on with lots of laughter, arguments, and general silliness. Just another family dinner for the books. While the girls get stuck cleaning the kitchen while Mike and Mom "neck" their goodbyes outside on the porch, I take Roan up to my old room. It's been converted back into Aunt Karen's office. I've been officially moved out for less than a week, and she's already put everything back in its place.

It doesn't matter, though.

I just need a wall, some darkness, and Roan.

As soon as I push him against said wall and flip the switch off, our mouths meet for a kiss. His smile can be felt against my lips and I love it. I'll never tire of kissing him. Of teasing and taunting him. Of loving him.

"Someone's needy tonight," he teases.

I nip at his bottom lip. "Not needy. Just grateful."

"Grateful, huh? For what?"

"You."

"Me in general or a specific part of me?" He punctuates his words with a thrust of his hips so I can feel his dick through his jeans.

"All of it. Your dick. Your annoying cocky ass. Your big fucking heart."

"Wow, rat, you should put that shit on a Hallmark card. We could be rich."

"Nah, it's all for you, rat lover. Pure poetry just for you."

"So romantic."

I grab at his belt buckle. "I can show you how else I can be romantic."

"With a blowjob in your aunt's office? Oh, my heart."

"You're a smartass," I grumble.

"Your smartass."

"Yeah, yeah. I guess I'll keep you."

He kisses me and I feel that sexy smile again. "I guess I'll keep you too."

I hope you enjoyed Hollis and Roan's story!
Continue reading about these hot bad boys in Little Hornet
where you'll get Jordy's book!
Start *Little Hornet*!

Enjoy the entire Horn River Hornets series today!

Horn River Bully (Book 1 – Roan's Story)
Little Hornet (Book 2 – Jordy's Story)
Mr. Angry Hornet (Book 3 – Cal's Story)
River Knight (Book 4 – Trey's Story)

**** The Horn River Hornet series all have interlinking storylines. They shouldn't be read as standalones. The first book in the series, Horn River Bully, is the only MM story. The others are MF. The Horn River Hornets is now a complete series!****

About the Author

K Webster is a *USA Today* Bestselling author. Her titles have claimed many bestseller tags in numerous categories, are translated in multiple languages, and have been adapted into audiobooks. She lives in "Tornado Alley" with her husband, two children, and her baby dog named Blue. When she's not writing, she's reading, drinking copious amounts of coffee, and researching aliens.

To see the full list of K Webster's books, visit authorkwebster.com/all-books.

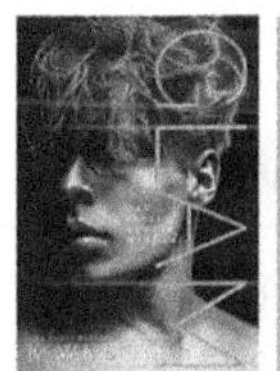

THESE PLUS MORE...

FREE SHORT STORIES

DOWNLOAD HERE

Happy Reading!

JOIN MY NEWSLETTER
at authorkwebster.com/newsletter

JOIN MY PRIVATE GROUP
at www.facebook.com/groups/krazyforkwebstersbooks

Follow K Webster here!

Facebook: www.facebook.com/authorkwebster

Readers Group:
www.facebook.com/groups/krazyforkwebstersbooks

Patreon: patreon.com/authorkwebster

Twitter: twitter.com/KristiWebster

Goodreads:
www.goodreads.com/author/show/7741564.K_Webster

Instagram: www.instagram.com/authorkwebster

BookBub: www.bookbub.com/authors/k-webster

Wattpad: www.wattpad.com/user/kwebster-wildromance

TikTok: www.tiktok.com/@authorkwebster

Pinterest: www.pinterest.com/kwebsterwildromance

LinkedIn: www.linkedin.com/in/k-webster-396b7021

Excerpt

Little Hornet

Roux

Seventeen Years Old

What's taking her so long?

I check my phone for any missed calls or texts but come up empty. Char was supposed to get here early so she could help me with my makeup. Early and Charlotte don't belong in the same sentence, though. She's late for everything.

Of all days for her to be late, this one is the worst.

Kayden is coming over.

I cringe knowing he'll see regular me. Not the me when Char works her makeup and hair magic on me. Ughhhh.

I'm especially nervous about today because it'll be just the three of us. No parents. No overbearing brothers.

Speaking of overbearing brothers, I can't help but smile. They may drive me nuts, but Hollis and Roan are total couples' goals. Who knew a gay wedding could be so freaking cute? I thought Roan would throw a fit and not let Hollis get his way, but something about Hollis has always gotten to my brother. He gives in to his happiness. After all the hell my brother has dealt with in his life, he deserves to be happy. He deserves Hollis. He deserves to be at the beach right now with his new husband on an adorable honeymoon.

I sigh dreamily.

One day I'll get married to someone awesome like Hollis.

Kayden is awesome.

Oh my God and freaking hot, too.

Like the hottest guy in our school.

I keep waiting for Char to tell me she's suddenly in love with him. She's not interested, though. This week she's dating Ryan Cunningham. Who knows who it'll be next week.

Crunch of tires on gravel has me rushing over to the window. I frown when I see it's just the mailman. Deciding to kill some time, I prance down the stairs and meet him at the box. He hands me the stack of mail and I sit down on the bottom step to go through it all.

I flip through some bills before finding an envelope from my dad. Eagerly, I rip through the envelope and smile at the silly card. It has Elsa from Frozen on the front. He started writing to me not long after Jordy went to prison. I think Dad thinks I'm still the little girl he left all those years ago. I'm not bothered by the fact he sends me childish cards. It's the thought that counts. Roan isn't thrilled that Dad writes to me, but he stays tight-lipped about it. Inside the card are seventeen wrinkly dollar bills. So silly, but it makes me smile.

I love you, Roux.

Dad's writing is messy, but I can make it out. I'd hoped he would have written a little more, but I'm still happy. I'm just tucking away the money back inside the card when I notice another letter from Oregon State Penitentiary.

I expect Dad's messy handwriting.

Not his.

Neat. Precise. Edgy.

Jordy.

My heart stammers in my chest. I haven't spoken to him since the incident. It's like he closed himself off from us. Just took the punishment like it was his alone to bear. I know it kills Roan, even almost three years later.

Why is he writing?

Because of my birthday?

I rip open the letter, eager to see what sort of birthday card he got me. A simple white card with a hand drawn kitten on the front. Inside, his neat writing looks like art. So beautiful.

Before I can read his letter, the thump of a bass on a car rattles every window in the near vicinity. Flutters erupt in my stomach. He's here. Oh God. I stand quickly and watch the black Dodge Challenger cruise down our street and into the driveway. A second later, the car shuts off and he climbs out.

Kayden Wheelhouse.

He's no longer the tall, lanky, shy boy from middle school. Somewhere along the way, he filled out and grew into this man. At seventeen, he's every bit as big as my brother. Kayden works out a lot with his brother, so he's super cut. I drool over his biceps all the time. Char likes to tease me that I'm more in love with Kayden's biceps than I am with him.

"Hey, Roux-Roux," Kayden says, his deep voice warming me in all the right places.

"Oh, hey, Kay," I chirp. "How's it hangin'?"

How's it hangin'?

Lame.

I am so lame.

Where is Char?

I need her coolness to save me right now.

He smirks as he saunters over to me and pulls me to him

for one of his friendly hugs. I try not to sniff him like a creep. "I think you grew taller since you turned seventeen," he teases, patting the top of my head.

"Ha. Ha." I roll my eyes at him. "I seriously doubt I grew in two days."

"I think you did." His eyes roam down my front, lingering on my breasts. "Yeah. You did."

I'm shocked at his words and can't formulate a response.

He's kidding. He has to be. No one flirts with me. Especially not Kayden. He's my best friend aside from Charlotte.

Before I can figure out what to do or say, his phone rings. He answers and then walks away as he speaks lowly on the phone. My hands are shaking. I need to calm myself down before he comes back over here and I do something stupid like throw myself at him and beg him to give me my first kiss.

I sit back down on the bottom step and pick up Jordy's card again to read it.

Little Hornet,
I know you still hang out with that kid.
Well, don't.
He's bad news. His brother is fucking Rex Wheelhouse.
So end your little friendship. It's better this way. Safer.
If I find out you're still his friend, I'll have to deal with it.
You do not want me to deal with it, Roux.
Later,
Jordy

I read his letter again to make sure I'm seeing this right. He doesn't speak to me for years. Years! And this is what he finally says to me. Hot tears burn my eyes as I crumple up his stupid card.

How dare he!

Kayden has been nothing but nice to me. He's one of my best friends. Jordy doesn't get to make assumptions about my life and try to control it from freaking jail. I want to scream at him, but he refuses to take visitors.

I hate him.

I hate him so much.

"Everything okay?"

Standing, I nod rapidly and avoid eye contact. "Great. I should call Char and see what's taking so long."

Kayden gently grips my chin in his fingers and tilts my head up so I'm looking at him. Dark brown eyes. Messy black hair. Perpetual smirk. God, he's so hot.

"I told her not to come." His grin widens. "Thought the two of us could hang alone for a change."

I blink at him in confusion. "What?"

"Don't act surprised, Roux," he says, lowering his face to mine. "We were always inevitable."

His lips press to mine and I gasp in shock. He tastes like his energy drinks and Chapstick. All I can do is part my lips and let him kiss me with his eager expertise. When his hand slides to the side of my neck, shivers run down my spine.

Kayden Wheelhouse just kissed me.

Oh my God.

I should be enjoying this moment, but all I can think about is Jordy's angry scowl. He wrote to me to tell me to stay away from him, and yet here I am doing the exact opposite.

Pushing thoughts away from Jordy so I can enjoy this moment, I smile up at Kayden.

"Inevitable, huh?"

He pecks my lips. "Yep."

"What now?"

"I'm going to take you upstairs and kiss you some more, Roux."

"Oh."

He laughs. "You're cute."

"So are you." My cheeks burn at my bold statement.

Together we walk up the stairs, but my mind is once again back on Jordy. He's bullying me through a stupid letter. It's ridiculous. Why does he even care who I date? It shouldn't matter to him. He's in prison.

Breathe, Roux.

He's. In. Prison.

There's nothing he can do from there.

Right?

Read *Little Hornet* next!

Printed in the USA
CPSIA information can be obtained
at www.ICGtesting.com
LVHW011159151023
760905LV00016B/638